LUNA NUNA

STORY
BY
KU HARVEY

The Romantic Ruin of the Most Celebrated Coin
. . . from the ashes of the historic 2022 LUNA collapse

BOSTON
BOOK
RESERVE

KU HARVEY

is a national bestselling author of Harbird-22 and Luna Nuna,
originally published in Korean. He navigates the confluence of
language, both an academic discipline and an artistic ambition.
He received his master's degree from Harvard and
bachelor's degree with the highest honors from Berkeley and
won the Robert J. Glushko Prize.

"If you want to know about birds,
you have to study their wings.
And if you want to know about humans,
you have to study their language."

A quote from his college commencement speech that he lives by—
though he cringes a bit every time he realizes he said it himself.

Please visit his website

www.langua.ge

for more books, writings, and reflections.

Boston Book Reserve
115 Mt Auburn St, Cambridge, MA 02138
Printed in the United States of America

ISBN 979-8-9880233-2-6

To Dad and Mom,
who taught me the solemnity of money
yet shielded me from its weight.

Act I

chapter block
01.0

A coin for his dream. A character for his ruin.

He adjusts the chronograph one final time. May 15th, 2022, 20:29:02, Pacific Standard Time. In that instant, two eclipses aligned across the boundless California sky: one, a rare celestial Lunar eclipse; the other, a calamitous terrestrial *Luna* eclipse.

Let the former captivate the curious astrologers, gazing at stars and planets. As for us, untroubled by celestial mysteries, riveted instead to the worldly ambitions and desires, to the tangible passions of our fellow men, and to the mysteries woven in human frailty and triumph alike—we shall explore the latter.

I consciously refuse to look at the moon, for it reminds me, in its silent enormity, that we play no part in nature's choreography, that humanity is but a passing whisper.

I fiercely cling to my creation, held in the grip of defiance, rejecting the simplicity of humanity reduced to a predictable machine, shorn of ambition, denuded of grandeur.

I shamelessly indulge in the illusion that, in our smallness, we are somehow unique among creatures, somehow exempt from the indifference of the cosmos.

The blazing California sun once beckoned us to brave the unknown, and I merely obliged. But now the hands of my chronograph lie still. As the sun sets and the moon rises, I sing only at the twilight of the Luna eclipse.

This is not a story of coins, but of characters.

•

—Even Steve Jobs, you know.

—What about him?

—Jobs was meant to be an artist, not a business guy. But then he came to California, and well, the weather just wasn't right.

—Dude, where else has better weather than here?

—Exactly. That's the problem—it's *too* perfect. Art requires cogito, and cogito craves shadows. But Stanford—this endless plain, this benevolent sun—offers no such darkness. Jobs didn't have the weather for music; he had the weather for building Apple. The sun left him no choice.

—Oh sure, that's not the dumbest theory I've ever heard.

—I'm telling you, man, it's true. Why were the greatest rock bands born in the rain-soaked streets of London? Why did the great literary giants emerge from the freezing brink of St. Petersburg? It's inevitable. The heavens have spoken — that we, the sad Stanford souls, are here to forsake art and build the next big thing.

—Okay, I'll indulge your bullshit later. *The Crypto Christ* is gonna walk in any second, so could you please shut up now? Did that art school girl dump you or what? Geez.

The chatterbox guy suddenly clamps up.

—Oh, wait, no way—she really dumped you? Haha!

—I think people are meant to look at the moon, not the sun. We're metaphysically drawn to the shadows.

—Yes, sure, man. Whatever you say. Maybe that's why iPhones have Dark Mode, huh? For heartbroken people like you, haha.

—Exactly. It's cosmic. That's why the Do Not Disturb sign is a little crescent moon icon. Jobs was still haunted by the shadows of art, you know?

The nonsense banter of third-year computer science majors, was laced with a strange, palpable anticipation. Beneath the jokes, however, an undercurrent of tension pulses through the room. Tonight is the monthly gathering of the Stanford Blockchain Club, held in the William Gates Computer Science Building, where every seat is taken—an unusual sight. Typically, a hearty 70% of the members would have opted for the charms of beer and casual chatter, but tonight there's an unspoken gravity. Dinners, drinks— all postponed. They sit in a rare, collective stillness, as though awaiting the arrival of someone.

—Alright, save the tears for a sob session later tonight. But really, zip it now—an important guest incoming.

—Who're we even waiting for? You said Crypto Christ or something?

—…Why are you even here, seriously?

—I thought we were hitting the pub, but then you guys dragged me into this cryptic crypto club thing.

—Just hang on for ten more minutes. Do-hyung Moon was supposed to be here at 9.

—Wait, his last name is *Moon*? Damn, it's like he was born for this crypto game.

—How can you not know Do-hyung—I mean, Do? He's the guy behind LunaCoin—the *Crypto Christ*.

—Oh, *that* LunaCoin? Didn't know his name, but I certainly won't forget now. It's like, *Just Do It*, right? Haha.

—No, it's pronounced D-O. Like, you know, the extinct Dodo bird?

—Ah, good to know. But is he actually showing up? He's, what, 40 minutes late already?

—Well, unlike that art school girl who stood you up last night, he's actually gonna come. Trust me.

—I hate you.

Another student, overhearing their silly exchange, cut in with a tone more solemn than the rest. He certainly doesn't seem to be a fan of this Do guy.

—Honestly, if Do had a shred of decency, he wouldn't even dare show his face here tonight. After all that happened? In fact, he should be in jail.

—Decency? Are you even serious?

—Yes. Decency? Accountability? Ever heard of those? He should answer for the apocalypse he caused. People lost their entire savings—hell, some even lost their lives because of the LunaCoin crash.

—Biden or Trump doesn't apologize when the value of the dollar drops. Look, I lost like four grand. But I don't complain because I invested at my own goddamn risk and because LunaCoin was a once-in-a-generation idea.

—Biden didn't *invent* the dollar. Do actually invented a currency—and blew it all up.

—Exactly! That's my point! How many people get to say they invented *a money*? That's next-level badass, right?

—Oh, please. He's a con artist. Smart as hell, but do you even know how much LunaCoin is worth today? Nada. Zero.

—Almost zero. Not totally zero—yet. And gosh, here we go again. Ever since you got into law school, you're all high and mighty. What's next, extra credit as the future D.A. cleaning up all the crypto crimes?

—I'm just saying, look at how many people actually lost everything. We're in this Stanford bubble. It makes you lose touch with reality sometimes.

—Yeah, sure, just blame it on Stanford.

The students scroll through social media and video feeds as they wait for Do. The torrent of cries and anguish over LunaCoin's catastrophic collapse unfold on their screens. The deeper they scroll, the more intense it becomes—a cacophony of confusion, screams of outrage, a chain reaction of despair.

Numbers corroborate the magnitude and severity of their pain. In the span of 48 hours since the collapse of LunaCoin, $32 billion worth of cryptocurrency has disappeared into the ether. And no, that's not a typo.

And no, that's not a typo—32,000,000,000 dollars, gone.

These days, however, no one steps out into the plaza; no one steps out to the open square anymore, baring their disillusionment under the open sky. Instead, each remains confined within their private chambers, separated, offering no consolation, forming no solidarity, merely echoing back self-deprecating memes and jaded comments. And so, even as desperate cries, hyperventilating gasps, or last words flash across their screens, they register only as flat decibels, barely piercing the flattened depths of the glass surface.

—Hey, check out those guys up front, in the suits. Are they even students? They look like they are about to take someone out.

—Holy crap, haha, yeah. Maybe they're Russian hitmen hired by billionaires who invested in LunaCoin.

—Or worse, North Korean operatives. You know Kim Jong-un always has his hackers swiping millions in crypto. But if he stole LunaCoins, all of it would be worth exactly zero.

—Hey, how about that, our future D.A. of Santa Clara County? Isn't that a silver lining? Better to crash LunaCoin than let Kim Jong-un make a dime off it.

Tonight, it isn't just the Stanford Blockchain Club students and a few suited mystery men filling the room. Venture capitalists of Sand Hill Road, professors with free parking permits at the school thanks to their Nobel Prizes, Ph.D. students, and major media reporters have all gathered—for the man and the unprecedented turmoil sparked by his grand invention, LunaCoin.

—Apologies, everyone. It seems Mr. Moon is slightly delayed with another engagement. I'll check on the situation and update you shortly.

The Club president, visibly anxious, sends a silent plea skyward for Do to arrive swiftly. As if in answer, she dashes back into the room after a moment, breathless yet buoyant.

—Everyone! Thanks for skipping dinner to be here tonight! I can't see a single empty seat. I think it's time to introduce our much-anticipated guest. I'm sure this is who you've all been waiting for.

Blue eyes, brown eyes, black eyes—all turn, in sync, toward the front of the room.

—Now, please welcome the Crypto Christ himself, the most influential figure in the global crypto scene right now, and a former Cardinal, Do-hyung Moon, the CEO of LunaCoin!

The students break into applause, charged with ambition and thrill as he steps forward. Reactions split between his fans and his critics.

—Wow, so he actually got the nerve to show up tonight.

—Told you he would. The guy wrecks a global financial system and strolls back to alma mater, haha. That's my man there.

—Hey, everyone.

Do greets them briefly, his voice steady but weary.

—Sorry to keep you waiting.

The media painted him as a voracious force, a destroyer of a global financial market, but here he looks just as human as any of them. Beneath the polished veneer, there are wounds far deeper than the exhaustion etched on his face.

—So tonight, I...

Just as he reaches for the microphone, however, a sudden shift sweeps through the room.

—Mr. Moon.

The suited men move in, closing the gap to the podium with a practiced precision.

—This is the FBI. We have a warrant.

The students freeze, stunned.

—What the...?

—Wow, I did not see that coming.

Turns out, the guys in suits were indeed scarier than any hired gun.

—Mr. Do-hee-young Moon? You are under arrest for securities fraud, wire fraud, and commodities fraud involving your algorithmic stablecoin, stock-mirroring assets, and the Anchor Protocol. That's quite a resume, Mr. Moon?

One agent intones, smirking briefly, actually amused by the list of his charges.

—It's pronounced *h-yung*, not *hee-young*. Might want to try again. You wouldn't want to mess up prosecuting me with those bogus charges because you mispronounced my name.

Do corrects the agent, returning the smirk with an extra hint of mockery.

—Alright, *D-O-H-yung*. You have the right to remain silent. Anything you say can and will be used against you in a court of law.

The FBI agent plays along, mimicking and accentuating the unfamiliar Korean pronunciation to the best of her effort.

—You guys will never understand the money I created. Because it's not *any* money.

Do calmly remarks.

—That's something we'll get to the bottom of at the court.

The agent's partner cut in, grasping Do's wrists and securing them behind his back with a firm click of handcuffs.

The lecture hall sat in a breathless, collective silence. The arrest has been executed in plain sight, and there is no dodging it now. Phones flash to life. Students tweet. Journalists type furiously. Within seconds, the internet is ablaze: *Do-hyung Moon, the CEO of LunaCoin, arrested at his alma mater, Stanford.*

With a poise that borders on the surreal, Do, his wrists chafing against the cold metal, raises his voice to the crowd.

—Sorry to keep you waiting. Unfortunately, I will have to exercise my constitutional right to remain silent at this time.

The architect of crypto's greatest experiment follows the agents out, his figure receding and leaving a shockwave of disbelief reverberating through the lecture hall.

—What the heck just happened?

—Look at him. He doesn't even flinch while the Feds drag him out.

—He knew this was coming, and he deserves it.

—Or he knows he'll walk free soon enough.

—No, look at his eyes. It's neither of those. You guys are all wrong.

Then the heartbroken student cut in with yet another silly line.

—Huh, really? What is it, then?

—...It's the eyes of a lover who has just let a loved one go.

—Oh, like you'd know anything about that, huh?

—I do.

—Haha, shut the hell up with your romantic crap. Let's go grab a beer and cry about that in the pub. I guess today's drama is a wrap.

While they laugh at the ridiculous romantic musings, the student, long critical of Do, finds himself unable to let the disgraced CEO depart without asking one last question.

—No… this can't be it.

He calls out to Do's retreating figure.

—Mr. Moon!

Do glances back, a brief flicker of acknowledgment. And the student, summoning a question torn from the visceral depths within, releases his first and final inquiry.

—Did you know?

And Do—the benevolent creator of LunaCoin—chooses, for but a moment, to forfeit his right to remain silent.

—Yes, I knew—that Luna would rewrite the story of us all.

chapter block
02.0

—Private Do-hyung Moon, reporting for duty, sir!

Even as he stood with a crisp salute, there was something subdued in his voice, a note weighed down by disillusionment. Fresh out of high school, Do had chosen the path least expected of him—enlistment instead of the Ivy League.

All Korean boys are equally bound by the duty of military service. No exceptions. Yet, as always, some boys are more equal than others. Do, too, had entertained the idea of deferring his enlistment. With an Ivy League acceptance, he could have drowned in the haze of campus parties and later apply for a more prestigious, comfortable assignment in KATUSA[1]. But life often finds ways to mock our grand designs.

Here he was—on the frontlines of the DMZ[2], facing the perpetual tension between North and South Korea.

—Alright, I'm Captain Kim. Nineteen years old, huh. Looks like you enlisted early?

—Private Do-hyung Moon! Yes, sir, that's correct!

—Any reason you left the college section empty?

—Private Do-hyung Moon! I haven't enrolled in a university yet, sir!

Captain Kim squinted at his file again. It wasn't unusual to see high school boys enlist right after graduation, but they were rarely from elite institutions. Yet there it was, in bold beneath the

---

[1] Korean Augmentation to the United States Army

[2] Demilitarized Zone

blank college section—the name of Korea's number one elite school: Sudo High. A place Captain Kim could only dream of sending his son. And here stood one of its graduates, without a college acceptance, reporting for duty at nineteen—while others his age were out celebrating their acceptances and learning to flirt with the dangers of early privilege.

Do wasn't here on a patriotic whim. Before the musty military uniform and his status as a mere private, he had been something much more. At Sudo High, he was a towering presence —the best of the best. His ambition gleamed in his eyes, his determination hard as steel, his belief rooted in a mantra he held sacred: we don't study to learn; we learn to win. Do wasn't a student in the scholarly sense. He was a competitor. His study habits were more akin to Michael Jordan's ruthless hunt for victory than to Isaac Newton's quiet contemplation. Every exam, every result was another notch in his belt of conquests. His victories piled high, each one reinforcing his identity.

And so, when the ultimate goal—an acceptance to the best university in the world—slipped from his grasp, the impact was earth-shattering. This wasn't a mere setback. It was a betrayal. Harvard was his due. Or perhaps Stanford, Yale, or Princeton. And no one doubted it, least of all him. But the system, in its cold indifference, sometimes seems arbitrary. He read during his sophomore year that elite American universities, in their quest for diversity, often reject Asian students with perfect SAT scores, considering them "uninteresting." Never in his wildest dreams did he imagine his application would fall into that category.

Perhaps he should have concealed his ego in the application essay? Or perhaps he should have let it burn bright for all to see? The rejection was more than just a letter—it was a rupture, a tearing apart of the future he had built in his mind. He was betrayed not just by the institutions but by the very ambition that had fueled him.

Do had an unusual, nearly masochistic way of processing pain. He found that the most effective way to silence one pain was to add another on top of it. So, fueled by a simmering bitterness, he made an impulsive decision weeks ago. He visited the military conscription website. Active duty? Click. Apply? Click. Date? Click. Complete? Click. While his friends lazily clicked the "Defer military service" button, he chose to punish himself by committing to serve his country.

And before he could second-guess himself, the military congratulated him with a text, informing him of his enlistment date. In his eighteen years, this was the first "acceptance" that didn't require a competition. On paper, Do was just another face in the crowd—indistinguishable, a nobody. In spite of or because of being a nobody, he felt a strange relief. The illusion of choice is often the root of resentment. Before the rejections, he would have scoffed at such a notion. But now? Now, the military felt like exactly the place for someone who had grown tired of chasing a destiny that only seemed to evade him.

—Do you know what position you'll be assigned to?

—Private Do-hyung Moon! I have no idea, sir!

Most fresh recruits spoke to Captain Kim with an instinctual hesitance, their voices catching in the presence of authority. This kid, however, was somewhat different. His edge went beyond the brains and connections conferred by Sudo High. Beneath the respectful tone, the Captain could feel the lethal edge that uniforms and ranks couldn't dull. Do's ambition simmered in each syllable, dangerous and barely contained. Captain Kim saw no need to remind a ticking time bomb that it had a fuse, so he assigned Do to a relatively cushy, isolated position.

"DMZ Signal Patrol Unit." That was his assignment. Do didn't have such an extensive background in cryptography or telecommunications, but neither did any of the other conscripts. The assignment would keep him occupied and out of trouble—hopefully.

Once the orientation was complete, Do pushed open the door to the barracks with a sigh.

—Whoa! New recruit in the house! Shouted a figure who, judging by his voice, appeared to be a senior soldier.

—Hey, rookie, this is Sergeant Yoon. Came the interjection from a nearby corporal, nodding toward the man with the gruff tone.

The barracks smelled of dampness after four consecutive days of rain, the air thick with the odor of sweat, mildew, and must. The soldiers within were raw, unrefined—people that Do had never encountered before. These men made him painfully aware of his own detachment.

—Reporting in, Private Do-hyung Moon!

—How old are you? Sergeant Yoon asked.

—Nineteen, sir!

—Damn, you're just a baby. Okay, kid. Here comes a very important question.

Sergeant Yoon leaned in, eyes gleaming with a predatory glint, mischief dancing behind his grin.

—Yes, sir!

—Do you have a *nuna*[3]? If she's pretty, even better. I've always had a thing for older women, you know.

Sergeant Yoon chuckled, a vulgar undercurrent in his voice. Do, despite the absurdity of the question, stood as stiff as a statue. He was only relieved that he didn't have an older sister.

—No, sir! I'm an only child, sir!

—Ah, you boring piece of shit. Sergeant Yoon grumbled. Alright, a less interesting question. Where are you from?

—Gangnam, Daechi-dong, sir!

—A rich kiddo, huh. You look like you should be herding cows on some farm, but yeah. The way you talk and act does scream private boarding school, haha. So, where do you go to school?

—Private Do Hyung Moon! I haven't gone to college yet, sir!

—The fuck? Are you kidding me? Who doesn't go to college these days? Even an idiot like me made it to college, haha.

---

[3] A Korean term or endearment used by a male to refer to an older sister or an older female friend with a close relationship.

Sergeant Yoon laughed, the sound harsh and coarse, echoing off the barracks' walls.

At this, a soldier with glasses chimed in.

—Sergeant Yoon, he's probably one of those guys who enlisted to study for his exams.

—Study? The Sergeant scoffed, his brow furrowed.

—Yeah, you know, some guys fail their college entrance exams, so they come here to study to retake the exam a year later.

It's a reasonable guess, Do thought, though incorrect. He had already aced his SAT with a perfect 2400. No, what he needed now wasn't more studying—it was to rewrite his essays, veil his bitterness toward the schools that had rejected him, and manufacture the kind of passion that would make him seem like the most intellectually curious applicant in the world.

—Man, I usually can't stand you Gangnam kids, all high and mighty from those fancy schools. I was so ready to make your life here a living hell, especially with that smug look on your face. But man, now I just feel sorry for you. Still, rookie!

—Private Do-hyung Moon!

—Wait, so your name's Do-hyung *Mun*? Let's see here... Alright, I'll give you a great Nickname. Mun... Muuun-do... Muuun-do? Hmm... Oh! Got it. From now on, your name is Mundo. Like Dr. Mundo. I'm Challenger rank, by the way. Top Mundos are annoying as hell, so it suits you.

—Excuse me?

Do blinked, his brain struggling to keep up with this ridiculous thread of conversation.

—Mundo. Dr. Mundo. You don't play *League of Legends*? Dude, if you couldn't even get into college, the least you could do is be good at playing games.

It's spelled M-oo-n, not M-u-n like the Model UN, you dumbass. Of course, though you've probably never heard of *MUN*, Do thought, clamping his teeth shut.

—Sergeant Yoon, didn't you only make Gold rank in the PC League? Challenger in mobile League doesn't count, man. Another senior soldier teased, smirking.

—Shut up, you little rat. Anyways, Mundo, listen up. The army may have gotten softer, but this isn't the place for you to study. I'll be watching you.

Sergeant Yoon then jabbed a finger toward the bespectacled soldier.

—Hey, Yohan!

—Yes, sir!

—Doesn't this guy seem like trouble?

—I'll make sure to keep an eye on him, sir!

—You better. If he ever screws up, it's on you.

—Understood, sir!

Do could have brushed off this idiotic Sergeant Yoon, but it was this bespectacled soldier, Yohan, who really annoyed him. Study for the exams? Retake the SAT? Did he really think Do was here for something as trivial as test prep? My ambition runs deeper than your stupid glasses could ever comprehend.

—I'm Yohan Lee, by the way. Nice to meet you. I'm a Private, too—just been here a couple months earlier, hehe.

With Sergeant Yoon now out of sight, the bespectacled soldier's voice softened, carrying a genuine warmth and innocence that hadn't come through before.

—...Private Do-hyung, Moon. Nice to meet you, sir.

—Haha, no need to put "sir" for me all the time. And hey, don't worry too much. Once you settle in, you'll have plenty of time to study for the exam. I'm studying for the CPA exam on the side, too. But first, focus on getting through the basic duties. It'll make your life easier.

Maybe Yohan isn't such a bad guy, Do mused. Still, he had no intention of making friends here. He had come to the military to escape, not to connect. That night, as the barracks darkened, the soft, muffled sound of someone crying filled the air. It must have been one of the new recruits, a fellow comrade, overwhelmed by it all. But Do? Do had already emptied himself of tears long ago. Only exhaustion remained, a consuming emptiness.

.

A week had passed. Private Do-hyung Moon had settled into the rhythm of barracks life, learning the mundane routines from Private Yohan Lee. Not that Do cared much—what he learned slipped through him like water through a sieve, barely held before it faded. When he spoke, it was usually with a sigh. Cleaning toilets, doing laundry—none of it bothered him as long as he was left alone. But tonight was different. The duty roster had him on night watch, paired with Yohan.

—Private Lee, we're on night watch together tonight. May I ask what the night watch duty is?…

—You know it's the first time you've ever asked me about anything, right? Haha. I was starting to think you didn't even have a curiosity bone.

—…My apologies, sir.

—Oh, what? No need for apologies, Mundo. I mean, I'm kind of glad you asked me something, hehe. You always seem so serious, barely saying a word. Just thought I'd try talking, that's all.

—Yes, I understand.

Do found himself wondering, though—how did Yohan manage to stay so kindhearted in a place like this, surrounded by low-IQ and low-EQ animals like Sergeant Yoon.

—But hey, Mundo, I gotta warn you. Night watch is no joke, alright? Brace yourself. We're about to spend a few hours in the coldest corner of purgatory, my friend.

What now, are we expected to fend off North Korean soldiers with knives at the border? Do thought, suppressing an eye roll.

•

Yohan and Do were stationed at the top of the mountain with five rounds of ammunition, two grenades, enough KitKats to last a siege, and an extremely old military radio that looked like it had survived the Korean War itself. They weren't out on any heroic mission—just standing there, freezing down to the bone.

The first hour passed without much to complain about. The bullets hanging from his side and the grenades weighing in his pockets were unsettling, sure. But the small heater offered some warmth and the KitKats a brief yet luxurious indulgence. For that one hour at the guard post overlooking the DMZ, Do could even feel a flicker of the romanticism of history—the strange, misplaced gravity of standing on the edge of something so significant.

But Yohan's words rang true. By the time the third hour rolled around, the heater's warmth was gone, the chocolate long eaten, and whatever romance had briefly stirred in the cold, it too had frozen solid.

Goddamn it. Do almost wished for the knife fight with North Korean soldiers at this point—at least it would offer a quicker, more decisive end than this excruciating cold. This was a slow torture. Russian soldiers didn't defeat Hitler; the unyielding Russian winter did. History lessons were all Do could think about as he sat there, the cold gnawing at his bones, every breath crystallizing in the air before him. Was this what real life in the DMZ was supposed to be?

—Nah, this is just regular guard duty. Actual training's way tougher. But yeah, we'll be regularly frozen to death up here. See that military radio? Guard it with your life. Yohan said, breaking the silence with a nonchalance that grated on Do's nerves.

—Sorry, come again, sir? Do blinked, his disbelief settling into the marrow of his bones.

—That radio. That's why we're here. Yohan nodded toward the aging piece of equipment.

Do stared at the outdated piece of equipment, disbelief settling in. This thing? This ancient relic is the reason we were freezing to death on this mountain? Was he supposed to cling to it like a mother cradling her child? Unless it held the key to Korean reunification, he couldn't understand why they had to endure this misery for it.

—Damn... this never gets easier. The cold is killing us. Here, Do, take this extra heater. Yohan offered, his breath clouding in the air as he spoke.

—Private Lee, can I ask why we need this radio? Do shook his head, refusing the heater; his head was already hot.

—What do you mean, why? It's for communication.

—Communication...? Do's voice was tinged with disbelief.

—Yeah. Think of us as human walkie-talkies. We're carrying this radio to keep communication alive.

Do's hands itched with a visceral urge to hurl the radio down the mountainside. He wanted to understand, to rationalize why he was here, why he had to babysit this damned radio. Yohan's explanation only stoked his frustration. Back in high school, Do and his friends talked about their bright futures, the grand contributions they'd make to society. He had mapped out a future that glittered with purpose and ambition. Maybe arrogant, elitist even—but no one ever doubted his potential.

But now? Now he was reduced to a human walkie-talkie. The cold had numbed his skin, but inside, rage simmered. It wasn't just the radio. It was everything. It was the waste of his potential, the mockery of the grand future he'd envisioned for himself. The weight of the absurdity pressed down on him, threatening to choke the very air from his lungs. *How had it come to this?*

—Do, are you okay? You don't look well. Warm up your hands and cheeks. Yohan must have sensed the turmoil in him.

—...Private Lee, can I ask you something?

—Ha, yeah. Maybe hearing you complain might be better than freezing in silence.

—Why are we carrying this radio? Do's defiant tone had already pushed the boundaries of his rank, even for Yohan's standard. He should thank the freezing cold for numbing the tension.

—I told you. It's our main mode of communication.

—It's fucking 2022.

Do wasn't even aware he had sworn in front of his senior—a slip that could've easily landed him in big trouble. But Yohan let it slide, perhaps recognizing the deeper frustration behind it.

—Private Lee, we have cutting-edge tech everywhere. Why are we stuck here with this outdated piece of crap? Do's voice cracked with frustration.

—...Do, I get you. When you first join the military, all of this seems pointless. But there's always something to learn from it.

Learn? Do's mind recoiled at the word. Learn what? What could there possibly be to learn here, freezing on a mountain with a military radio that belongs in a Korean War museum? Yohan's attempt to console him only made his anger flare hotter. Oh, or is this what you tell yourself to get through this purposelessness, Private Lee? Convincing yourself that there must be some hidden meaning in this meaningless role-playing?

I know, damn it. None of this is your fault. I know you aren't the Secretary of Defense. I know you are probably the best guy in the entire barracks. But I honestly want to just shoot every damn North Korean soldier, you, me, and yeah, maybe the Secretary of Defense, too. He thought, fury pulsing. Because I hate every last bit of this.

•

Five hours passed, and with them, every semblance of resistance. Physiology triumphed over psychology, as it always does when the body is pushed beyond its limits. The DMZ's cold wasn't passive; it was an active force, eroding his will and extinguishing every ember of defiance burning inside him. Do's fire was no match for the creeping frost.

Do even tried to follow Yohan's lead, telling himself the same comforting lie that there's something to learn here. Instead, every time he tried to wrap himself in this false belief, the cold bit harder, as if punishing him for daring to search for meaning in it.

For the first time since he joined the army, a tear slipped down his cheek, freezing the moment it touched his chest.

If Sergeant Yoon had been there, he would have slapped the defiance out of him—maybe then Do might feel something in his numb cheek. But Yohan, despite everything, didn't scold him.

Yohan too had been here before, had faced the same suffocating futility when he first climbed up to the post with the military radio. And so their conversation died down, replaced by a heavy, frozen void they shared.

—...Hey, Mundo.

—Private Do-hyung Moon...

—Cold?

—...No, sir...

—I sure am. Phew, let's head back to the barracks.

—Sorry?

—The night watch is over. Time doesn't exactly fly up here, but at least today's done. Haha. Let's head down.

Do blinked, barely processing Yohan's words. But knowing the shift was finally over, a faint relief flickered inside him. Only the heavy exhaustion of having made it through stayed with Do. In the end, survival was the simplest of human desires.

As they began their descent, Do picked up the radio—the same cursed object, the weight of meaninglessness. The way down was even harder than standing guard.

•

—Sucks, doesn't it?

—Excuse me?

—It sucks. Everything here sucks. It's okay to say it, Do. No one's listening but me. Anyway, good job on your first shift.

Yohan handed him a steaming cup of ramen still in its plastic package, untouched by a bowl. Even if the plastic was leaching chemicals, the taste mattered more right now. This was "ppogeuli," the quick ramen cooked directly in the bag—a tradition only Korean soldiers would understand, only those who know the grind of this life. The hot broth flooded his veins, reigniting his circulation. Forgive Do for not being able to describe this godly taste or instant ramen with more eloquence. The heat coursed through Do's hands, thawing what cold had frozen still. And with his blood boiling again, this insistent young boy had to ask that question one more time.

—Private Lee.

—What? Want more ramen?

—No, sir. Thank you. It's really good. And... I'm sorry. About earlier, at the post...

—Don't sweat it. My first shift pissed me off too. I thought, "Did I really get dragged here just to be a human walkie-talkie?"

—Did you say anything?

—Are you crazy? I'd get my ass kicked by Sergeant Yoon, haha.

—I see... but... Can I ask you the real reason we have to drag around this stupid radio?

—It's a top military secret. If I tell you, I might get sent to jail for leaking classified information.

—I see...

—Haha, I'm kidding. There actually is a pretty good reason.

—Really?

—Yeah, really. Look, we're on the DMZ, right? Practically neighbors with the North. So the chances of war breaking out are much higher. And what would happen if war broke out?

—...We'd all be dead?

—My gosh, Mundo, really? Yes, likely, but we'd still try hard not to die too fast. Why do you always jump to the extreme? Geez.

—Ha, sorry. A small laugh escaped Do's lips.

—That's the first time I've seen you laugh. Anyway, if war breaks out, what's the first thing the enemy would go for?

—...I guess they'd try to seize the command center.

—Not bad. But why? Because the ramen here is excellent?

—Haha, no... I mean, yes. The ramen is excellent, but they'd prioritize going after our communication systems.

—Bingo, Mundo. If the North hacks or destroys our communications, the whole command structure falls apart. We're thrown back to the Stone Age in the worst possible place. So, what's our backup plan? This old-fashioned military radio. Why do you think that is?"

—...Because even if one radio goes down, the others still work. Even if one gets hacked or taken out, the rest will keep working.

—Exactly! Like I said, everything seems pointless at first, but there's always something to learn.

Huh, the absurdity of military radio was still there, but maybe —just maybe—there was a sliver of purpose hidden behind it. The explanation did click, more viscerally than intellectually. It didn't matter how obsolete the machine was; it still held the power to bridge gaps between life and death, chaos and order.

—Yes... I guess that's true. A little.

—Haha, there's that "little" at the end. But you're right. Ninety-nine percent of this is just killing time, and maybe one percent is learning.

—Yup... I guess it is.

—You were one of those geniuses back in high school, right?

—Hmm?

—I mean, smart kids are always the ones who question everything, who can't accept it until it makes sense.

—Maybe... Yes, that's true, haha.

—How's the studying on the side going? You probably haven't had much time for it yet.

—No, not really. Actually... I'm not here to retake the Korean college exam. I took the SAT, and well, that's taken care of. I just need to write a better essay this admissions cycle.

—Really? Did you go to international school or something?

—...Sort of. I went to the Sudo High.

—Hold up—Sudo High? That's where all the genius kids go, right? How did you... I mean, why didn't you get into college? Is that even... possible? Shit, sorry, that was dumb. I mean, insensitive.

—Haha, no, it's fine. Actually...

Sharing ramen in the dead of night had a way of breaking down defenses—not between the two Koreas but between two comrades. Worn out as he was, Do found himself opening up. For

21

the first time since leaving Sudo High, his thoughts softened, slipping away from their usual sharp edges.

Before the reveille sounded, Yohan patiently as Do spoke of his unspent ambitions, of the fire he had yet let to relinquish. In the quiet, cold night, with the steam of ramen rising between them, Do felt that maybe his bad luck at being stationed here wasn't so bad after all.

•

It was an uneventful day, but not an empty one. One hundred days had passed since Do had become a protector of DMZ. One hundred days in which time had lost its old rhythm, the routine of soldiering swallowing the boy whole. Every day was a continuation of surreal monotony.

—Mundo, you've been here a while now, huh? You're up for your hundred-day leave next week.

—Thank you. I wouldn't have made it without you, Private Lee.

—Man, saying something nice like that doesn't suit you at all, haha.

Do was more excited about his upcoming leave than he'd let himself admit.

—Is that the mobile League of Legends game Sergeant Yoon's always playing?

—Huh? League? Nah, this isn't a game, man. This is way better for killing time here.

On Yohan's tiny phone screen, Do saw sharp blue candlestick charts nosediving. Was it the stock chart? Whatever it was, it didn't look promising.

—Nah, this isn't stock. It's Bitcoin. Ever heard of it?

—Yeah, isn't it some kind of digital money?

—It's badass digital money.

—But Private Lee... aren't those kinds of things mostly scams?

—I was a little skeptical too, but there's this block-something technology behind it, so it's supposedly secure. Anyway, Mundo. Yohan brushed off the skepticism.

—Yes, Private Lee?

—When you go on leave, could you pick up a couple of books about Bitcoin for me? I'll pay you back.

—Sure. Just grab anything with "Bitcoin" in the title?

—Yeah, and you should try it too. You can make some quick cash at first, haha. But honestly, it's not just about the money. Unlike the stocks, it trades 24/7. And when it takes off, it really takes off. When it crashes, it crashes hard. The dopamine rush is insane. Honestly, I think I'm addicted to Bitcoin just for the dopamine.

—Haha. Doesn't that make it tougher though?

—For regular folks, sure. But we're soldiers. We're living in this dopa-mine-zero zone—or DMZ.

—That's clever.

—Ha, thank you. They say the DMZ's the first place that'll break into war, but in reality, we're just staring at an empty border with a few North Koreans milling around. Bitcoin is like a healing tonic, a dopamine fix to keep me sane.

—So, I just need to open a stock account to get started?

—No, no, you need a wallet. A cryptocurrency wallet. It's like your mobile bank account for crypto. Set it up when you go on leave.

—Yes, sir.

—Heh, you know what actually? Scratch that. It's your first leave. Don't worry about this money stuff. Worry about getting laid or something, haha.

—Haha, yes, sir.

—Damn, can't believe you've been here a hundred days already. Remember our first night watch duty? I was low-key worried you'd pull a gun on me or something.

—Come on. No way. I would never do that, especially to my Private Lee, the very model of respect.

—Look at this slick operator, haha. But seriously, even on day one I could tell—you're gonna do something big. I'm kinda jealous of that. You know what you're capable of.

—Not really. You are the one who got stocks and Bitcoin going for you.

—Pssh, who cares about that? I just want to make some quick money. I only joined the military 'cause I couldn't pay tuition without a scholarship, and my jackass professor gave me a B out of spite last term.

—Oh… still, getting a scholarship is impressive.

—Not as impressive as graduating from Sudo High. Anyway, enjoy your first leave. Just don't do anything crazy, like going AWOL, haha.

—No worries, sir, I would never go AWOL.

chapter block
03.0

Do inhaled deeply, savoring every ounce of South Korean air outside the DMZ. Yes, he had weekends and holidays in high school too. But back then, he willingly threw those precious breaks into the flames, mere fuel for his ambition. Only now, after having the freedom forcibly stripped away, did he truly understand its true worth.

Collapsing onto the old mattress in his Gangnam studio, Do relished the softness he had longed for. After regaining a bit of stamina, he decided to do the most delightfully unproductive thing this generation could do: Instagram.

It took a bit, because he had to reactivate his account for the first time in months. He took a deep breath, bracing himself for the inevitable flood of updates. Soon enough, familiar faces began to fill the feed. It was comforting, at first, to be surrounded by these images from his past, thrown into a world of familiarity.

Then—*damn*. He should've stopped scrolling. Those familiar faces disarmed him, vulnerable to what came next—a painfully endearing photo of @junema_gic.

It was none other than his dear June Ma. She was standing in front of the fog-draped Golden Gate Bridge.

—Why do you wear glasses when your vision is sharp enough to count freckles on my face?

Do had once teased her. They were in the study hall around 1 a.m. Sudo High School allowed—more like encouraged—students to cram there until 3 a.m. So with their right hands, Do and June scribbled down notes; with their left, they secretly reached for each other, fingers intertwined, their couple rings brushing softly against each other's fourth fingers.

—Because of my dark circles, dummy. There aren't even lenses.

—Heh, didn't know that.

—Look, you could poke your finger right through! Just don't poke my eyes, hehe. June laughed in the most adorable way.

—You two! Keep it down. The supervisor would scold the couple.

He just never had the right timing to tell her how much he loved those dark circles, how her eyes sparkled behind those thick, lensless frames. He wished he had.

A tightness gripped his chest, regret surging through him. After the brutal string of rejections—from Harvard before Christmas, then Stanford and Yale after the holidays—he reached his breaking point. He cut himself off, vanishing from everyone's lives, especially hers.

June, gosh—I missed you. I missed you so much, and you look even cuter than before. Should he message her? He clicked and enlarged her cliched Golden Gate Bridge Instagram photo, a wave of endearment washing over him.

But he shouldn't have. When Do clicked her username @junema_gic to probe further, he was taken to the top of her Instagram profile. Two photos were pinned there. One was the Bridge photo. The other… was a photo of a letter.

A letter that began with the C-word. *Congratulations*. Not like the ones he'd received, the ones that started with the dreaded T-word. *Thank you for applying, but unfortunately…* And there, on the letterhead, was the proud tree logo of Stanford University, emblazoned in bold Cardinal Red.

@junema_gic: Stanford Class of 2020. Thank you to everyone who helped me along the way.

Her caption was as straightforward and confident as she had always been.

Of course. *Of fucking course.*

Of course June got into Stanford. A cold knot twisted painfully in his stomach. He should have known better when she posted that Golden Gate picture. And then another question nagged at him. Wait, who took that picture? If it had been her parents, they would've been in the picture too. Was there someone else with her? And why does the photo somehow carry a subtle warmth, a touch of affection he couldn't ignore?

He felt defeated, because he loved June's ambition as much as he loved June herself. He couldn't even name the emotion—longing, obsession, jealousy, self-loathing—an amalgamation of all coursing through him. So, all he could do was to deactivate his account.

"Why are you deactivating your Instagram account?" Instagram's automated question blinked on the screen. He ignored it and pressed the deactivate button again, but Instagram insisted he provide a reason.

Why on earth would you want like a 500-word essay explaining my reason for deactivation? Frustrated, his fingers shook as he typed out a long-winded rant in the space provided for just a few words.

@do_llarmoon: ...I'm deactivating this fuckin account because I screwed myself over by voluntarily locking myself in the DMz, because of all the opportunities I failed to seize, because my relentless drive answered every damn question wrong. i'm pathetically lost... But to think of it, it's kinda fucking unfair? if just one letter of acceptance had arrived, one shred of proof that I was right, that I was enough, everything would have been fucking fineee!!!!

Maybe I should've written my college application essay this candidly, he thought wryly. Knowing that no one at Instagram would read his rant, he found it easy to vent. With a heavy sigh, Do completed his impromptu essay for deactivation and tapped the "Temporarily Deactivate Account" button again.

But another Instagram notification flashed. "You can only deactivate your Instagram account once a week. Try again in 7 days."

—Oh, fuck you! You couldn't have told me that earlier?!

Do let out a frustrated scream, throwing his phone against the wall before picking it back up. The sound of impact was brief, but the helplessness lingered. He picked the phone back up, his hands moving in a pattern he had done a thousand times. He felt more useless now than he ever had in the barracks.

.

After a couple of hours wasted in the mindless abyss of web surfing, Do recalled Yohan's words about Bitcoin. Maybe a little dopamine hit would keep him from spiraling back into thoughts of June.

He found a Reddit post that gently walked him through setting up a cryptocurrency wallet. Click, click, click.

Donzo.

Do exchanged about 10,000 won for 22 Bitcoins. Watching his money transform into digital currency wasn't anything new—it was just like purchasing game credits in League of Legends. What he really wanted to know was whether he could actually buy something with Bitcoin. Reddit had a list of things people had bought with cryptocurrency: movie tickets (but he had no one to go with), brand new Nike shoes (but he can only wear military boots), and adult videos (which he scrolled past quickly). Then he saw it. Pepperoni pizza. Okay, let's go with this.

But this was Seoul. And Korean pizza places—unlike their U.S. counterparts—aren't accepting Bitcoin in spite of the tech-forward beacon its government aspired to be. Neither were the movie theaters or shoe stores. The only thing he could actually buy with Bitcoin was… adult videos from foreign websites since the internet knew no borders.

Do decided to make a purchase—yes, out of sheer curiosity. Click, click.

Ding. A notification popped up on his phone. *Wow, that was fast.* The transaction was a little too instantaneous. The guy on Reddit said it would take a few minutes. Do quickly swiped open the notification, expecting to see confirmation from his Bitcoin wallet—but perhaps too quickly.

It wasn't the Bitcoin wallet app. The notification came from Instagram app—specifically, from the username he knew all too well: @junema_gic. A DM[4] from June. Too late to disappear again.

@junema_gic: are you there Do
@junema_gic: when did you even deactivate your account??
@junema_gic: hey i can see you read this. you know there's a thing called read receipt right??
@do_llarmoon: heyy… erm june
@do_llarmoon: hi
@do_llarmoon: uh arent you in san fran now?
@junema_gic: san fran?
@do_llarmoon: oh nono nvm
@junema_gic: wait you mean my insta pic? ohh that was from the admit day

Admit Day. Right. You're the admitted one. I'm the rejected one. He almost typed it, but quickly erased it.

@junema_gic: im back in seoul
@junema_gic: you still living there right??
@junema_gic: i'll come over
@do_llarmoon: ? what

---

[4] Direct Message

@do_llarmoon: you coming over now? like now?
@junema_gic: yeah?
@junema_gic: its a 10 min walk
@junema_gic: you are on military leave rn right? you arent like
@junema_gic: AWOL or sth right?
@do_llarmoon: how do yuo know awol?
@junema_gic: i googled.
@do_llarmoon: oh no, no… not AWOL… haha I'm on my first leave. yeah
@junema_gic: k. will be there in 15
@do_llarmoon: uh june you wanna grab some coffee or something?
@do_llarmoon: and btw I haven't had the time to clean the place… sorry or maybe give me a sec to tidy up and i will DM you again
@junema_gic: i wont stay long
@junema_gic: dont bother

Do's heart raced not with excitement but with dread. The kind of fear that coils tightly in your stomach when you're about to be seen for what you really are. He wasn't going AWOL, yet her DM message felt like the cold, insistent knock of military police who came to catch him. His ex-girlfriend, who had accomplished everything she set out to do, was now coming to visit him—a man who seemed to be sinking deeper into nothingness. Instead of changing into civilian clothes, he stayed in his musty uniform, the scent of dust and barracks clinging to him as though it could somehow shield him from her judgment.

•

Ding-dong. The doorbell rang, followed by another Instagram DM notification.

@junema_gic: im here?

Do opened the door with great hesitation.

—...Hey, June.

—Hey.

Her face was as familiar as ever, yet her voice felt distant, foreign, carrying a quiet authority stronger than Captain Kim's—though June had never been the type to assert herself over anyone.

—...Look, June. I'm... I'm sorry. I don't even know where to start. About everything. For not staying in touch, and all the other things... whew. You uh... wanna come in?

—I told you I won't stay long. And why are you still in your uniform...? Did you just get off leave?

It felt like an interrogation to Do.

—Uh... yeah. Yeah.

—...That must've been tough.

A tingle of sympathy in June's voice. *Tough.* That single word of sympathy softened the knot of fear in his chest, reminding him that June was never there to judge or expose him but to soothe him—perhaps. June was that kind of person.

—June... I don't know how to make up for, like, disappearing on you for months. But when all the rejection letters came... you know how close I was to getting in. I just couldn't handle it.

—...And so you decided to go to the DMZ right away.

—I'm... I'm going to reapply to all the schools that rejected me.

—I heard from Mr. Sun that you didn't even finish applying to the rest of your schools. Is that true?

—I don't think I was wrong.

—...Hasn't the army changed you at all? I'm glad, in a way.

—I wasn't wrong about college. But, June, I was wrong about you. I should've at least called you. But I missed you, June. I really did...

Do stepped forward, intending to hug her, but sensing the distance between them, he stopped short. Instead, he stretched out his hand, cautiously intertwining his fingers with hers like they used to in the sacred Sudo High study hall. But as his five fingers brushed her five fingers, they were met with something unfamiliar. His eyes darted downward—a ring on her fourth finger. But it wasn't the one they had once matched together.

His chest tightened, his breath catching. *What... what is this?* Should he even ask? His gaze fell to the ring once more, then flickered back to her face. *Is that the ring you bought with whoever took that Golden Gate Bridge photo?* He didn't need to voice the question; the faint flinch in her body as his fingers grazed the ring already answered it. If he asked, it would open a door he wasn't prepared to walk through.

What about you? Wouldn't June ask him that? He conjured an imagined June in his mind, volleying questions back at him. *You vanished before Christmas and ghosted everyone.*

That's different! his mind howled, desperate to defend his silence. *I had to run because my world was falling apart. You got into Stanford. You're moving on, starting over, leaving everything behind.* In the privacy of his thoughts, he crafted an answer, spitting back at this phantom.

—Oh, hey there! Didn't see you standing here. Are you on your first leave?

The guy next door greeted, opening his door to take out the trash and spotting Do in his military uniform.

The interruption snapped both of them out of their silent exchange and back to the present. For Do, the weight of the situation crashed down on him all at once. He stood there, in his musty uniform, with no acceptance letters to his name, while June —dressed in stylish Off-White T-shirt and cute Miu Miu gray cotton hoodie—was on her way to Stanford. And that ring. That unfamiliar ring on her finger felt like a noose tightening around his throat.

—Do, you know there are still schools accepting late applications, right? With your grades, you could get in almost anywhere. Or you could transfer later.

—Ha, yeah. And you'll go off to Stanford and live happily ever after. Meanwhile, I'll be lucky to scrape into some safety school. Right?

—You are not hearing me.

—Well, then don't talk down to me like you are my senior. You think I haven't already gone over every possible option you just rattled off?

—Ha… June shook her head.

—Actually, no. Sorry, you are right. You *are* indeed my senior now. Maybe I should start calling you *nuna*, since you'll be a freshman at one of the finest universities in the world, and I'll be forever stuck in high school. No, it's worse. I'll be stuck in the goddamn DMZ!

—…Do. We're no longer in the kind of relationship where I'm going to indulge your sarcasm.

—So that's why you came here, right? To end things.

—Do.

—Yeah?

—Those days back in Sudo High were tough, weren't they?

—They were… but not because of you. It was because of Mr. Sun and…

—And because of your unquenchable ambition.

—…Yes, that too. You were the only… yeah, sure.

You were the only bright part of my time at Sudo High, June. Do was going to say that. But just like how he couldn't bring himself to tell her how cute her dark circles were under the lensless glasses, these words faded into nothingness, disappearing before they could be spoken.

—…It's over, isn't it? Do said, almost to himself.

—No. It's just that high school was one chapter, and now it's finished. We've graduated, Do.

That bittersweet smile. That selfish sweetness.

—I skipped the graduation ceremony, you know.

—Ha, yes. How could we forget that? The look on the principal's face when he called your name for valedictorian and you weren't there.

—A valedictorian who got his ass rejected by Harvard, Stanford, Yale. Who is, therefore, less than a leper.

—Yes, that's… that's how you see the world all the time.

That comment hit Do rather hard.

—...June, I knew this day would come.

—Oh, did you?

—Yeah. We're both the top of class—the valedictorian and the salutatorian. But we were different, too. I always knew that once you got into the school you wanted, your fire would burn out.

He unfurled the bitter truth he'd been holding back.

—That fire? It was never your own. It was just the fire Mr. Sun lit in for you. And look at your true colors—a cheerful hypocrite—pretending those brutal high school days were some beautiful memory. But I'll show you. Even if those pricks at Harvard decide to take me back, I'll never lose my fire like you did. I'll get into whatever fucking school I want, and I'll prove I was right.

She stood frozen, stunned by the cold fury of his unhinged rant. *Say something, June. Please.* Do's tirade had cut deeper than she expected, bruising her pride and leaving her momentarily speechless.

—Whoops, sorry to interrupt again! Hey, let's grab lunch sometime!

The guy next door reappeared from his trash run, cheerily breaking the tension between them.

—...I see.

June calmly remarked.

—That's it? "I see?"

—Yeah, that's it. You know I was always the more realistic one, right?

—...Yeah. You were. And you are. I'm the unrealistic, delusional one, so I will never succumb to reality. I'll never seek anyone's permission for anything.

—Good luck with that.

—Thanks.

—I'm leaving.

She said in a soft, trembling voice, gathering her emotions along with her things.

—You are?...

—Yes, I am.

—...Take care, June.

—You too, Do.

●

After June left even earlier than expected, Do remained holed up in his apartment. A half-eaten pepperoni pizza—not bought with Bitcoin, but with cash—sat cold on the floor. The room was still, thick with the remnants of her presence. He spent hours lying down, mindlessly trading various cryptocurrencies. Buy, sell, buy, sell. It wasn't about making money. Money never excited him, especially not now. Trading was simply a way to chase an instant dopamine hit—but even that was far from enough.

Too emotionally drained to lie still, he opened his laptop and sighed. He typed random phrases into the search bar, over and over, unsure of what he was looking for. His search meandered to mindless distractions—street fights, subway altercations on YouTube. He chuckled, like some primitive creature drawn to primal violence, the scenes dulling the edges of his thoughts. The people in the videos, and he himself, seemed no better than animals.

He shifted his pillow into a neck rest and, numbed by the hours of passive consumption, logged onto a porn site using a VPN. Bitcoin was listed as a payment option. Normally, a video cost 10,000 won, but with Bitcoin, it was only 20 BTC. Since he bought 22 BTC with 10,000 won, it's a 2 BTC discount. Perfect.

Wait... he glanced at the chart. The price of Bitcoin had surged by over 20%. Was this normal? He quickly checked the charts again, but before he could finish, the price plummeted again by 25%. The cost of the video remained at 20 BTC, but the value fluctuated between around 9,000 and 12,000 won before the 15-second preview even ended.

Well, this volatility matches my emotional rollercoaster perfectly. Seems like the right payment option. Click, click, purchase. 20 BTC—transaction complete. Click, click, purchase.

20 BTC—transaction complete. Bitcoin's price had surged by 18% just as he clicked, meaning he somehow ended up paying an extra won when you think of the exchange rate. Still, the crypto payment went through smoothly. Wow, so I can actually buy things with this digital money... though it's not exactly what I'd call "stable".

Unfortunately for Do, the porn only tangled his feelings further. Soft whispers of love, loud moans of affection. The couple on the screen were clearly in love with each other.

What the fuck are they doing? Do they think they're starring in La La Land or some sappy Korean drama? Porn is not supposed to be a goddamn love story. Maslow's hierarchy of needs, anyone? Porn is supposed to satisfy base desires, not this fantasy of love! Do shouted inwardly, bitterness lacing his voice, tinged with mania.

But who was there to listen? Do slammed the mute button in frustration, but the image of the loving porn stars lingered. His mind, already fragile, betrayed him, and he connected their adoring expressions to June and whoever her new lover might be. Fed up to the back teeth, he slammed his innocent laptop shut. Another wave of self-loathing washed over him.

Back when he was with June, they forged a triangle: him and June at each corner, with their shared ambition to reach the world's top universities at the pinnacle. We'd transcended mere physical desire for something greater, nobler. Or... was this lofty Platonic ideal just an ineffective defense mechanism? June's soft lips and the gentle dew left on them after their kiss floated through his mind. I shouldn't have preached myself about Maslow's hierarchy of needs. *Oh, fuck. Everything's just so fucked up.*

Only one thing was clear. The triangle they once forged and shared had collapsed, leaving behind a single, solitary line—from Do to his seemingly unreachable ambition.

If I called her, would she have turned back? Would she have taken off that new ring on her fourth finger? No. He knew the answer. She would've nonchalantly said something like this: Do, high school's over. We've graduated. Well said about not needing anyone's permission. I wholeheartedly agree. This is the beginning

of a new chapter, one where I don't need anyone's permission—
especially yours.

Ok, enough of this imaginary back-and-forth. June… I only
forgot to say one thing out of jealousy.

Congrat-fucking-ulations. You earned every bit of it.

I really mean the latter part, at least.

•

—Private Do-hyung Moon! Reporting back, sir.

—Hey, hey, hey, Mundo's back! Wait, but no donuts?

Sergeant Yoon narrowed his eyes at Do.

—Oh, I'm really sorry, sir… I'll bring some next time.

—No pretty nuna with you and no donuts… damn, what are
you good for, huh?

—Come on, Sergeant. You just carried the game with Top
Mundo, haha. Cut him some slack, please? Yohan chimed in with a
grin.

Everyone in the barracks knew Sergeant Yoon was terrible at
League, so it was obvious Yohan had thrown the match to give him
this rare taste of victory. But Sergeant Yoon, as simple-minded as
the Dr. Mundo champion he so adored, took the bait. His stern
expression cracked just enough to reveal a flash of self-
satisfaction.

—Fine. Mundo, you know I just crushed Yohan's Top Lucian
earlier, so I'll let it slide. How dare you bring a ranged champion to
the sacred Top lane! But seriously, don't forget the donuts next
time, rookie.

—Yes, sir! I'll make sure not to forget.

Sergeant Yoon waved him off, his heavy frame landed with a
dull thud—the sound of a man who had mastered the art of sloth.
Private Moon moved through the barracks, greeting his superiors
with a mechanical politeness that belied the turmoil beneath.
Maybe except Private Yohan Lee.

—Private Do-hyung Moon, reporting back, sir. And thanks
for covering me, Private Lee.

—It's all good, Mundo. How was the first leave? Wasn't it the sweetest 48 hours in your life?

Instead of confessing how close he'd come to going AWOL, Do handed Yohan the Bitcoin books he had asked for.

—Whoa, thanks! Must've been a hassle on your first leave, huh? Sorry about that.

—No, not at all. And just like you said, I made a Bitcoin wallet too.

—Oh, really? How was it? Fun, right?

—Yes. I actually made a couple of purchases, and it was… interesting.

—Wait, purchases? You actually bought something with Bitcoin?

—Yeah… a pepperoni pizza.

—What? There's actually a pizza place accepting Bitcoin? Where is it? I swear all those Pizza Huts and Papa John's don't take Bitcoin.

—Well... uh, yeah. A pizza place near my place just started accepting it.

—Oh right, Gangnam kids, huh? Those trendy pizza joints there must be picking up on it. You didn't, like, buy porn or something, did you? Haha.

—N-no, sir.

—Haha, just kidding. And like I said, no need to sir me. But man, the Bitcoin price is fluctuating too much. I might just cash out next week and throw it into Tesla—at least their chaos comes with wheels.

—That sounds like a good idea, sir.

—Oh, by the way, while you were on leave, Corporal Park got injured playing soccer… I know, tsk. So you and I have to cover for him tonight. It's night watch duty again. Tough break, huh? Right after you got back.

—No problem, sir.

—Damn, Mundo. You start to sound like a real soldier. No soul left in your voice or your eyes, haha.

●

Another soul-crushing night watch duty. Do gripped that cursed military radio like a lifeline in the bitter, unforgiving cold. The icy wind howled relentlessly, slicing through every layer of clothing as if his uniform were made of paper. His breath hung in front of him like frozen smoke, disappearing into the freezing void. His body ached, his skin burned from the cold, and it felt as if his bones were turning to ice. The DMZ was a battlefield against nature itself.

As part of their post-guard duty routine, Yohan handed him a steaming cup of ppogeuli. And a Marlboro Ice Blast cigarette, too. Same ramen, but always a new blessing. The noodles were still boiling, the steam rising like salvation, thawing Moon's frozen face just by holding the cup close.

—Here, eat this. It'll warm you up. Yohan said.

—Hew… thanks… Do muttered, his voice barely audible through his chattering teeth. He glanced at the cigarette Yohan offered, the cool menthol a cruel reminder of the frigid air surrounding them.

—I know. *Ice Blast*, ironic, huh? Hah. Go ahead, take a smoke. Yohan said. Up here, it's either ramen or cigarettes that'll get you through this kind of cold.

—…You know what, Private Lee, I'll save it for when I really feel like I'm going to shoot myself. Do replied.

—Alright, suit yourself. Good thing that you are not there yet. Yohan smiled.

With every sip of the hot ramen broth, Do could feel life slowly returning to his frozen limbs. Without Yohan's small gestures of kindness—mostly food—Do wasn't sure what he would've done. He was teetering on the edge.

Perhaps Do should've surrendered his first hundred-day leave. Tasting freedom only to lose it right after—no, tasting love only to lose it right after.

What time is it? By now, June had surely flown off to America. Oh, right. The timezone difference—he forgot about the gracious Pacific Time. She must have already landed at SFO, stepping out into the generous warmth of the California sun.

Six hundred and sixty six days, from reveille to lights out. That was how long he had left to serve—guarding an ancient military radio, frozen to the core in the dead of winter. As Solzhenitsyn wrote it, an extra day was added because there was a leap year.

chapter block
04.0

@do_llarmoon: Stanford Class of 2022. Thank you to everyone who helped me along the way.

Of course, you should know by now that Do didn't mean a single word of it. If he thanked anyone, it was himself. For his tenacity, for his relentless determination, for his ability to turn obsession into a guiding light. After Yohan completed his time and left the DMZ, there hadn't been anyone to help him along the way. Only that ancient military radio had stayed with him until the end as a hollow companion—like the more burdensome version of Wilson the Volleyball in *Cast Away*.

He stood post in the DMZ for more days than he cared to remember. He stopped counting long ago. It was about surviving another night, another hour, another bitter gust of wind. He rewrote his college essays in those stolen moments, layering on the feigned humility that his time in the DMZ was supposed to have instilled in him. When he finally finished his service and received his honorable discharge, the letter of acceptance he'd yearned for arrived soon after.

He reactivated his Instagram account and posted a picture of the acceptance letter — just like someone did two years earlier. Then, in a move he knew was petty, he unfollowed @junema_gic, only to follow her again. It was an empty gesture, nothing more than a notification sent her way.

The reactions from old friends poured in immediately, congratulatory DMs flooding his inbox—friends who hadn't bothered to ask how he was when he'd been rejected from all the Ivies. So Do knew better. He hadn't endured the grueling hours of DMZ, hadn't fought his way back to the top of the academic world, just to bathe in the shallow praise of social media.

•

The annual Sudo High School Alumni Reunion took place in early summer. It was a convergence of worlds—the returning alumni, from their U.S. campuses on summer break, mingling with the recent graduates soon to depart for their own journeys. The air buzzed with pride, anticipation, confidence—an air of having made it. They gathered at the Conrad Hotel in Yeouido, where the soon-to-be college freshmen wore suits, remnants of last year's Model UN competitions, as if to declare their readiness for the next level of the game.

Do was there, too, raising his champagne glass with the younglings. But the thirst that gripped him had long since transcended theirs. He wasn't one of them anymore.

A line from his favorite novel drifted into his thoughts. *The bliss of acceptance. But take care—it is no Gatorade after a pickup game with friends; it is the seawater sipped alone, an eternal thirst, yet thirsting anew with every salty swallow.* It was an apt description. No matter how much expensive champagne he drank, the thirst persisted.

Across the room, he spotted her. June—who hadn't yet liked his Instagram post, who hadn't sent a congratulatory DM or text—stood among the crowd, effortlessly distant. Should he go over and say hi first? Does she even know they will soon be classmates again at Stanford? He weighed the perfect moment to close the distance between them, but she was quicker. She caught his eye first and gave him a brief, polite smile—more a formality than anything—before turning away, stealing the moment he thought he controlled.

Tsk. Well, June, we'll have plenty of chances to run into each other in Palo Alto, he thought bitterly, biting down on the rim of his champagne glass.

Brimming with awe and admiration, younger students secretly glanced at Do. Would they still send him the admiring gaze at him if they knew what he was really thinking?

Yup, likely. Three years ago, these same students had watched him, mesmerized, as he stood on stage during their first Class Day at Sudo High, telling his story as a model student and soon-to-be valedictorian. And his acceptance to Stanford, albeit belated, after completing military service—it added even more flavor to his legendary feats.

—Yo, Do-hyung!

A somewhat familiar voice pulled him from his thoughts. Jay, fourth-ranked in their class back in their Sudo High days. Now at Brown.

—Hey, Jay. Long time no see.

These four words barely scratched the surface of everything that had happened since they last spoke. Jay, like the younger students, had no idea of the torment that simmered beneath Do's polished exterior.

—Man, so you really pulled it off in the end, huh? I knew you would.

—Haha, thanks. How's life at Brown?

—Rhode Island's nice. Small though. But the RISD girls are pretty, so no complaints. Dude, we should all meet up for Thanksgiving in New York.

—Cross-country from Stanford? That's a bit of a trek, haha.

—Haha, true. Or we could do it in Seoul. By the way… you and June…?

—We're on good terms. Or not-so-bad terms. But I don't see many people from our year here, besides you and her.

—Yeah, Ban Cheney and his boys were supposed to come today, but I heard they bailed when they found out you'd be here. Probably jealous. He's always been ticked that he couldn't beat you, and here you go proving it again.

—Haha, haven't heard his name in a while. It all feels kind of distant now. Was Mr. Sun able to make it here today?

—Oh, you didn't hear? No, he couldn't make it. Lucky me. But honestly, he would've been over the moon to see you. Oh, wait! Harvey! Rosa! Over here! Come on!

Two younger students approached Do timidly.

—Do-hyung, this is Harvey and Rosa, fresh graduates finally escaping Sudo High.

One of them piqued Do's interest—the one called Harvey. His excitement to meet Do was palpable, but there was a fine distinction in the kid's eyes. Unlike the others who looked up to Do as if he was some celebrity, Harvey looked up to him as if he found a kindred spirit, a fellow outsider, a man of unquenchable ambition.

And the kid was right. Do wasn't the Bill Gates type, feigning benevolence and telling people what they want to hear. No, he was more the Steve Jobs type—letting raw ambition and obsession radiate, even if it made people around him uncomfortable. Do recognized that look in the kid's eyes instantly. It wasn't admiration; it was recognition.

And this Harvey kid seemed to be the only one, apart from Do himself, without the Sudo High Class Ring on his finger. Or perhaps he'd never received one?

—It's a pleasure to meet you, *sunbae-nim.*

Harvey addresses Do with all the politeness he could muster. I'm Harvey. You probably wouldn't remember, but I actually saw you at the Class Day three years ago. And since then... well, so much has happened... I know you've been through a lot too... oh, sorry, I'm rambling.

—Are you... the one who dropped out of Sudo High and said you were going to Harvard?

—Yeah? Yeah! Oh, how did you...

Do smiled softly, rather uncharacteristic of him.

—Mr. Sun came to my barracks once, to the DMZ. We mostly talked about us, but he talked about you too.

—Oh... I see.

—It's okay. It was no one's fault. It was just inevitable—the way Mr. Sun ran Sudo High. And you know how he is. He's probably thrilled right now, seeing all these acceptance letters flooding in. "The desperation has finally blossomed into greatness!" he'd say, hah.

—Haha, yeah, that sounds like him.

Both took awkward sips of champagne, the bubbles fizzing quietly between them.

—So… are you going to Stanford? Harvey cautiously asked.

—Yeah, that's the plan. Have you ever been to Stanford?

—Uh… no. I've never been.

—I mean, I know nine out of ten Koreans would choose Harvard because, well, it sounds better. But do you know the biggest difference between Harvard and Stanford?

—Erm… probably the weather?

—Haha, besides the weather.

—I'm… I'm not so sure.

—The building names.

—The building names?

—Yeah. Most American universities name their buildings after historical figures or donors. Kennedy School, Adams House, William James Hall…

—Right, the Widener Library.

—Exactly. He was the one who died on the Titanic, right?

—Yes, Harry Widener. The Titanic guy.

—John Adams, John F. Kennedy—they're all giants. But they also only exist in history books—or in movies. Now look at Stanford's building names. The Gates Building, the Knight Center, the Yang Building. And these days, the Jensen Huang Building counts too. These people may have aged too, but they're still alive and kicking.

Harvey nodded, half-convinced, half-confused.

—Of course, people can see it differently. But I think of it this way. Harvard's buildings are named after people who ruled the past. Stanford's buildings are named after people who rule the present.

—Ah… I see your point.

—And honestly, I don't plan on graduating. I'm not heading to Stanford for a degree—I'm going there to start a business that will change the world, though perhaps not for the better.

—Like Zuckerberg?

—C'mon, you. Zuck's a Harvard guy. But yeah, he was smart enough to head to Palo Alto, knowing California was the only place to plant his ambition. He's the case in point that school doesn't matter anymore. No matter how great the school is, the essence of it never changes.

Before Harvey could ask what he meant by the essence of school, Do was already answering.

—In school, you always have to wait for someone's permission to succeed. And I'm so fucking done with asking for permission. School gives you steps; I want wings.

chapter block
05.0

When Do first stepped onto the campus of Stanford, he almost believed utopia had come to life. The cardinal red banners fluttered against the vibrant orange of the buildings, while Rodin sculptures stood scattered across the sprawling, manicured lawns. Here, the great minds of the world convened—renowned scholars, former presidents and cabinet members—mingling casually in the student cafeteria. Legendary venture capitalists lingered in nearby offices, ready to fund the next world-altering idea, just a few minute bike ride from his dorm. Every day, he rode under the shade of palm trees, basking in the Californian sun, his spirit swelling with the limitless possibility that this place promised. That was his freshman year.

Now, this was his sophomore year. The initial enchantment had dulled, replaced by an inevitable inertia. The promise of utopia had given way to the grind. He had declared his major in computer science, but his codes only amounted to a handful of neatly arranged websites and an impenetrable parade of compilers. This disgruntled sophomore was on his way to CS106: C++ Programming held in Hewlett 200. He was less interested in the subject than the name of the building—Bill Hewlett, the founder of HP. What he craved was something monumental, something that would etch his name into one of the school's buildings someday.

After enduring the morning lecture, he made his way to Panda Express, absentmindedly shoveling orange chicken and fried rice. His next lecture was at the Jen-Hsun Huang Engineering

Center. This class was his favorite, though. CS183C: Technology-Enabled Blitzscaling. This time, not just because of the building name. It was taught by none other than Reid Hoffman, the founder of LinkedIn, the PayPal mafia, a veritable god among the Silicon Valley elite. Unlike typical academic courses, Hoffman's class was an arena where titans of the tech world appeared on a weekly basis. Two weeks ago, it was Eric Schmidt of Google. Last week, Reed Hastings of Netflix. Each figure loomed larger than life, their very presence an exercise in self-restraint for Do, who struggled to maintain composure.

At the start of every lecture, Do scrutinized them, searching for cracks in their god-like personas. Are they mere mortals after all or are they truly deities? He felt the invisible barrier between him and their world slowly dissolve. By the time the lecture ended, he was electrified, certain that he had absorbed the very magic that made them titans. Their magic coursed through him, urging him to launch his own vision onto the world stage and imprint his legacy on the NASDAQ.

Do's delusions of grandeur were also fed by his proximity to greatness. Just last month, Evan Spiegel, a former classmate, dropped out of Stanford to launch an app called Snapchat. And it very soon became the tech industry's darling, even challenging Facebook.

The moment he stepped outside of the building after the lecture, however, Stanford's scorching sun hit his face, and the hot wind that followed crashed over him, bringing him back to earth and breaking the spell of his soaring ambitions.

Why not me? Do asked himself. Why couldn't I turn my delusions into reality? This thought gnawed at him, restless and relentless.

Cryptocurrency was the talk of the town, and Do dabbled in his own cryptocurrency project—though indistinguishable from the dozens of others, each one hoping to become the next Bitcoin. Reid Hoffman's lecture today was about money. Naturally, Hoffman would talk not about how to make money but about how to *make* the next money. Today, he invited a Wall Street titan. Do took his usual seat—second row, slightly to the right of the center. It was the perfect spot to focus, but more importantly, to be seen.

—What's good, Do?

His new friends didn't call him "Mundo." Apparently, League of Legends never reached the cultural dominance in the U.S. that it had in Korea. His professors and TAs struggled to pronounce "Do-hyung" during roll calls, so he dropped the "hyung." He was simply "Do." Again—no, not like *Just Do It*. Yes, like the extinct Dodo bird.

—What's up, Nik.

Nikitas Petrakis. From Greece. Top of his class at a prestigious Greek science high school, national debate team member, and a silver medalist at the International Philosophy Olympiad. A typical Stanford student.

—You should've come to Jerome's party last night, man.

—Yeah, shoosh. Something else came up.

—Hey, Do. A familiar voice, one that caused a small ripple in his chest.

—Oh... June. Hey, hi.

Maybe it was her. Maybe she was the reason for this persistent hunger. More than a year passed since their breakup and unlikely reunion at Stanford, followed by a whirlwind of angry texts, i-do-love-you texts, a second breakup, and breakup songs. Yet June always seemed unaffected by the drama, greeting him with the same cool and detached decibel. Maybe it was her. But no —Do tells himself that his ambition was driven by something far larger than the ghost of an old love.

—I get it, Do. Nik teased, his grin mischievous.

—The hell are you talking about?

—All great startups are born out of an ex-girlfriend, right?

—Oh, shut up, man, haha.

—So, how's that Bitcoin project coming along?

—No more Bitcoin. I think I should dig deeper into this thing, the stablecoin.

—What's that? Doesn't sound very stable when you slap "coin" at the end of it.

49

—Hah, true that. It's like Bitcoin but with a price fixed at a dollar.

—Okay, if it's really that stable, perhaps Kim Jong-un can adopt it as North Korea's national currency. They can hack it from other countries anytime when they need a quantitative easing. So, then, how's your stablecoin project going so far?

—It's going great.

—Sure it is, heh.

—Okay, fine, it's killing me. Remember when the Y Combinator guy—Sam Altman from last month said to start small, with a minimal viable product, and scale from there once it's proven?

—Yeah, but I guess your coin project is like... it's like VMware. You don't need a market. You don't need customers. The product itself creates its own market and customers.

—Yes, exactly! Like Steve Jobs said—people don't know what they want until they see it. Nobody knew they needed an iPhone until it existed. I just—I need to create something so good that it bypasses permission. People will crave it. They won't even think to question it.

—Well, I saw you pushed a new commit last night. Was that for the bridge functionality or... oops, Hoffman's here. Let's talk more later, haha.

—Yup. And there's Ken Greenspan. I don't get why Hoffman invited a hedge fund guy, though. Shouldn't he have invited the Ethereum or Ripple guys?

—I think so, too. But dude, look at him. Have you ever seen human eyes that shiny and blue? Did you ever play *Yu-Gi-Oh* back in Korea?

—Yeah, back in elementary school. Why?

—Dude, if the Blue-Eyes White Dragon became a human, that guy's eyes would be it.

—Haha, oh my lord, shut up, Nik. If he heard you, he'd bury you in billion dollar bills.

Do laughed, maybe a little too loud. His voice must've carried across the room, as June shot him an annoyed glance. Good, he thought, let her notice me.

—Afternoon, everyone. Today's esteemed guest has flown in all the way from Wall Street. Let's give a warm welcome to Sitadel's founder and chairman—Mr. Kenneth Greenspan.

A billionaire introduced another billionaire. Applause filled the room.

—Thank you, Mr. Hoffman. I debated wearing a Patagonia vest on my way here. Greenspan said, smirking. But I figured you students would see right through that. So I stuck with the usual Brioni.

When billionaires speak, even their breathing seems to spark laughter and admiration, Do mused, his mind drifting away from the lecture—back to his project, back to the restless ambition gnawing at his core.

—Mr. Greenspan, could you share a bit about how you got started—perhaps not just the Sitadel days, but dating back to your college days? Hoffman asked.

—Well, sure, though I might have to date back quite a bit, haha. I wasn't doing anything particularly remarkable before college. Grew up in Florida, did well enough in school, math and software were my things. Got lucky enough to get into the best school in the world.

—Oh, Stanford? Hoffman teased.

—Oh no, the exact opposite. Just a small, sad old college in New England.

The room erupted in brief laughter at his smug, self-deprecating joke.

—So at Harvard, I heard you ran into some trouble in your junior year? Hoffman asked.

—Yeah, most young people today don't know about it…

—Sorry to interrupt, Mr. Greenspan, but you're not even fifty yet.

—Haha, compared to today's young entrepreneurs, though, I'm ancient. But for the record, everyone, Mark Zuckerberg wasn't the only student breaking Harvard's rules to start a business.

—Oh, please share with us what kind of rule you broke.

—Sure, back in my day, Harvard's rules were much stricter. They had a policy prohibiting running any form of business inside the dorms.

—That sounds frustrating just hearing about it.

—Right? And this was pre-internet days. To you guys, that sounds prehistoric. Back then, there was no way to check stock prices in real time as there was no Internet whatsoever.

—But you couldn't just skip class and hang out at the exchange on Wall Street either.

—No, I had to maintain my grades for Plan B, which was becoming employee number 100 at some Wall Street firm. But then it hit me—there actually was a way to check stock prices in real time without leaving the campus.

—What was that?

—You Stanford students are so tech-savvy, so you might laugh at it. But the technology I employed was… none other than a satellite dish.

—A satellite dish?

Hoffman sounded amused. Or at least he pretended to be, because these billionaires probably already knew every detail about one another.

—Yep. But the problem with satellite dishes was…

—You have to set it up somewhere outside.

—Exactly. You can't just stick a satellite dish inside your dorm room. But I was determined to install it, no matter what. So, naturally, I put it up on my dormitory roof.

—A dorm roof? Wow, haha, I'm guessing the housemaster wasn't exactly thrilled?

—Nope. Well, he only found out later, because I didn't exactly ask for permission in advance, haha.

Do caught that word—*permission*—and something clicked inside him. So, there were others before me who faced the world with the same playbook. Greenspan was decades ahead, but the essence remained the same. The blue-eyed billionaire continued his college trading saga.

—I ran the cable down the wall, through a hallway window, and into my room. Once I had it hooked up, I could check stock prices in real time. After that, I started arbitraging convertible bonds for profit.

It was a familiar tale—the boy genius breaking the rules to become a billionaire. Yet, no matter how many times it was told, it never lost its allure. And to season it a bit more, June was listening even more attentively than before, which made Do's own attentiveness amplify in proportion.

—So, Mr. Greenspan, you didn't face any punishment for violating the rules? Installing a satellite dish, running cables around the dorm—that's practically setting up your own private exchange at Harvard! Haha.

—Oh, there were consequences. The housemaster got a little upset, sure. But I wasn't going to ask for permission when I could ask for forgiveness later once I become successful. And I think I have—to a certain extent.

Greenspan replied with a touch of rote humility, and Hoffman smiled with a rote affirmation.

—Of course you did!

—Appreciate it, haha. Here's what I learned and what I hope you all will take away. If I had gone around asking permission to install that satellite dish, Sitadel wouldn't exist today. Instead, I made profits with my little satellite gig, built Sitadel, and eventually donated millions to Harvard so students could live in better dorms without worrying about tuition—or the dorm roof. I believe that is a happy ending for everyone.

Not bad. Actually, more than not bad. Do absolutely loved the idea of not asking for permission, even if Greenspan's utilitarian philosophy didn't particularly resonate with him.

Now came the part where the Q&A began—the part where idiots inevitably waste everyone's time with ridiculous questions. Do opened his laptop and resumed coding.

—Hello, Mr. Greenspan. I'd love to intern at Sitadel and help bridge finance and computer science. What kind of interns are you looking for?

—Hello, Mr. Greenspan. Do you consider yourself self-made?

Seriously? Is there some unwritten rule that the dumbest students are always the ones to ask the first questions? Do thought, his fingers tapping away at the keyboard.

But the next question wasn't so dumb. In fact, it was precisely the opposite.

—Hello, Mr. Greenspan. Do you think the dollar can be replaced?

—Hmm. I think it's unlikely. Although Yuan has certainly become a force to be reckoned with.

Greenspan's answer sounded somewhat off-topic. The questioner tilted her head slightly, an almost imperceptible gesture that hinted at more.

—My apologies, sir. Maybe I wasn't clear. Do you think money itself could be replaced by a different kind of currency?

The accentuation on the "different" was unmistakable. She meant the cryptocurrency.

—Hmm, that's a good question. And I like that you didn't call crypto a "new" currency, but rather a "different" one.

A flicker of amusement passed across Greenspan's face. It looked like he tested her if this was another stupid question wasting his expensive time—and her question passed the test.

Do looked back and saw the voice of a question. A girl stood with quiet poise, her bobbed hair framing her face neatly. She wasn't tall, but she exuded a confidence that belied her stature. She had a beautiful olive skin tone, a rare blend of heritage—somewhere between Asian and Latinx—that added to her enigmatic presence. She wore thick rimless glasses—functional, not fashionable, certainly not to conceal dark circles. Her eyes glinted behind frames, a captivating sharpness in them that commanded attention. And what stood out most was her auditory presence than the visual. Her accent flowed smoothly, each syllable placed with precision and deliberate rhythm that made her voice compelling.

Though interest flashed in his eyes, Greenspan's response carried a trace of cynicism.

—Let me be clear on this, though. There will always be only one real currency—the fiat currency, the dollar. For centuries and likely long afterward, money is money. It's immutable. We trade it. We trust it because of its intrinsic value.

—But what if blockchain technology could fundamentally redefine what it means to be a currency? The bespectacled girl pressed on.

—Look, cryptocurrencies like Bitcoin and Ethereum— they're all the rage, especially among the younger crowd in places like this.

Greenspan's gaze swept the room, his words steady, as resolute as the old, powerful fiat currency he defended.

—Yes, indeed. But I think blockchain is more than just a passing trend.

—I have to say, I view Bitcoin as a 'jihadist against the dollar.' It may sound extreme, but cryptocurrencies lack the stability and the economic foundation of real money. They have no inherent substance, and without that, they lack the most critical element of currency—trust.

Greenspan's answer was meant to quell her rising tides of dissent, but she still didn't back down one bit. Almost all students —tech-savvy enough to light up at blockchain's mention—nodded in tacit agreement with the message of the brave young girl. Yet, none dared to challenge the messenger on the opposing side—one of the world's most successful hedge fund managers.

—But I believe that, with blockchain, we can achieve something mankind has never managed to accomplish before.

The crypto Joan of Arc continued, unflinching.

—Oh, and what could possibly be that?

Greenspan's curiosity piqued, though laced with skepticism.

—Programming the trust.

—…Haha, I see you're definitely a computer science major.

Light laughter rippled through the room, but neither the girl nor Do joined in. Her answer was simply too good for laughter. *Yeah... Programming trust.* That's a brilliant point. That was indeed the raison d'être of blockchain.

Sensing the electric current in the room, Hoffman leaned in, ready to stoke the flames of debate.

—Remember, everyone, this isn't just a Q&A—it's a debate. Challenge your fellow students, challenge Mr. Greenspan. The idea of reshaping currency has the potential to spark something revolutionary.

June, who had been nodding in sync with Greenspan's points, seized the opportunity to enter the fray, countering the bespectacled girl.

—I respectfully beg to differ with the idea that crypto can replace fiat. As Mr. Greenspan said, money isn't just about technology; it's about trust—economic and social trust. Trust isn't a few lines of code, and it can't be executed with a keystroke. If money could be reduced to data, then tulips could've been money too, like during the tulip mania. And at least tulips had intrinsic value as beautiful flowers.

Oh, gosh. June... not the tulip analogy again. That's just so lame. Do could feel his irritation rising. Was it her argument or just her presence that provoked him? Perhaps both.

—I *respectfully* beg to differ. Crypto is not a tulip. It's not going to crash and burn like during the tulip mania. And I honestly think that analogy is overused and inaccurate.

Do interjected, his voice rising, compelled into the fray.

—Well, I beg to differ again, *respectfully*, mister! They're indeed very similar—starting with the lack of fundamentals to wild price volatility.

June's voice struck back, the heat of debate spurring her on. Nik, sitting beside Do, smirked, clearly enjoying what was beginning to look more like a lover's quarrel than an intellectual debate on the future of money.

—Stocks on NASDAQ fluctuate, too. Do shot back.

—Sure, but those stocks have financial statements—underlying value and numbers to justify the price swings to a certain extent. Comparing crypto to traditional stocks is apples and oranges. So, back to the main point—do you really believe a mere piece of data, or tulips for that matter, can ever replace fiat currency?

Do was formulating a sharp retort for his ex-girlfriend. But the bespectacled girl reentered the ring of debate with a simplicity and elegance that eclipsed anything he had prepared in mind.

—Stable tulip.

—Excuse me? June blinked, visibly taken aback.

—Then how about a *stable tulip*? A tulip valued at one dollar, and it stays that way.

June regarded the girl as though she'd just uttered an absurdity. But Greenspan's expression shifted. He leaned forward, gripping the mic, intrigued by the girl's proposition.

—Are you talking about stablecoins?

—Yes, sir. The stablecoins. I agree with the volatility issue she raised, but with stablecoins, that's not a problem anymore. You don't have to worry about your coin being worth one cup of coffee today and a house tomorrow. Stablecoins maintain a consistent value. Bitcoin and Ethereum dominate the headlines now, but the future of cryptocurrency extends beyond them. Tether, for example, has already surpassed a market cap of 10 billion dollars, and it's still growing—although, to be fair, Tether has its own issues.

She cleared her throat and continued, reasserting her point.

—If cryptocurrencies like stablecoins can mirror the stability of fiat currency, why can't they replace it entirely?

Stablecoins. Do's mind latched onto the concept. Stablecoins, as she'd articulated, can maintain a stable value, usually tied to the U.S. dollar through collateral. Tether was one such example, pegged to the dollar, ensuring that 1 Tether equaled 1 dollar. No wild price swings, no volatility—it offered the convenience of crypto with the stability of traditional currency. In theory, it was the perfect blend of old and new.

—That's a solid point.

Greenspan acknowledged his dissenter, giving her due credit.

—Thank you.

And she accepted his compliment with quiet confidence. Do found himself nodding along too, truly appreciating her insight—not in a bid to one-up June this time. He was genuinely intrigued by the crypto Joan of Arc. Detecting the heightened energy in the room, Greenspan decided to probe deeper and threw an agenda.

—Stablecoins like Tether are indeed interesting, but let me ask you this. Does anyone know *how* 1 Tether could equal 1 dollar?

Do's competitive side flared. As he'd mentioned to Nik at the start of the lecture, his own cryptocurrency project was fortuitously pivoting toward stablecoin, so he wanted to show Greenspan—or maybe June—that he understood the intricacies involved.

—Tether is pegged to the U.S. dollar by holding reserves of fiat currency and cash equivalents. Each Tether token is backed by assets, guaranteeing 1:1 redemption.

Do replied, confident in his answer. Greenspan nodded.

—That's right. The pegging. But is pegging really the essence of Tether?

—Yes, the blockchain technology behind the pegging... I believe that's the essence of stablecoins like Tether.

—No, I'm not simply talking about the technology. I am asking about the *real* essence. Let me put it this way: if the essence of Tether is pegging, then what is the essence of pegging? Distill your thinking to the very core.

Greenspan countered, his voice carrying a deliberate edge. Do faltered. He sensed a trap being set.

—Let's say 1 billion Tethers have been issued. To keep their value at 1 dollar per Tether, what has to happen?

—Erm...

Before Do or anyone could respond, Greenspan continued.

—There must be 1 billion dollars to back those Tethers. Without that collateral, the value collapses. Tether doesn't generate its own value. It's entirely dependent on the U.S. dollar. So, what's the real essence of Tether? It's the U.S. dollar.

Damn... he's right.

—No matter how innovative Tether might appear, it's a derivative of the dollar at its core. Without the dollar, Tether wouldn't exist. So, do you really think Tether—or any other stablecoin—is capable of replacing the dollar?

Greenspan's words were calm but landed with weight. The room fell silent, and Do felt the blow. He reeled from the realization that stablecoins, for all their innovative edges, weren't standalone inventions. They were inextricably linked to traditional currency.

The hedge fund king hadn't dismissed cryptocurrency out of ignorance; he understood it more profoundly than anyone else in the room, perhaps except the bespectacled girl.

Damn, I should've just shut my mouth. Mortified by the total defeat in front of the class—and in front of June, no less—Do consciously turned away, unwilling to meet her eyes. Sensing the room's tension, Hoffman, ever the skillful moderator as well as entrepreneur, intervened to soften the blow.

—Haha, well, that was a spirited debate! Who knows— maybe someone in this room will redefine what money means some day. Speaking of which, let's hear from you all. How did you first get into cryptocurrency? Samantha, have you ever used Bitcoin, Ethereum, or stablecoin?

—Uh... I once bought a Hawaiian pizza with Bitcoin. And yes, pineapple *does* belong on pizza. Samantha quipped.

—I secretly ran a mining program on the lab computers. Please don't report me. George confessed. It blew my mind that you could create money using just a few lines of code. Well, not exactly a few lines, but you get the point.

—Our campus is all about tech, so there's definitely a shortage of love here. I'm sure a few of us have used Bitcoin for... certain love-related videos. Oh, don't laugh—I know you guys have all been there.

Nikitas's candid confession earned chuckles from the audience, even coaxing a smile from Greenspan. Amid the laughter, Do was quick to see his chance for redemption. He needed a better reason for how he came to use crypto apart from pizza and pornography. He needed a story. Something profound. *Oh, right!* The Korean boy on a quest to reclaim his pride cleared his throat, raised his hand, and let his sharpened resolve take center stage.

—Yes, Do? Hoffman gestured toward Do.

—I started seriously thinking about cryptocurrency... while I was serving in the army.

—Oh, that's interesting. Thank you for your service. Hoffman responded.

—Thank you. It was actually the Korean army. I was stationed in the signal patrol unit at the DMZ.

The mention of the DMZ was a suitable beginning to catch everyone's attention. Especially for the American students, the DMZ was a distant, almost mythic place—something from war documentaries, a no-man's land frozen in a tense standoff. Do continued his parable.

—Every night, as a private, I'd stand watch on a mountain for four or five hours straight. Armed with five rounds of ammo, two grenades, and a bunch of KitKats. But the most important thing was this old military radio, which looked like it was pulled straight from the Korean War. It seemed like the most useless thing in the world, even heavy. But I slowly grew attached to it in the freezing, lonely DMZ guard post. Kind of like Tom Hanks with that Wilson volleyball in Cast Away.

Classmates laughed.

—Interesting. What was the old military radio for? Hoffman asked, his curiosity piqued as well.

—At first, they wouldn't tell me why I was lugging that ancient thing up the mountain. But then I found out—there is no central communication system among bases in the DMZ. Everything relies on these military radios. If war breaks out, the first target will be the telecommunication system. North Korea could hack, destroy, or disable all our networks.

Hoffman leaned forward, intrigued, though unsure of the connection.

—That's a uh, fascinating story, Do. But how does it relate to blockchain or cryptocurrency?

—Well, I realized I was basically part of a human peer-to-peer mesh network along the Korean border. Hundreds of soldiers, all decentralized, each playing a role in keeping the system running. Which is the essence of blockchain.

—Ah-ha!

Hoffman's eyes lit up, the analogy clicking into place. And Do continued, gaining momentum.

—Think about it. The U.S. dollar is like a highly advanced communication network—centralized, efficient, tightly controlled. Issued and managed by a central authority that grants permission for its use. That's its strength. That's where it gets its stability and trust — its intrinsic value.

He paused, letting the room absorb his words. Then, locking eyes with Greenspan, he pressed on.

—But that's also its weakness. Everything depends on the permission from the top. Now, take that old military radio I carried. It was slow, outdated, almost primitive. But if North Korea destroyed our central command or if our captain turned out to be a North Korean spy, the communications would still work just fine. Why? Because we soldiers—me, my superior, my superior's superior—are all independent nodes of the network. Even without the central hub, the network stays alive.

It was unusual for a student to speak at such length in front of a guest like Greenspan, but Do was on a roll now, and he couldn't stop.

—As Mr. Greenspan pointed out... the things that don't require permission to operate—that's what's valuable. Stability and trust, through decentralization. And the stablecoin is the embodiment of that idea, in the form of money. And that's the true intrinsic value of cryptocurrency—the value we should all recognize.

He was fully engrossed in his own argument now, and the room was with him. The class was captivated by his impassioned take on the philosophy of decentralization.

—So, erm, with all due respect to Mr. Greenspan's points, I believe stablecoin does have the potential to become a full-fledged currency. Because with stablecoin, stability isn't just about price; it's stability through and through.

His thoughts—shaped by nights spent on freezing mountains and honed in solitude—had been knit into a coherent, powerful message. The grand finale of today's lecture came from a 20-year-old student from Korea. The room was still absorbing Do's DMZ-to-stablecoin parable.

—What's your name?

And then Greenspan asked, breaking the quiet.

—Oh, Do-hyung Moon... sir. Just Do.

—Mr. Moon. I still think this cryptocurrency or stablecoin craze isn't all that different from tulip mania centuries ago. And at Sitadel, we don't hire people based on one clever answer.

—Y-yes.

—But sometimes, a single answer can change a life. In fact, that's what investing is—a perfect answer at the perfect timing. I found your philosophy very intriguing, and I like smart people who challenge me.

—I agree. That was indeed an excellent answer, Do. Hoffman nodded in agreement.

Is this really happening? Do thought, pulse quickening. The titans of Wall Street and Silicon Valley—praising me?

Greenspan stood, checking the time.

—Well, it's unfortunately about time. This has been truly enjoyable, everyone. I may not be a legendary VC like Mr. Hoffman here, who can help grow your company from infancy. But if you do become big enough to go public on NASDAQ, come find me at Sitadel. Especially you, Mr. Moon.

—Haha, Mr. Greenspan, thank you so much for joining us today. Some of my students and I will see you at TechCrunch tomorrow. Hoffman said.

—Yes, I'll see you all there. And thanks again for hosting this wonderful event.

—Everyone, let's give Mr. Greenspan a big round of applause. And don't forget, next week, we'll have Sam Bankman-Fried, CEO of FTX, as our guest. The reading list will be sent out tomorrow!

Applause filled the room, but Do was still in a daze, barely registering the sound. *Especially you, Mr. Moon.* Greenspan's words still echoed, reverberating with a weight that settled deep. He had stepped into a room of giants—and walked out with their attention. Moments like these leave a mark, become a part of you, and change you irreversibly. Once touched by such gravity, there's no return to the ordinary—whether for better or worse.

chapter block
06.0

—Go Cardinals, go!

It was the Big Game—Stanford's annual football rivalry with UC Berkeley. For both schools, this was the event of the year, a fierce showdown between Cardinals and Bears. Stanford was playing away at Berkeley. Do halfheartedly joined his friends to the north of San Francisco for the match.

—Go Bears, go!

—Let's go Bears! Boom-boom, let's go!

The Berkeley cheering squad exploded with energy, their chants overpowering the rival chants.

—Wow, is that Berkeley's cheer squad? They're so, like, overly energetic, haha.

This is Aaron Kim, Do's not-so-close friend.

—Probably because they've lost to us three years in a row. They sound desperate. Another friend added.

—Or it's probably the bear-beheading ceremony someone posted online yesterday? The video got like 3,000 likes. I thought a bit too much, haha.

—Oh yeah, haha, saw that on your Instagram. Why did they make it look so real?

Suddenly, loud cheers erupted, snapping the crowd back to attention.

—Yo, was that a touchdown?

—Looks like it. Does that mean we've won? Actually, wait, this kinda sucks.

—How come? We just won.

—Ha, well, for the Berkeley-Stanford Korean Student Association meetup tonight, the winning school has to buy dinner. Apparently, losing the game *and* footing the bill ruins the Bay Area Korean camaraderie.

—Hey, I had nothing to do with Stanford's win today. The Bay Area spirit can shoot itself. Where's dinner? Eureka Pub?

—Nah, they moved it to Berkeley Social Club.

—Great. A Korean Student Association meetup at a Korean restaurant.

—Haha, Berkeley Social Club isn't exactly legit Korean food, though.

Aaron turns to Do.

—Do, you coming to the KSA meetup after this?

—Hmm? Uh… not sure. Do wasn't inclined to spend his capital on useless things.

—June might come, too, you know. Aaron grinned.

—Oh, shut up, haha.

Even though he tried to laugh it off and not to notice, Do was acutely aware of her presence a few rows behind him, just slightly to his left. Aaron, ever the bearer of the unsolicited news, told him that June was dating someone new—a junior from Rhode Island, majoring in Symbolic Systems, yada yada. Not that Do had any plans to speak to her at the KSA dinner. He just didn't want her spending the entire evening with that guy, though he knows full well he has no business for her dating affairs.

As another roar surged from the crowd, Do glanced where June sat. Fortunately—or unfortunately—he didn't catch her face with its tiny Stanford "S" logo painted on her right cheek. But his gaze landed on something else—a new silver round object glinting on her ring finger. *Nice design, huh? Swarovski?* He winced internally. He could feel his pulse quicken, a familiar churn of emotions. Damn it, why the heck did I look back?

Aaron noticed Do's visible unease and chuckled.

—Bro, I'm the one heading to the military next semester, so your odds of finding a new love are way better than mine, probabilistically speaking.

—Ha, you had to pull the military card. Fine, I won't complain.

—I'm telling you, Do, you were smart to get this military stuff over with early. Gosh, I heard someone even cut his own Achilles to avoid conscription. Sucks that I don't have that kind of courage, haha.

—…Yeah, I guess. Since you will soon become a proud member of the Korean Navy, better start practicing your swim strokes if you plan to go AWOL.

—Ha, don't remind me. I've been hitting the campus pool nonstop for that combat swimming at boot camp. Check out these shoulders—getting huge, right?

Aaron went on, flexing his pathetic muscles.

—It's great to get in shape when there won't be a single pretty nuna in the Navy. Or maybe there is, but odds are dismal.

Aaron continued whining. Do, of course, was sincerely not interested in Aaron's misfortune.

—Yeah, tragic.

—By the way, June asked me about your coin project the other day. Stable money or something? What's that about?

—Wait, June asked you about my stablecoin project?

An unanticipated flicker of excitement.

—Uh, yeah. Heard her new boyfriend is the VP of the Stanford Blockchain Club or something.

Aaron certainly had one talent: being a killjoy, likely on purpose.

—Huh, okay. Sure. Because those blockchain club guys are definitely the century's experts on blockchain and stablecoins.

—Haha, sorry, man. Didn't mean to make you feel worse.

—Nah, it's fine. But seriously, stablecoins are legit. I don't think June would get it anyway. Most crypto people just hype their coin, write shitty whitepapers, pump prices, and bail. But stablecoin? It will be the new currency, man. Do makes an emphatic speech, though mostly for himself.

—Yeah, yeah, totally. Uh, I read on my LinkedIn feed that Binance—or was it Gemini—is doing something similar. You saw it?

—What?!

Do's heart sank. He quickly pulled out his phone and searched it up. Binance had just announced a stablecoin called BUSD.

Oh, but hew. A relief washed over him. It was not the kind of stablecoin Do had in mind. It was just another Tether—a stablecoin pegged 1:1 to the US dollar.

—Man, you almost gave me a heart attack.

Do said, glancing sideways at Aaron. He certainly did have another talent—playing dumb while skillfully getting under people's skin with that stupid grin of his.

—Oh, my bad, haha. I don't know jackshit about coins. So, it's different from what you're working on, right?

—Yeah, totally different. They're just stacking dollar reserves and pegging their coin to it. It's never the same.

It prompted Do to reflect on his plan. The fact that crypto giants like Binance were moving into the stablecoin space only reinforced his belief that his project had potential. Yet from another angle, if only the giants were entering the field, was he—a lowly college sophomore—charging down a road that wasn't his to take? Most startups began with simple apps that users love right away, building upward from there. Here he was, however, imagining a new decentralized bank, pursuing what felt like a fantasy, wondering if he was stumbling forward without any real steps to hold him up.

The final whistle of the Big Game blew, and the stadium swelled with chants of "Go Cardinals." Do glanced back at June again. She was chatting and laughing with that honorable Stanford Blockchian Club VP guy. And that tiny Stanford "S" logo painted on her beautiful cheek crinkled with each smile.

Do's own mood crinkled too. And she was already a senior, about to graduate and step out into the real world. He felt like he was perpetually a step behind, forever late to every chapter of life.

—So, Do, you are not coming to the KSA dinner?

Aaron asked. Do held back from saying the KSA dinner can go fuck itself.

—Uh… nah. I think I'll skip it and work on my project. But let's get hammered in your dorm next week before your farewell party. Do said.

—Oh, hell yeah. Hey, Do, and if your coin project takes off, let me know. I'll jump in as a seed investor for you, haha.

—Ha, yeah, I'll let you know if that day ever comes.

•

Do bolted from the stadium, weaving through the endless stream of crowds spilling into the streets like a massive migration. With so many people packed into one place, taxis and Ubers were nowhere to be seen. Bus lines stretched infinitely, and with traffic control in place, the whole situation was a nightmare. BART? No thanks. By the time he got off, his throat would be coated in dust.

Thank god he brought his laptop. He gave up on joining the herd back to Palo Alto and decided instead to wait it out in Bear territory until the chaos cleared. Swimming against the human current pouring out of the stadium, he made his way back to Berkeley campus.

Searching for a place to work, he soon realized he'd been wandering in peaceful oblivion, strolling for half an hour across the moonlit campus. The crowd had long since thinned, leaving only the crisp rustling of leaves in the breeze. He visited Berkeley before, but never in the quiet of evening.

Do was—how to put it—*defamiliarized*. It carried a certain romance of nature, one not found in the neatly arranged symmetry of Stanford.

As the sun dipped lower and the campus grew quieter, the evening air settled over the now-empty pathways, and he found himself winding through silent, tree-lined paths. The trees at Berkeley were also different, almost irreverent. At Stanford, everything was structured—trees that looked as if plucked straight from the school's logo, perfectly shaped, perfectly spaced, postcard-ready in every detail. But here, at Berkeley, the trees grew in whatever direction the sunlight nudged them, wild and free. Alone, each might not be the prettiest sight, but together, they created a presence, little groves scattered like a miniature Muir Woods across the campus.

Ahead of him loomed Berkeley's iconic ivory tower. To his left, a grand building caught his eye; it turned out to be a biochem library. And even better, no student ID was required for entry. *Guess this is the spirit of the commune.*

Inside, the library was hushed, filled with studious scholars, each one claiming a little world of their own. No one here seemed to care that a football game had just unfolded outside. They typed away, heads bowed, immersed in their work, completely absorbed in their tasks. Blending in with these focused minds, Do finally felt at ease.

•

—Excuse me, hello?

A voice interrupted his thoughts, and Do turned to see a girl who looked oddly familiar.

—Hi there. I'm afraid this library is only for Berkeley students.

The girl spoke, and it wasn't in English. Her words carried the charm of imperfect yet earnest Korean.

—What? Oh, oh, I'm so sorry…

Do stammered, feeling caught off guard.

—Especially today, since we lost the Big Game, Stanford students are definitely not allowed here. Her tone was rather playful, almost teasing.

—Oh... right. I'm sorry. Wait, are you with the Berkeley Korean Student Association?

Do asked, trying to make sense of the moment. Instead of answering, she responded with her own question.

—How is the stablecoin project going?

—Huh?... You're not, like, following me or anything, are you?

Do now looks even more confused now. He wasn't joking—he was pretty serious.

—Heh, I am afraid you are not that big of a deal—yet.

She smirked, clearly reveling the asymmetry of information. And Do laughed along. This could have been intrusive, but it somehow didn't feel intrusive at all. Was it the slightly off but attractive way she spoke Korean?

—Then, may I ask your name too? It's only fair we're on even ground. Do asked.

—My name?

—Yes.

—First name's Luciana, last name's Kim.

—Oh.

That's a beautiful name, Do thought.

—Why? Luciana Kim asked.

—I wasn't expecting you to give your name so easily. Where have we met? You look really familiar. If I knew when you learned my name, I'd probably figure it out.

—Well, technically, it was Ken Greenspan who asked for your name.

Ah! The realization hit him like a lightbulb flickering on.

—Oh, oh! Hey! Now I remember! You're the stablecoin girl from Hoffman's lecture! Hey!

His face lit up with sudden recognition, reacting with perhaps a little too much enthusiasm.

—Nice to meet you again, DMZ guy.

Luciana offered her hand in greeting. Do almost made a lame joke about "DMZ standing for Do Moon Zone," but decided against it.

—Sorry, I didn't recognize you at first because, well, we first met at Stanford, not here... I guess the context threw me off. The anchoring effect.

—Anchoring effect?

—If we'd run into each other in San Francisco or anywhere else, I would've remembered instantly. But seeing you on rival territory, sort of threw me off.

—Well, I appreciate that you're keeping the Big Game spirit alive. And though it did take you long enough, thanks for remembering me.

—Thanks for saying hello first.

They again shared a brief, easy laugh.

—Wow, it's uh, really good to see you. So you go to Berkeley?

—Yeah, you're not the only one encroaching on rival territory. Even Google employees and Berkeley students sneak in to attend Hoffman's lecture series sometimes. Luciana smiled.

—Funny how we run into each other again here. Oh, yeah. What happened with your... erm, thick rimless glasses?

—You remember my glasses? A delightful astonishment. Haha, I am wearing super thick contacts today—my eyesight's terrible. And my friend complained about face-painting the Berkeley logo on my cheek with my glasses on. Though it was kinda for nothing, heh.

It wasn't lost on Do that the glasses weren't the issue. *You're cute with or without them,* he thought but kept it to himself because, yes, it's too soon for that.

—Oh, and uh... Do fumbled a little, unsure of his next question. You're not heading to the Korean Student Association meetup tonight, are you?

—No, I prefer to just work on my own projects. I don't think they even noticed my absence. I've only been there twice during my entire undergrad years.

—Yeah, I get that. The meetup's just a waste of time. So... uh, yeah. Like you said, I'm working on this stablecoin project. I assume you're also working on some cryptocurrency project?

—Some freelance dev work. Blockchain projects are hot right now, and they pay well.

—What tech stacks are you using?

—Mostly Solidity, Rust, Go, et cetera—depends on the project. She replied with a shrug, her tone casual but confident.

—Wow, you know your blockchain. Yeah, I've been trying to learn and code in Solidity myself, but it's no joke. You erm... are you, by any chance... how do I say it, interested in a not-so-profitable blockchain project? Do asked cautiously, hope creeping into his voice.

—That's why I came to say hi to you, DMZ man. Although technically, you came to *my* campus, heh. So, you want to talk about your coin project?

—Yes! Yes, of course! Do sounded elated, perhaps over-elated. Uh, how about we head down to Starbucks and grab a coffee? Iced Americano, maybe? I saw one just down the street earlier.

—That's funny.

Luciana said, a playful lilt dancing in her voice.

—Hmm?

—You know, Korean students—I mean, Korean-Korean students—I heard they're known for two unique cultural traits. One is that they love to go to Starbucks and order an Iced Americano.

—Haha, that's not inaccurate. What's the other? Do laughed softly at her playful jab.

—How old are you?

—Me? I'm 21. Do unknowingly gave his Korean age, different from the international system. Likely because they were speaking in their mother tongue.

—Yeah, that's the other. Age is one of the first things Korean-Koreans ask when they first meet, haha.

—Wah, so you are running a little Korean stereotype test on me, huh? Do asked, a grin tugging at his lips as he leaned into the banter.

—I've always wanted to. Never had a chance to meet an *authentic* Korean guy, heh.

Luciana admitted, her eyes gleaming with something like mischief.

—Well, it's my honor to pass the Korean-Korean stereotype test. Then please let me ask how old you are?

—I'm 22. In Korean age.

—Oh, so you are *nuna.*

—Mmhmm. Just barely. If I were just a few months younger, I might have had the chance to call you *oppa.*

—Oh my, please. Do winced at the mention of *oppa,* laughing softly. I cringe at that word, despite the fact that *oppa* is indisputably Kpop Terminology 101 at this point.

—Haha, exactly. *Oppan Gangnam Style,* right?

—Geez, please don't remind me. And I just happen to come from that place—the birthplace of oppas and nunas.

—Wah, really? I always wanted to visit Gangnam.

—I'd be happy to show you around if you ever visit Korea, but there's really nothing except overpriced coffees, haha. Do said, though secretly, he imagined walking those streets with her, showing her places he never thought much of before.

—That's sweet of you. I want to, since I've never been to Korea.

—Didn't know that. Do blinked. You are, uh, let me guess actually, Korean-Latinx mixed?

—Wow, how did you know? Most people don't get that on their first try.

Her expression shifted to one of pleasant surprise, as though he had passed another silent test. *Because of your beautiful olive skin, magnetic eyes, and striking lips...* He swallowed back the words and chose a safer answer.

—The V-B accent.

—What about that? Luciana tilted her head.

—I took a sociolinguistics class last semester, and they said both Asian and Hispanic speakers tend to pronounce "v" closer to "b." I noticed it.

—Ho, you are quite observant. I mean, there's not much raw data of my pronunciation yet since we've talked for five minutes.

—No... I, uh, heard and registered every syllable when you spoke at Hoffman's class.

Do tried, unsuccessfully, to mask his crush on her, bubbling beneath his words and fighting the instinct to let his fascination slip.

—Aha.

Luciana's lips curled into a smile—just enough to show that she noticed his effort. She found this Korean-Korean guy rather cute.

—So you are a second-gen Korean? Do asked, steering the conversation, though his mind lingered on that smile.

—Yup. Born and raised in Koreatown—in the city of Los Angeles.

—Ah, I see. You don't have the uh, LA accent, though.

—Yes, the LA K-town has an accent of its own. The subtle nuance in her tone suggested that there was more than what met the ear.

—And you spoke Korean quite flawlessly. So I'd say you're more than qualified as an authentic Korean haha.

—Hm, *quite* flawlessly? She raised an eyebrow, a playful challenge in her voice.

—Minus the quite, if you ask me. And Do played along.

—Heh. Well, let me show you how *inauthentic* I can be— how about we skip Starbucks and sit on the grass instead? In case you didn't know, here at Berkeley, you can sit literally anywhere. Let's find a spot.

•

The moon and stars hung overhead as they sat on the grass instead of at Starbucks. The dusk made their names feel even more intimate, as if each syllable carried more weight than usual.

—You've probably heard this a million times, but...

Do began, his voice slightly tentative yet sincere.

—Yeah?

—Luciana is such a beautiful name.

—Heh, thank you. And I like your name, too.

—The first or the last?

—Eh, the latter. Not that I dislike the former.

—Aha, *Moon*?

—Yeah, that's a super unique surname. I mean, I know your president has the same surname, haha. But when I was little, I thought every Korean person's last name was Kim. My dad's Kim, my mom's Kim, my neighbors were Kims.

—Haha, like *Inconvenient Kim* or something? That's a TV show name, right?

—*Kim's Convenience*, duh. She corrected. And it's a Canadian show, by the way.

—A Canadian show, really?

—Gosh, you.

She rolled her eyes, playfully exasperated.

—Haha, I don't dislike my last name. But I don't like my first name—it's way too short.

—Well, "Do" is a pretty versatile name. Just D-O it. D-O or die, hehe.

—My god, I never thought of "do or die," but thanks. He groaned in mock horror.

—You are very welcome. D-O.

—Yes, please think of Do as in the extinct Dodo bird.

—Did you practice that line?

Luciana laughed, the sound light and warm, carried by the night air.

—Yes, there were, uh, versions of it. I practiced this one before my student visa interview at the US Embassy. It sort of stuck afterwards.

—Hahaha, oh my. Well, if I shorten my name drastically, it would be Lu. Like Lululemon. *Dodobird and Lululemon*. Hmm, that's something.

—That is indeed an oddly alliterative combination. So, do your friends call you Lu?

—No, but they might start now, thanks to you. She gave him a sideways glance. What about you? Your friends call you Do?

—Yup, my full name is *Do-hyung*, but no sane American is capable of pronouncing *hyung*, so Do it is.

—Oh, I know what *hyung* means! It's like an older brother, right? Like the male counterpart to *nuna*?

—Exactly, haha, a male version of *nuna*.

—Shoot, I didn't pronounce that so well, did I, haha. Guess I'm not an authentic Korean after all.

—Haha, no you are. You pronounced that cringeworthy *oppa* perfectly.

—I'm so flattered.

—And I am perfectly like you calling me Do. Do or die, it's already growing on me.

—I know, right? Haha.

Do hesitated for a beat, then, half-joking, half-serious, asked.

—Luciana, would you mind if I call you *Nuna*? I figured, erm, well, at least one of us should have longer than one syllable.

Heh. Luciana looked at him with a soft affection in her eyes. When I saw him in Hoffman's class, I just thought he was another ambitious Stanford kid, she mused. But I like how his ambition is softened by that boyish mischievousness, the kind that makes his drive feel endearing. So yeah, if someone were to call me *Nuna*, yeah, it would be someone like you, Dodo birdie.

—We'll see about that.

She replied, her voice teasingly coy.

—Too soon?

Do put on an exaggerated crestfallen expression, furrowing his brows dramatically. She let out a quiet laugh, shaking her head.

—Well, you are alright. Since I never had a younger sibling, and since I did always want to be called Nuna when I was young, so… I suppose I'll allow it.

—Hehe, thank you, Nuna.

Do smiled without any reservation. Their laughter blended into the quiet of the night, a clicking harmony of shared humor and a budding connection. It had been a long time since Do felt this kind of lighthearted but unmistakably romantic atmosphere. As he glanced at Luciana—I mean, *Nuna*—a warmth stirred within him, the eyes of a man falling in love.

—Haha, so... Nuna, shall we talk about stablecoins?

—Huh, sure. Let's skip the small talk and dive right in, the moment after I let you call me *Nuna*. Luciana raised an eyebrow, her tone teasing.

—Sorry, haha. I'm terrible with pacing.

—I'll give you a pass this time.

—Much appreciated. So, Ms. Kim, Do said, switching to a more formal tone with a wink.

—Yeah, Mr. Moon?

—Do you believe in coins?

Luciana chuckled softly at his silly introductory line.

—What are you—a crypto missionary from the Korean Church of Bitcoin?

—In a way. Korean Church of Stablecoin. Do smiled.

—No. But then her response came unexpectedly terse.

—Huh?

—I believe in blockchain technology, but I'm not really sold on coins as its ultimate application. Sure, they're a major use case, but the coin is not the essence of the blockchain, I think. And because of those crazy ICO[5]s and the illusion of quick fortune they create... I don't blame anyone who thinks coins are a form of depravity.

—I kind of agree with that.

—But you want to create a coin, don't you?

—But I'm not doing it to make money.

—Is that even possible?

—It is. Do said it quite firmly.

—You cook to make money, you write to make money, but you're telling me you're creating *money* not to make money?

—That's exactly it.

—Hmm. Even Tether makes money off fees, doesn't it?

---

[5] Initial Coin Offering

—Tether is a decent idea, but it's not the true essence of a stablecoin.

—There's no stablecoin more stable than Tether in the current market, though.

—Yeah, it's stable. Stability is their whole and only identity. In the end, all they're doing is piling up cash reserves and issuing coins backed by that cash. That means it's still at the mercy of whoever controls that cash.

Do doesn't back down an inch.

—...That's true.

—So that's not really blockchain, right? Tether's just another bank in disguise.

—I agree, to an extent. Luciana nods at his philosophy.

—If the Fed Chair is unhappy about Tether, she can make it go away. Hypothetically speaking, of course. Speaking of which, wasn't Janet Yellen a professor here?

—Yeah, I tried to get into her class once but couldn't. Ratemyprofessor.com says her lectures were boring but still super packed, haha.

—Haha, I believe that website. So like, if someone very persuasive or if someone who majored in hypnosis sneaks into her office and successfully convinces her to shut down Tether, it might actually happen.

—Gosh, haha. I doubt she is an easily persuaded person, but okay, I get your point.

—Just hypotheticals. But that's why Tether isn't a true stablecoin. And Greenspan was right about that.

—You mean the part about intrinsic value being tied to the U.S. dollar?

—Yes, the part I was being played. Thank god the lecture didn't end there. I'd just be another idiot who got schooled. And I wouldn't have been able to impress you. You probably wouldn't have bothered talking to me, heh.

Do glanced at Luciana, who almost gave him a gentle lie but ended up smiling instead.

—You're not much of a liar, are you? He grinned.

—Haha, I'm unfortunately not. So, Do—then how is your stablecoin going to be different from Tether? I can tell you're onto something big.

—I appreciate you saying that. Yes, the stablecoin I'm dreaming of will never involve a dime of U.S. dollar. Not that I have anything against the dollar; it's just wrong in principle.

—Hmm... instead of fiat currency, then you're planning to use Bitcoin or Ethereum as collateral?

—You're ahead of the game, as usual. But no, even more than that.

—More? But collateral is still necessary. If it's not fiat, and it's not crypto, what would back it?

—An algorithm.

—An algorithm?

—Yeah. A stablecoin where the price is maintained purely by an algorithm. No collateral, no permission needed. That's the true essence of a coin, in my opinion. The only, real, coin.

Crickets chirped softly in the background. Luciana found Do's conviction, almost stubborn, somewhat... charming, to her own surprise.

—Oops.

A cricket leapt from the grass toward Do's face.

—Haha. You okay?

—Ha, here we are talking about changing the world, and a little bug comes along and ruins the moment, haha.

—It didn't ruin it. This is interesting.

—Really?

—*Really.*

She repeated herself, as if affirming a shared conviction—though what that conviction was remained unspoken, undefined. Their attention lingered on each other, and as the last light of the sunset bathed the Berkeley lawn in a golden hue, they synced their ambitions instead of romance.

—I have to say, though, the idea of an algorithmic stablecoin could be a bit too dangerous. She said, a note of caution in her voice.

—Dangerous?…

—Of course. It's actually very, very dangerous.

—…It's not like we're talking about Oppenheimer's atomic bomb project here, though.

—No, if we were, we'd already be recruited by some secret government agency—or worse, locked up.

—Together? Do grinned, mischief lighting up his eyes.

—Unfortunately for you, no, haha. We'd probably each get our own solitary cell and die there alone. Luciana smoothly returned his grin.

—Wait, wasn't Oppenheimer also a professor at Berkeley?

—And so was the Unabomber.

—What's with all the dangerous professors here? Well, I guess, since you learned from them, we'll just have to do something dangerous together.

—Actually, we often learn the opposite. You study dangerous professors to learn what *not* to do. Hence, the real dangerous students are at Stanford—like Elizabeth Holmes?

—Woah, Nuna. That's really mean.

—I wasn't making any direct comparisons, haha. She teased him further.

—Haha, well, since we've both taken the obligatory history lessons of our respective schools… I'll take on the dangerous stuff, then.

Do shifted his position, sitting up straighter.

—So, Nuna. Let's get back to the main agenda.

—Yes?

—Would you be, uh, slightly interested in joining my stablecoin project? I haven't settled on a name for the project yet, but would you?…

Do hedged his invitation with as many qualifiers as he could muster, cushioning against a possible rejection.

—…Hmm.

—I will ask again in a simpler metaphor. Will you please be my Wozniak? No school alumni pun intended.

—Haha, I love Woz. And it's a good metaphor.

—Right? I mean, it's only fitting that I meet my Wozniak on the Berkeley campus!

—And that makes you my Jobs?

—I try to be. I aspire to be. I will be your Jobs minus being a dick. Or I can be the Woz if you'd rather, but you seem much more technically talented than me.

—Yeah, I think I am more Woz than Jobs. They were both brilliant and creative, but while Jobs was always reaching for the stars, Wozniak kept his feet firmly on the ground.

—Feet on the ground?

Luciana bent down, her fingers gently brushing the soil beneath the grass.

—The Valley's full of people who think the sky's the limit—people dreaming of the moon. She said, her gaze lifting to the moon and the stars, where the stars began to shimmer.

—True. Elon Musk is dead set on getting to Mars.

—But unlike them, I want to keep my feet on the ground. Both feet, firmly planted. This idea of creating a stablecoin purely with an algorithm—it could work, sure, but...

—I haven't done it yet, but I'm telling you, it's possible.

—But creating it isn't the end.

—I agree. You build it, grow it, change the world with it.

—No, you build it—and then you keep it safe.

Luciana punctuated the last word. Do, puzzled.

—...We're still talking about a stablecoin project, right? Not, like, a nuclear weapon? What do you mean, keep it safe?

—Money isn't going to blow anyone up. But if people don't have it, it can take their lives away.

—...Yeah, I guess that's true.

For the first time since meeting Luciana, Do couldn't fully agree with her insight. Yet, he pretended to, his ambition blurring the edges of his disagreement. And Luciana, sensing the slight discord, let it slide, intrigued enough by his ambition to continue.

—Nuna, since we're on the topic of Jobs and Woz, let me borrow a thought from the former for a second.

—Go for it.

—Before the iPhone came out, people didn't know what they wanted, right? But once they saw it, they realized their hidden desires. Same with this stablecoin. You don't know it, I don't know it yet. But once we make *that* coin, we'll know. And when we do, the masses will too.

—…Not a bad answer.

For the first time since meeting Do, Luciana couldn't fully agree with his conviction. Yet, she pretended to, her curiosity outweighing her concerns. And Do, sensing the slight hesitation, admired her insight too much to press further.

Their differences, however, didn't breed tension. Instead, it nurtured a sense of mutual respect. They shared a quick smile, as if the gap between them was something to be celebrated. The night deepened. Beneath them, the grass, and above, the leaves of clustered trees reflected the streetlights, casting shadows of rich, dark green.

—I didn't know Berkeley at night was this quiet. This serene.

Do murmured.

—Stanford's not?

—It is. But the grass is different.

—The grass, how?

—The grass at Stanford is perfectly manicured, almost artificial. But here, the grass grows wild, straight out of uneven soil. It's real, you know? And, well, full of bugs, too.

As he spoke, Do's fingers grazed the soil beneath the grass, tracing the spot where Luciana had brushed just moments before. His hand inched closer, wordlessly, metaphysically inquiring if it might entwine with hers. Luciana's hand gave a subtle nod, a delicate consent, her fingers opening slightly, and the artery in his hand pulse with quiet ecstasy.

Without disturbing the terrestrial order, their hands met in a soft, clandestine kiss.

•

As their hands came together in a soft kiss, the night grew just a shade deeper, as if aware it was now the keeper of their small secret.

—…So, how are you getting home?

Luciana's voice slipped into the quiet, her tone light and casual, yet somehow grounding them back in the present.

—…Do I have to?

Do asked, his playful sincerity hanging between them like a question he genuinely wished had no answer.

Luciana smiled at his boyish reluctance. She didn't mind him lingering a little longer, but...

—I like tonight's coincidence, Do.

Luciana said softly, her words wrapping around the moment like the night itself.

—I *love* tonight's coincidence, Nuna. he echoed.

—But if we're going to work together, it might be a little early to switch genres—from *The Social Network* to *La La Land*.

It was too apt a metaphor for Do not to laugh.

—I understand. And I agree. So does that mean I could assume you're interested in my stablecoin project?… Erm, if that's the case, I suppose I'll need your number. For, well, you know… purely *work* purposes.

His voice had softened, suddenly shy as he stumbled over his own intentions.

—Heh, for work or for something else? She tilted her head.

—You're making me say it. Fine, for asking you out too.

Do admitted, his face flushing slightly as they exchanged numbers.

—Alright, it's really late now. You should call a taxi soon, or they'll charge you extra. Or take Lyft—they're cheaper and better.

—Actually… I like Uber.

—Oh boy, how are our preferences this different already? Haha, why Uber over Lyft? She asked, laughing at the absurdity of their fledgling disagreement.

—Haha, well, because Travis Kalanick was a true hustler. Hang on, let me call one before we debate this.

Luciana laughed as she watched him blush over a phone number but stay adamant about his ride-sharing preference.

—Okay, done. Do said. I mean, any middle schooler could've thought of a ride-sharing app, but Kalanick's the only one who refused to ask for permission from taxi unions and governments. Lyft? They just followed the road he paved.

—I gotta ask you before your beloved Uber arrives. What's your grudge against asking for permission? Greenspan seemed to have a similar grudge.

—Ha, sorry. I tend to get unnecessarily serious about this stuff.

—No, I'm actually curious.

He hesitated, then shrugged.

—Maybe I'm just a natural rebel. I don't like other people deciding my life for me. Or maybe I just dislike authority. You know how hackers are—they always seem to despise centralized systems.

Luciana gave him a knowing look. *Is that all?*

—We've only known each other for, like, five minutes, but that seems… a little uncharacteristic of you.

—Does it? He chuckled. Haha… yeah, maybe yeah. I think you're right.

—I mean, I think I know why I like blockchain, if you're interested in hearing my personal motivation, that is.

—Of course, Nuna!

Do quickly opened the Uber app to cancel the ride. Much as he loved the convenience and the philosophy of it, he'd cancel a hundred Ubers if it meant one more precious minute in Luciana's company.

—Oh, for god's sake, don't, haha. You'll have to pay the cancellation fee. And it's not that grand of a story.

—Sorry, heh. Do mumbled, grinning sheepishly. He canceled his cancellation request. Still, every word she spoke carried its own quiet grandeur to him.

—And I actually mentioned this back in Hoffman's class. Do you remember by any chance?

—I definitely remember, though I'm not sure if this is the answer. It's because... it's because you can *program trust*?

How could Do forget the words spoken by someone he already adores and admires so much? Luciana nodded, her smile soft but knowing.

—Yes. The intrinsic value of the dollar is trust, said Mr. Greenspan. But people talk as if trust is as stable as a stablecoin. It's not. Trust can be as volatile as the price of Dogecoin whenever Elon Musk tweets. People cheat. Money cheats.

There was a faint edge of something personal in her voice, but Do chose not to pry. He respected the boundary of her silence.

—Do.

—Yes?

—Blockchain is a fascinating concept.

—Of course!

—No, I mean it in a slightly different way. She emphasized, her eyes narrowing with intensity. If I join your project, it's because I love blockchain. Not because I love money. There's a huge difference. Her words carried weight, and she let them land without apology.

—I understand, Nuna.

Do replied, sensing the gravity of the distinction she made.

—Listen, every new computing platform starts out worse than the one before it. When smartphones came out in the age of desktop computers, people laughed at the tiny screens and slow speeds. But smartphones had something computers never had. You know what that was?

—Uh... erm... Cameras?

—Exactly! And?

—...Not sure, exactly.

—How could you call Uber just now? Luciana nudged Do to solve her riddle.

—Oh! The GPS.

—Yes! The camera and the GPS. The camera in the smartphone gave birth to Instagram. The GPS in the smartphone allowed you to call an Uber just now. Blockchain is the same.

—Right, it's worse than smartphones in many ways, but…

—But it can program trust. It can program trust! Computers, smartphones—no computing platform so far could ever do that. You don't need to trust people or money. You just trust the math.

Do didn't need to add anything to her brilliant insight. Her words lingered in the air, crystallizing their shared vision. Just then, headlights cut through the dark as the Uber driver pulled up to the curb.

—Well, looks like your Uber's here. I guess Uber is actually a little faster than Lyft tonight, haha.

Luciana's tone lightened, a brief reprieve from the depth of their conversation. Do, for his part, silently wished for a flat tire—anything to extend their time together.

—Nuna, I…

—We can talk more later. It's really late now. You should really get back to Palo Alto.

—No, wait. Nuna, I've gotta say this. Do's voice softened with sincerity. You've opened my eyes, even though we've only known each other for like an hour. Thank you. I mean it. And I want to work with you—to build the permissionless stablecoin with programmable trust. Next time I see you, if you accept my date, I'll be more prepared.

—…Sounds like a plan, haha. Now you should really get going. I think your driver's getting annoyed, not understanding all this Korean.

—Haha, alright. But I'll see you soon. Really soon. Goodbye, Nuna. Take care.

Do switched to English to add a few more words.

—See you, Do.

He disappeared into the night, the Hyundai carrying him across the Bay Bridge. Luciana stood, brushing the dirt from her pants, watching the car pull away—but she didn't wave.

In the car, the Korean boy, smitten with love, gazed out the window. His aversion to permission had always felt instinctive, but now its origin had crystallized. His ambition was betrayed by the permissions of others—permissions he sought but never needed.

People were replaceable; ambition wasn't. But he felt no need to cry about what happened in high school anymore, because Nuna was his new ambition.

chapter block
07.0

This microcosm embodies the quirky brand of nationalism. I'm talking about the Stanford Korean Student Association.

These privileged students had lived among a vibrant mosaic of races, blending effortlessly without prejudice or comparisons. Yet, whenever they reconvened at the Korean Association with other Korean-Korean students, they invariably retreated into a narrow world of sly competition and silent judgment.

Tonight was a farewell party for Aaron, who was finally heading off to the Navy after a year of endless whining. Perhaps when people like him left for military service, this Association could adopt a broader perspective.

—Do! I've been hearing some interesting rumors about you lately. Aaron said, ever the connoisseur of gossip, even on his last night in the U.S.

—Interesting rumors?

Do replied, a trace of irritation coloring his tone.

—A friend of mine from Berkeley—he told me something interesting. Hmm... something going on with Luciana Kim, perhaps?

—How do you, like, how do you even know all that?

Do noticed June, seated nearby, suddenly perked up. Well, Aaron, you sly dog, maybe you're not so useless after all, Do thought.

—Come on. You can never underestimate my gossip connections, haha. So, you two seeing each other or what?

—...And just how does your friend know Nuna?

—Oops, sorry. I didn't realize you were on *oppa-nuna* basis already.

—Oh, shut up, haha.

—Well, I heard Ms. Luciana Kim is a certified computer genius. Remember Noah from last semester's CS230? The nerdy guy who wouldn't shut up about being in Mensa? He's serving at KATUSA. I pray I don't meet him during the joint military drills, haha.

—Yeah, good riddance.

—I know right? Well, that nerd went to a Caltech hackathon one time and got completely owned by Luciana.

—Huh, really?

—So, are you guys dating?

—Well, I did ask her out...

—Damn, that's fantastic! Haha, I actually saw her once when I was catching up with my friends at Cal. She'd honestly look prettier without those thick glasses.

—I don't need your assessment of her looks, thank you.

Do's expression tightened as he shot Aaron a pointed look.

—Oh, man. I was only uh... just making an observation.

—She's pretty with or without glasses.

Do couldn't let Aaron's passing comment linger. And it really had nothing to with jealousy—his ex-girlfriend's good old lensless glasses to cover dark circles or whatsoever.

Now, when Do thought of glasses, only images of Luciana's bright black eyes and the endearing folds of her eyelids stirred in his mind. *Guess I've fallen for her more than I thought,* Do thought.

—Ah, of course, man, haha. You two make a great couple. Hey, Do, have a drink. This is some expensive stuff.

Aaron backtracked with practiced ease, as he handed a glass of deep, blood-red wine into Do's hand.

—Thanks.

The wine hit harder than expected, but as it slid down his throat, it carried a subtle aroma that made the burn more pleasant than painful.

—How's that? Smooth, right? That's almost $3,000 a sip. Chateau Lafite, 1982.

—What? $3,000 for one sip?

—Well, yes, haha. My mom sent it over from a winery as a farewell gift. I mean, in a few weeks, I'll be trading this for unfiltered Navy water. Gotta cleanse my system while I still can.

—Haha, it's not that bad these days.

—Oh, I don't buy that for a second. I'll be dragged around, and I'd need to save up a year's salary just to buy a single bottle of a decent wine. Keep me in your prayers, alright? Haha.

Do silently prayed Aaron would be stationed in the DMZ, stuck with that ancient military radio. But Aaron would likely end up coasting through his service in the most comfortable land-based Navy assignment he could find, so the prayer was unlikely.

●

After the discharge, Yohan was living a typical yet challenging life like most twenty-somethings. The job market was tough. He made it to a few interviews, only to face rejection after rejection. To cover living expenses, he worked part-time at a convenience store and a bookstore, which at least gave him time to study on the side. With what little he saved, he dabbled in stocks and crypto. His returns were modest but promising. If only I had a larger initial capital, he often thought, occasionally even toying with the idea of becoming a full-time cryptocurrency day trader. But just as he was weighing that option, he received a job offer from his dream company. Ecstatic, he donned a cheap suit and headed to his new job in Yeouido's buzzing financial district. The office was perched on the 30th floor of the IFC Seoul[6], with a view that opened right onto the Han River.

---

[6] International Finance Center Seoul

After a month of on-the-job training, Private Yohan Lee earned his promotion to Employee Number 222. As a productive member of the company, the long-anticipated reward arrived—his first paycheck. There's a tradition in Korea: you buy red thermal underwear for your parents as a symbol of gratitude. At exactly noon, while standing at a crosswalk after an early lunch, he checked his phone and saw that his first salary—3 million won[7]— had been deposited. This was different, a world apart from the scattered wages of part-time work or the occasional crypto gain. He felt a warm surge of pride, a mark of new beginnings.

Yohan hurried back to the IFC building. Instead of heading up, he took the elevator down to the IFC Mall below, scouring for the red thermal underwear. But in a mall where shirts didn't go for less than 100,000 won[8], affordable red long johns were nowhere to be found. Thankfully, he finally came across a pair of maroon-colored underwear at UNIQLO. It wasn't precisely the red of tradition, but it would do. His mother had insisted he save his first paycheck, not worry about gifts. But how could he not thank the person who meant the most to him?

He wanted to give his mother more than inexpensive red—I mean, maroon—underwear. As he mulled over what else to get, he remembered that his mother had recently become fond of listening to trot music on the radio. He also recalled the sideways glances on the subway when she unknowingly played her music a bit too loud on her phone, unaware that her cheap bundle Bluetooth earbuds had run out of battery.

Luckily, the Mall had plenty of upscale options for the extra gift—an Apple store, a Samsung store, Bang & Olufsen, Sennheiser. Yohan walked into the Samsung store and picked out the best wired earphones they had in stock.

—Welcome, sir. Are you looking for a specific series? Wired earphones are coming back in style with that retro vibe, but the

---

[7] Approx. USD 3,000.
[8] Approx. USD 100.

latest Galaxy Buds 2 have top-tier specs. I'd highly recommend the Bluetooth ones.

—Thanks, but I'm only looking for wired ones. They're just uh... they're easier to use. This looks very nice. I will get this one.

—Ah-ha. Of course, sir. Would you like us to gift-wrap it? The observant clerk caught on quickly that these weren't for him but a gift.

—Oh, I didn't know there was an option. Yes, please. Thank you.

The clerk nodded and disappeared behind the counter to prepare the box.

chapter block
08.0

The romance unfurled faster than the stablecoin. Perhaps the former was easier to cultivate than the latter? What began as future-focused discussions about cryptocurrency often veered into reflections on their pasts. Playful sparring over whether Bibimbap in Seoul or LA Koreatown tastes better. Recollections of high school crushes followed by childish jealousy. Weekend picnics in the Presidio, with a detour for selfies by the Yoda statue at Lucasfilm. Then a goodbye kiss as Do took Uber back to Palo Alto and Luciana took the F bus back to Berkeley.

On weekdays, they spent a considerable amount of time on the yet unnamed stablecoin project, often skipping classes, working at a WeWork office sponsored by Stanford's Student Startup Center. Luciana was the unofficial co-founder, coding shoulder-to-shoulder with Do. She was every bit the coding genius people said she was. Do sketched the architecture, and Luciana brought it to life, laying down each line of code like concrete poured for the foundation of a new world. Occasionally, Nik would lend a hand. Three of them forged ahead into the unknown. After sleepless nights of coding, the three together translated their technical visions into a whitepaper promising to shake the foundations of the old financial world.

Of course, it wasn't always smooth. No, it was anything but smooth. Turning love into shared ambition felt like a natural course of things, but turning ambition into love came with many complications.

They soon learned why most co-founders avoid romantic entanglements. A startup thrives on friction. Yet, after each heated argument, they grew hesitant, careful not to push each other too far. Real issues were sidestepped, their conversations edited for safety, their suggestions increasingly cautious, superficial even. And when the elephant in the room grew too heavy, one of them would slip away to Philz Coffee in Palo Alto, letting the sweet scent of a pumpkin scone cool things down without ever bringing them to a boil.

Last week was no different. Today, however, marked a small anniversary. Their 100th day together—a milestone for both the romance and the stablecoin. This tiny marker was enough to paper over the cracks, at least for now. They agreed to let the elephant in the room stand undisturbed and dressed up for dinner at a Michelin 2-star restaurant in San Francisco.

•

—Nuna, you know how San Fran is like the DMZ?

Do remarked as they walked into the restaurant.

—In what way?

—Well, Berkeley's packed with socialist hippies—that's the North. Stanford is overrun with soul-selling capitalists—that's the South. And San Fran, well, it's the DMZ sitting right in between.

—Oh quiet, DMZ boy.

Luciana laughed as she reprimanded his silly analogy.

They arrived at *Paguk*, a sleek contemporary Korean fusion restaurant whose name struck Do and Luciana as both curious and whimsical. "Pa" means scallion, and "Guk" means nation in Korean, so the name loosely translated to "Nation of Scallions." According to Yelp, the chef was described as "the master of coaxing the essence of Korean cuisine using scallions as his signature." Do couldn't help but wonder if the chef had written that mouthful review himself. Nevertheless, the Michelin 2-star plaque gleamed at the entrance, casting an air of prestige over the place. Despite the Korean theme, not a single staff member appeared remotely Korean. The irony wasn't lost on him as he exchanged a bemused glance with Luciana.

—Do you have a reservation?

Asked the waiter, whose stony demeanor suggested he had long ago grown weary of the city's endless flow of clientele.

—Yup. The name's Do-hyung, Moon.

—Doe-heyeung? Let me check… You said Doe-heyeung?

Do didn't even know where to start with correcting the pronunciation.

—No, it's Hyung. *H-y-u-n-g.*

—Yes, Do-h-hyounge… hmm, I'm not seeing it. Are you sure you booked?

Of course not, you probably scribbled down the most creative version of my name when I called yesterday, Do thought.

—Yes, I even called yesterday to confirm the reservation. The last name's Moon. No, not M-u-n-n. Not like Olivia Munn. Just the normal Moon. M-o-o-n, like the thing in the sky at night? Yes, yes, that's correct.

—One moment. Ah, here we are. Mr. Moon, welcome to Paguk. Thank you for dining with us. Tonight's special course is…

—See? They never get my name right until I give them my last name.

Do whispered to Luciana as they were escorted to their table, attempting to dissolve the awkward tension with a laugh.

—You could use my name next time. I mean, Kim's practically a global brand now, thanks to the supreme leader Kim Jong-un.

—Haha, true that. Kim Kardashian's somewhat helping the cause too. But I didn't want to spoil tonight's surprise.

—Makes sense, haha. How about next time we use an alias, a combination of our names?

—Like, Do Kim?

—Well, something like that. Or John-Doe-Kim?

—Oh, haha. That's clever, Nuna.

Do chuckled, rubbing his cheek affectionately against Luciana's.

—Mr. Moon, your table is this way.

The waiter gestured toward a small table near the center of the room, clearly not the window seat Do had requested.

—Wait, no. I specifically booked a table by the window.

—I'm sorry, but we're fully booked tonight.

—Right. And I'm one of those bookings. I made it clear I wanted a booth seat by the window. You can check with the manager if necessary.

Instead of fixing the mistake, the waiter cast a brief, judgmental glance at their outfits. Just because this was California, it didn't mean everyone strolled into high-end restaurants in flip-flops. Some corners of San Francisco were as particular as any place in Manhattan. Do's attire passed the inspection, but Luciana's casual blouse and off-the-rack shoes didn't seem to meet the restaurant's unspoken standard.

The waiter's tone was laced with that subtle derision—*why are you broke college kids dining here?* Normally, Do wouldn't have let it slide. His temper was a tinderbox waiting for a spark. But he held it together because it was the anniversary, because Luciana was next to him. At last, they were seated at the intimate, private booth Do originally requested, right in the corner, beside the window.

•

—Whoa, four courses for one meal?

Luciana peered at the menu, her eyes wide.

—Yeah, amuse-bouche, appetizer, main, and dessert.

—What's amuse-bouche?

—It's just an appetizer before the appetizer. A fancy name for a tiny bite, haha.

—Heh, my first time at a place like this. You think we'll make it through all four courses before we're stuffed and running out?

—Don't you worry about that, Nuna. Each course is served so small that we might need to hit Chipotle after this.

—Or a food truck. Mission Bay has some great ones.

—Sounds like a great post-meal plan.

They shared delicate, fragile smiles, the kind that masked the unspoken tensions both had quietly agreed to sidestep for the night. Tonight was not for complications, not for arguments, but for enjoying each other's company—hoping that, for this brief moment, everything else could wait.

—Nuna, listen. About a year from now, we'll come back to this place. Do proposed.

—Really? I mean, the Michelin stars and the decor here are impressive, but... I wouldn't call this the most comfortable place to dine in San Fran. She mused.

—I agree. But hear me out. Next time we visit, when the check comes, we'll pay using the stablecoin we created. By then, most Silicon Valley restaurants will be accepting crypto, right? *That same jerk waiter will ask, Oh, you're paying with that stablecoin? and we'll say, Yes, we created this.*

Luciana smiled at the thought, finding his proposal charmingly childish. Do had a way of talking about ambition as though it were romance itself—his fantasies of success often laced with dreams of making her proud. She found this ambitious mischievousness more than endearing.

—Heh, I like that. I like that very much. But—she teased—we'd better settle on a cool name for our coin before that.

—Couldn't agree more, haha.

—Because we can't just say *Oh, by the way, I'm paying with Tether.* It wouldn't have any flair in the name.

Looks like Nuna now shares her boyfriend's disdain against their main competitor.

—I know right? Haha, yes, I do have a name in mind, but... I would probably have to keep it a secret for now.

—Oh, come on. Why not tell me?

—I don't want to jinx it before we complete the project—you know, I don't want to *drink the kimchi soup first*, haha.

Do smirked, referencing the Korean idiom about not counting one's chickens before they hatch. It does make sense linguistically, because both kimchi and chicken soups are soul foods. Anyways.

—I like it when you pull out those ancient Korean idioms only my grandparents would use. Makes me feel like I'm talking to my grandpa. Luciana laughed.

—Oh, thank you. Now let's hope they don't actually serve kimchi soup as an amuse-bouche.

Do glanced at his watch, attempting not to look impatient as the delay in service stretched on.

—As much as I loved being Employee of the Month at H-Mart, I'd be pretty disappointed if they do serve kimchi soup, haha.

Luciana quipped, grinning. Unlike Do, she wore no watch and seemed to savor the waiting.

Finally, their amuse-bouche belatedly arrived—a crispy pan-fried tofu dish brimming with the rich aroma of scallions, living up to the restaurant's name. A stark contrast to the unfriendly service, the taste was nothing but inviting. Smiles spread across their faces as the flavors settled on their tongues.

—Woah, this is delicious. This is more than delicious!

Luciana whispered, the quiet exclamation slipping out with genuine delight. Do, captivated by how her cute eyes lit up with rimless glasses, barely tasted his own bite.

—Yeah, it's amazing. It's definitely worth the wait. And your reaction makes it twice as good, heh.

Do replied with a cheesy grin.

—Aww, seriously though, this is so good I almost forgot we were talking about our coin name.

—Aw, girl. Don't be mean.

—I'll stop being mean if you stop being cheesy. She teased with her twinkling eyes.

—Haha, fine, deal.

—So you're still not telling me the coin's name, huh? I do have a suggestion in mind.

—Really? Let's hear it.

—You know how the ticker name is super important, right? Those 3 to 4 characters—they've got to hold our essence.

—Right.

—So I wanted a ticker that's not only memorable but already popular. Something like L.A.

—Hmm, well, no dispute on the popularity front. But don't you think it might bring up too many other associations?

—That's my concern too. So the full name has to be really beautiful to balance it out.

—Any candidates on your mind?

—How about... *Land Arcadia*? Okay, before you say anything, haha, I know—it's not the easiest to pronounce. But it's the best option with the letters L.A. Better than Land Aether or Land Axis.

Do could sense how much Luciana's attachment to her hometown played into this choice, though he wasn't sure if that attachment was something she was comfortable sharing yet. So he didn't pry.

—Actually, I think the word *Arcadia* is really beautiful. And Nuna, you always seem to have this deep connection to Earth, haha.

—I mean, heh, ours is a stablecoin. Shouldn't it give off a grounded, stable feeling, like solid land?

—That's a good point, actually. So the ticker would be $LA? Isn't that taken already though?

—Yup, it's unfortunately already taken. So I was thinking, how about $XLA? Putting the "X" as the prefix—kind of like how Ripple does it?

But Do remembered something and quickly opened an app to check, and a faint, awkward smile spread across her face as he showed her the screen.

—Oh, no! How is it taken already? The $XLA was just taken four days ago?? Oh no... I thought of it five days ago. I was faster. Nooo...

—Haha. ICOs are crazy fast these days. Though, of course, not for projects done right, like ours.

—I know, right? Ugh, it's unfair... no.

He fully sympathized with her disappointment, but seeing her slumped with her head down, looking so adorably crestfallen, he just found her more endearing.

—Now I want to hear your name for our coin. You *have* to tell me yours, Do.

He would normally refrain from breaking his little superstition about jinxing the name, but making his cofounder slash girlfriend feel slightly better seemed like a more urgent task.

—Okay, uh...

A mix of pressure and enjoyment under her expectant gaze.

—No more *uhs* or I might just start calling *Do Oppa*.

—Ew, okay, okay, haha. Fine, here we go. It's called *LunaCoin*.

—*NunaCoin*?

—LunaCoin, come on, *Nuna*, haha!

—Aaah, *L-una*Coin?

Luciana's cheeks flushed, momentarily tinged with pink.

—Yes, I want to call our stablecoin LunaCoin. And the ticker is going to be $LUNA. It's not taken yet, fortunately.

Do broke his jinx, his eyes immediately searching for Luciana's reaction. And fortunately, it looked like Nuna really loved the name.

—Luna... Luna... woah.

She looked at him in wonder. For the first time since Do had fallen for Luciana, she spoke in the most uncharacteristically animated voice, almost like Janice from *Friends*, letting out a quiet but dramatic *oh my god* face. Seeing her temporarily break out of her usual calm character made her all the more lovely.

—Do! That sounds absolutely beautiful! $LUNA, wow. How is it even not taken already? Kay, we gotta work twice as hard and get this ICO done before someone else takes the ticker name!

—Heh, I'm glad you like it.

—I *love* it! But wait a sec. Hold on.

Luciana suddenly slipped into a playful detective mode, mock-serious as she interrogated the origin of the name.

—Please, Mr. Moon. Elaborate. How did you come up with the name?

—Em. Okay, but here's the thing: it's either going to be super self-conscious or super cheesy. Which version of the story do you want to hear?

—The real one, duh, she said, smirking.

—Haha, alright. Well… you know how crypto people always say "wen moon"? I first wanted to name it after the moon or moon-related stuff, but, well… that's also my surname, you know.

Do rambled on, his turn now, his cheeks tinged with the faintest flush of pink. He continued.

—Naming a coin after my own last name felt like, I don't know, another level of self-consciousness. So, I searched the Internet for a feminine name of Latin origin that means "moon"…

—Oh, so you just naturally searched the entire expanse of the Internet for the feminine name of Latin origin meaning "moon," huh?

—I absolutely one hundred percent did. And voila. It just so happened that "Luna" was the very word for the feminine name of Latin origin meaning moon! Very serendipitous. And it sounded pretty… well, like you.

Luciana gave him an "aww" face, eyes gleaming with affection but keeping her silence, knowing her expression said it all.

—Oh gosh, no "aww" face, please. So you wanted the cheesy version after all! Haha, so uh, yeah… that's how it ended up being called LunaCoin.

—Mmhmm?

Luciana raised her eyebrows, tilting her head with a look that clearly said, *Come on, there's more, isn't there?*

—Okay, you got me, Nuna. I wanted to name it after you— *Luciana Nuna*. And the natural combination, that even carried the meaning of the moon, was… none other than *Lu-Na*.

Do looked so earnest, his words spilling out with that extra verbosity that came whenever he tried to say anything romantic.

She couldn't help but laugh, charmed by his blend of silliness and sincerity.

—And so, maybe one day we'll come back here and pay for our meal... with LunaCoin.

—Come here.

Luciana kissed Do's cheek instead of the lips, just in case they accidentally share the scallion flavor.

•

As they shared a cheesy laugh together, the amuse-bouche plates were cleared and the appetizer arrived: scallion pancakes with oysters, reimagined with a Korean twist.

—Nuna, are you okay with oysters? Do asked.

—No worries. You?

—Not an issue with me, haha. I grew up eating oyster pancakes every Korean Thanksgiving. Perhaps they took inspiration from that.

With practiced ease, Do lifted a scallion pancake with his chopsticks. Luciana laughed at her boyfriend's Korean-Korean moment again.

—Hmm, I have to say, the oyster tastes like raw metal. A delicious metal, maybe copper. He said.

—Yeah, I can feel that deliciously metallic taste, too. Guess that's fitting, considering our grand project. The oyster tastes like licking the 10 cent coin. She said.

—Oh, what a coin-cidence, huh?

—Oh, that's clever, hahaha.

Their playful banter continued, smoothing out the earlier tension from the restaurant's icy service. The pressures of their delayed stablecoin project faded into the background. As they polished off their coin-tasting oysters, the mood felt lighter, warmer, as though they'd rediscovered the easy connection that had drawn them together at Berkeley.

It was time for the main dish. According to Yelp, this restaurant served the best "Hanwoo Wagyu with Scallion Sizzle" steak in the Bay Area. A redundant, nonsensical name really, since Hanwoo and Wagyu are essentially the same thing. But "Wagyu" was a more familiar exotic term and "Hanwoo" was a less familiar exotic term, so they put the names together to impress non-Koreans customers.

—Your Hanwoo Wagyu steaks are here.

—Thank you.

Korean Hanwoo BBQs typically include raw cuts to the table, where they are cooked on a grill right before you. But here, the steaks arrived pre-cooked, plated just like another high-end American porterhouse. The scent of scallion butter wafted up, rich and inviting—so no complaints here.

—Woah, listen to that sizzle of the hot plate. You ordered medium-rare, right, Do? Luciana asked, cutting into her own steak.

—Yup, the classic. Look at this pink inside. Do marveled, cutting into his own steak. You really should've ordered medium-rare too, not medi—

Do stopped as he caught sight of her steak—a dull brown hue throughout, utterly devoid of the rosy blush it should have had.

—Wait... Nuna, you ordered medium, didn't you?

—Mmmhmm... yeah...

She looked down at her plate. Upon the first slice, her steak revealed itself as hopelessly overcooked, brown to the core—so thoroughly well-done that even a charred steak might feel embarrassed by comparison.

—Excuse me? Do called out, raising his hand to signal the waiter.

—It's fine, Do. At least I won't taste metal this time, haha. Luciana joked, trying to wave off his concern.

—No, it's not fine.

He tried calling the waiter again, but his voice was drowned out by the raucous laughter from the table behind them—a group of venture capitalists in their signature Patagonia vests, their voices brimming with patronizing confidence. Do caught the waiter's eye at last, but the waiter looked away, pretending not to notice, retreating behind a veil of convenient ignorance.

Frustration surged in Do's chest. He didn't want to make a scene in front of Luciana, but there was no ignoring this. He stood, weaving his way to the front desk and finding the manager.

—How can I assist you on this fine evening, sir?

The manager's condescending voice was paired with a gaze that swept from Do's shoes to his haircut, assessing, weighing.

—*Fine evening…* right. Okay, here's the issue. My girlfriend ordered a medium steak, but what you've served is overcooked to the point that even well-done wouldn't do it justice. Could you please send it back and cook it properly?

The manager, dressed to the nines, took note of Do's controlled tone, aware of his attempt at civility. Rather than offering the anticipated apology, however, he took a long pause, examining Do's complaint with the air of someone indulging a trivial matter. And he insisted on checking the steak himself, heading over to their table as if he were doing them a favor.

—Well, my apologies. He began, making no move to take back the steak. But you may not be so familiar with our cooking style. Our first-time customers often think the steak is overdone, but I assure you, this is perfectly cooked to the medium.

—Are you… are you seriously going to stand there and tell me this is medium? Do's tone sharpened.

—Yes, sir. You ordered medium-rare, which, compared to that, makes this steak indeed medium. Our cuisine has contemporary Korean influences, so the steak may look different from what you're accustomed to.

—I'm from South Korea. You are not seriously lecturing me about Korean food, are you?

—Oh… no. No, sir. That is not my intention at all. If you feel the steak is overcooked, we'd be more than happy to prepare another one to your liking. It's already being handled in the kitchen, so please give us a few more minutes. The manager replied, his insincerity palpable.

Wow. That was about as condescending as it gets. His tone dripped with insincerity—since you two uncultivated creatures are being very sensitive, we'll throw you a little something to shut you up. The VCs at the next table had ceased their laughter, watching the exchange now as if observing animals in a zoo, reveling in the spectacle. Everything about this restaurant made Do even more agitated. Luciana, noticing his restraint, gave him a small, understanding smile. It held him back, though perhaps not for long.

•

When the steak finally returned, it was near-raw—more red than brown, practically pulsing with the passive aggression of the restaurant.

—I'm sorry, Nuna. We shouldn't have had to deal with this tonight—on our anniversary of all nights.

—No, I'm fine, Do. They're the ones being assholes, Do. Those condescending pricks.

She tried to match his frustration with some tempered resolve.

—Yeah…

—Let's just leave. And they're not getting much of a tip.

—I… yeah, okay. But let's… just wait a little longer.

—Why? Let's just go grab something at a food truck.

—I know, I just… uh… let's stay just a little longer.

Luciana gave him a quizzical look, not quite understanding why he wanted to prolong their time in this awful place. Well, here was why: when Do made the reservation in Opentable, he added a special anniversary dessert with their names lettered on it. Despite the terrible service from the start, or maybe because of it, he wanted to share that famous matcha tiramisu together with Nuna.

But, of course, expectedly, the dessert never came. Ten minutes passed, then another five.

—Do, let's just go. It's not worth it.

—It's fine. Don't worry about it. Just give me a second, Nuna.

With a determined breath, Do stood and marched back to the front desk, a purpose in his steps.

—How can I help you, sir?

Again, the faintest smirk curled the manager's lips. He knew exactly what was going on but was feigning innocence just to push Do's buttons.

—Oh, please. I need your help on so many things tonight.

—More than happy to assist, sir.

The smug face of the manager was so punchable—if only it wouldn't risk revoking Do's student visa.

—...Well, where should I even start? First, you serve my girlfriend a clearly overcooked steak. Then, you give her a clearly undercooked one, probably on purpose. And now, the dessert I requested is mysteriously missing. And please don't act like you don't know what I'm talking about.

Do could feel the weight of every eye in the restaurant on him. There's another old Korean idiom: *The loudest person wins.*

But not here. In a place like this, the loudest person always loses. A two-eyed man in a land of the one-eyed. The manager, unfazed, let Do's anger roll off him with a patronizing smile.

—My sincerest and most heartfelt apologies, sir. Unexpected delays do happen. Your dessert will be out shortly.

—I asked for special lettering on it, for our anniversary.

—Lettering, sir?

—Yes, I specified it in the Special Request section on OpenTable.

—Ah, my sincerest congratulations on your anniversary, sir. But you see, requests like that should be made directly to the restaurant, not through the app.

—And I did follow up with a call to double-check.

—Mm, yes, sir. It's a common mistake for first-time guests.

—You mean a common mistake at this particular restaurant?

—No worries, sir, we'll prepare the lettering for you, but it may take some additional time.

Do let out a long, exasperated sigh, feeling as though he were on the edge of surrender.

—Wow, you're really a master at passive aggression, aren't you? And not just that. Incompetent, too.

—Oh, sir. My sincerest apologies for the inconvenience. We're doing everything we can to meet your expectations. The dessert will be ready soon.

Sophistication. That's one way to put it—the kind that only years of finely-tuned arrogance could produce. Their "sincerest apologies" made Do sick, his face clenched in frustration. Just as he was about to lose it, Luciana grabbed his arm and pulled him out of the restaurant.

—Do, let's go. We don't need to stay in such an awful place like this.

Her voice was firm but soft, tethering him to reason.

•

Outside, they left behind a sigh as heavy as their evening had become. The cool evening breeze from the San Francisco China Basin helped lower Do's boiling blood pressure, albeit for a brief moment.

—Nuna, wait. What about the bill?

Do asked in an abrasive tone, edged with the residue of frustration.

—I already paid. Barely left a tip. They don't deserve one.

Luciana said, her own voice carrying an undertone of irritation.

—Why, why did you pay? Let me go back and take care of it.

—No! Why the heck would you go back in there? Forget it.

Her frustration was beginning to match his.

—Fine, I'll just transfer it to your account later.

—I can pay for dinner too, you know. Just buy me something at the food truck later.

—Wait, did they even serve you dessert?

—What dessert?

Her frustration tinged with exhaustion from the evening's nonsense.

—Oh, gosh, no, never mind. Forget it.

—Sir?

Just as they were reaching the peak of their frustration, the condescending voice of the restaurant manager sliced through the air once more.

—You left your phone behind.

He handed Do the phone with deliberate slowness and then added an extra sting of passive aggressiveness.

—We regret you didn't get to try our signature matcha tiramisu. We would love to welcome you back for another visit. Have a pleasant evening!

A wave of indignation surged through Do, turning into a rage so fierce that he was ready to storm back into the restaurant.

—No, don't go back in there! Do, Do! Calm down, Do.

Luciana pleaded, grabbing his arm again, this time with all her strength.

—They owe us a fucking apology!

Do spat, the words laced with indignation and pride.

—For what? You avoid stepping in crap not because you're scared of it but because it's crap. Just let it go. Come on, Do!

Her voice filled with a different kind of urgency now, because he might actually do something he'd regret.

—…Nuna, why aren't you taking my side? His voice was hoarse, his frustration spiraling into hurt, confusion clouding his thoughts.

—…What?

Luciana stopped, her hand loosening its grip slightly as she stared at him, stunned.

—Why are you not, like, aren't you angry at those fucking assholes?

—I fucking am! She shot back, her voice rising in response. But what am I supposed to do there? Are you saying I should've defended you in there? And for the record, I did! And I'm stopping you from punching someone and getting arrested!

—Yes! I mean, no! It's not about defending! We didn't do anything wrong. We're on the offense—they're the ones in the wrong! We have every right to get an apology from those sons of bitches. Are you… are you upset because I ruined our anniversary?

The words tumbled out, illogical and raw, the exasperation twisting into shame and spilling out in a hopeless, messy tirade. Do knew he sounded absolutely absurd.

—Do I... do I seriously look like I'm upset because of the fucking anniversary? You know better than that!

Luciana's voice trembled with a mix of anger and disbelief.

•

—...Nuna.

—What!

Her response was sharp, a reflex born from frustration.

—You know how beautiful and amazing you are, right?

—Is that compliment supposed to make me feel better?

She was baffled.

—No, but you always seem to avoid confrontation. Sometimes it's necessary. Why won't you—why can't you just get mad with me at those worthless bastards just once, instead of acting like you're lesser than them?

Are you even serious right now? Luciana shook her head in disbelief.

—Wow... you do know you are entirely talking out of sense right now.

—Maybe. Yes, ok, I am. But this is not the first time I wanted to ask this.

—Ask what?

—It's a pattern. I see this in my Korean friends in the States often. When other minorities get treated like this, do you think they just stay quiet and leave like nothing happened? No! But we always act like we're supposed to just fucking take it. That's why nothing changes. But you know what? I'm not gonna take shit and stay quiet!

Her lips tightened into a thin line, her patience tested.

—Did it look like the loudest person was winning back there? Maybe next time we should bring a megaphone and a drum to announce to the world how unfairly we've been treated?

—You know that's not what I meant!

—Then ask the real fucking question, Do. Are you upset because I didn't fight harder, or because your pride took a hit?

—They're the same thing! He yelled, as if she'd struck a nerve.

—It's not and you know it. She paused, her voice trembling, her words unsteady yet sharp. Do you think this is the first time I've dealt with those condescending motherfuckers? At least we're the customers here—they're the waiters. What do you think it would've been like if it were the other way around?

Her point hit him like a wave, and he swallowed his response, choosing silence over another outburst. Luciana continued.

—Do you think my dad didn't yell back like you? Whenever those condescending motherfuckers came to our diner and threw racist, sexist remarks at mom, he'd explode—just like you. When I was young, I thought that was brave. I didn't understand why mom would look scared. I used to think I'd be proud of my husband for defending us like that. But when I grew up, I realized it wasn't about protecting mom. Dad just couldn't let his fucking pride get hurt one bit. And when he couldn't control that temper of his, do you think it was just the customers he'd unleash it on? Luciana's voice cracked, the rawness of the memory clear.

—Nuna, I wasn't...

But his words withered in his throat. Do knew his words had already left a wound. His anger, so righteous moments before, had drained away, leaving him hollow, filled with a toxic mix of regret and self-loathing.

The weight of his own frustration now eclipsed by the shame gnawing at him. Gosh, if he had a glock, he wanted to go back to the restaurant, shoot the manager, and the waiter, and then lastly himself.

—I'm... I'm sorry, Nuna.

His voice was small, a whisper in the night.

—...It's easy for you to let it all out like that and apologize.

—...Nuna.

—Not tonight. I'll call you later.

She turned from him, as if gathering her composure, holding in the hurt. Her words were steady, but her eyes told a different story.

—Are you going back to your dorm?…

—Yes. Already called an Uber. It'll be here any minute.

—Can I go with you?…

She hesitated, then let her words fall quietly, almost reluctantly.

—…You know what's our problem, Do? It's not the restaurant, it's not the stablecoin project dragging on. It's that… we're so *different* sometimes.

That single word—*different*—pierced him deeper than any argument or insult ever could. She'd said it calmly, solemnly without any embellishment, a brutal honesty that left no room for evasion.

It was a mere drop compared to the torrent Do had poured out, but Luciana too backtracked slightly, wondering if she'd hurt him more than intended. She tried to soften the blow, but the truth lingered, suspended in the space between them.

—Do.

—…Yes? His voice was quieter now, tentative.

—Why are you always so angry?… Why do you see everything as a wall that needs to be knocked down? Why do you always feel like it's your job to fix everything?

—Because… because they *are* walls. Because what they did to us was wrong, and I can't stand to let that pass. I shouldn't have lashed out at you. But to them… how was that wrong?

His voice carried an apology, though it didn't abandon his conviction.

—Yeah, they're assholes. But so what?

—…How do you mean?

—I care about *you*. And maybe I do care about our fucking anniversary after all! So no, I don't want to spend it chasing down the assholes or proving points. In case you didn't realize, an anniversary is about celebrating us, not them!

Do couldn't say anything. She was right—painfully so. He had to admit that. His ambition burned too fiercely, a fire so intense that it couldn't be contained within, spilling over, searing everything in its path. So how could he hold her close, without setting her ablaze?

—Luciana?

Called a loud, raspy voice from the curb. A beat-up red Prius idled there, one side mirror missing and the front bumper barely holding on.

Great timing. Thank you, Uber—for always interrupting our conversation and deciding to show up so on time.

—Uber's here. Hop in, pretty girl.

The driver said, oblivious to the emotional weight of the situation.

—…I need to go, Do. I'll call you later.

Luciana spoke, her voice as weary as her eyes.

But Do couldn't let her go just like that, not like this. She needed space, yes, he understood that. He needed something, anything—to soothe the wound he'd left open before it scarred. He hurriedly climbed into the front passenger seat of the red Prius.

—I'm sorry, Nuna. I know you need some space, but please, let me come with you. Just that, nothing more… I'll sit here in the front. I won't bother you. I'll just watch the Bay Bridge go by. Please just let me stay until I know you're back safe.

Something in his voice, the plea wrapped in vulnerability, made her relent.

—…Fine.

•

A man burning with fire. A woman refusing to catch fire. The couple sat together—not side-by-side but front-and-back—staring out of the window, each lost in their own silence as the streets of San Francisco drifted past.

Once they passed the more congested Financial District, their talkative Uber driver no longer needed to constantly flick the turn signal, so she decided to give her two cents to these youthful lovers.

—Beautiful weather today, ey? I don't know why, but I just love when the fog rolls in thick like this in San Fran.

—Yeah... Do replied absently.

—I'm Susan, by the way. Nice to meet you.

—Hi, pleasure. I'm Moon.

Do was too drained to bother giving his first name and then correcting it.

—That's a lovely name, son. You're a college student, right? You look tired—heard college kids these days barely sleep with all the work. You go to school around here?

—Yeah, Stanford... he mumbled.

—Oh my! Stanford! I wish my daughter could go there too. She's at Albany High. She's thinking of San Fran State or Babson College—heard they're great for business majors. But still, we'll have to help with tuition and everything. The economy's rough, so I'm working Uber, Uber Eats, DoorDash... you name it!

—Yeah, it's tough...

Mrs. Susan's heavy Southern accent initially added a soft twang like syrup, warm and sticky, as if trying to coat the cracks between Do and Luciana. After half an hour, though, it grated on his already frayed nerves. Sitting up front came with its own unique toll, it seemed.

—You two dating, right?

She asked joyfully, undeterred by the lack of enthusiasm.

—...Yes.

—You two look like such a lovely, smart couple.

—...Appreciate it.

—Now, you know, every couple has its rough patches. They say a married couple's quarrel is like cutting water. A relationship is like Yin and Yang.

Do inwardly rolled his eyes. *Gosh, you have to do this now?*

—It's Chinese.

He said, his voice a bit sharper than intended.

—Sorry?

—The Yin and Yang—it's from Chinese philosophy. We're from Korea.

—Oh, oh, I'm so terribly sorry, dear! My mistake. Back in Atlanta—well, actually Decatur, not exactly Atlanta—I had a couple of Chinese friends. Siyue and Yifan, both from mainland China. The kindest folks I ever knew. Haven't ever had a friend from Korea, so I got mixed up. I'm really sorry.

Her sudden tangents—that rustic and unpolished earnestness —had an oddly detoxifying effect on Do, scrubbing away the tension left by the restaurant's pretentious air.

—...It's fine, no worries, ma'am.

Do replied, letting the comment dissolve. Yes, it could've been slightly tone-deaf, but he saw now Mrs. Susan's heart held no ill will. Besides, right now, all that mattered was holding on to the fragile thread of his relationship with Luciana.

—Oh, I love Korea! I watch cooking videos on YouTube, make bibimbap for my kids sometimes—they absolutely love it, haha. And, you know, the U.S. and Korea have a lot in common. Down in the South, where I'm from, it's like another United States. It's more than the accent; it's the food, the politics, even the sports. I guess it's similar in Korea, right? Just to be sure this time, you're from South Korea, not the North, right? Haha.

—Yes, I'm from the South, haha... and yes. It is very— *different*.

Do agreed, a bit too tired forcing a smile and not a yawn.

—My husband and I, we don't live together anymore. We stay in different places and spend weekends with the kids. After forty years of marriage, that's the one thing we figured out. Learning about Yin and Yang helped me understand that. Like, it was a profound moment that lingered with me for quite a while. That's why I mentioned it so carelessly earlier. Sorry again. But yeah, the Yin and Yang. They're different, but they're just relative to each other.

Her last sentence made Do tense up for a second. *Relative to each other?* Something clicked in his mind. The fleeting idea, however, flickered out just as quickly as it appeared. He shook his head, leaning back into the seat, trying to summon back the thought that had slipped away.

Meanwhile, Mrs. Susan seamlessly veered onto a new tangent—this time about Star Wars.

—It's like Luke and Anakin Skywalker. Sorry, haha, my kids are always watching Star Wars, and I can't help but make comparisons! So like, the other day…

•

The baton of ceaseless chatter was now passed to Luciana, who, with remarkable ease, picked up the thread, navigating Mrs. Susan's tangents with grace.

Silly you, Do thought at the front seat. You must be just as worn out as I am, yet there you sit, humoring Mrs. Susan so she won't feel the least bit slighted. Why must you always be so exhaustingly kind?

Silly you, Luciana thought at the back seat. You said you'd just stare out the window and wouldn't care, yet you keep glancing back, caring far more than you'd ever admit. Did you really think I wouldn't notice?

She had been upset with him earlier, and rightfully so. But looking at his puffed-out cheeks, like an obstinate child who refused to listen yet still cared about every word she might say—it softened her heart a bit.

The conversation with Mrs. Susan quieted as they hit a traffic jam once again before leaving the heart of the city. A mist enveloped the car. The glass façades of the cityscape shimmered. They gleamed not with the sterility of the Financial District but with the Pacific *grue* hues rippling like brushstrokes across the windows. It signaled that the red Prius would soon glide onto the Bay Bridge, bidding farewell to San Francisco.

Luciana was sneaking a look at Do's stubborn cheek. Then he suddenly turned, catching her off guard. She whipped her head away, feigning indifference.

—Yin and Yang…?

Do muttered, his gaze drifting out the window before resting back on her. *Nuna.* And then he called.

—…What?

Luciana replied, her voice carrying a slight, endearing pout.

—It's Yin and Yang… It's the goddamn Yin and Yang!

—What?

—Nuna, that's what we needed…! Mrs. Susan, I'm terribly sorry, but can you pull over for a second?

—Oh, sweetie. I'm afraid I can't change the destination once it's set in the Uber app. You'd have to call a new ride after I drop you off.

—-Oh, no, Mrs. Susan. Not that. I only need to get in the back seat and talk to Nuna.

—Aha. Of course, hon! Sure thing. Lucky you asked before we hit the Bridge. I'll pull over to the side.

—Thank you. Thank you so much. Nuna, can I sit next to you for a sec?

Mrs. Susan pulled over to the curb of Folsom Street. And Do, practically in one motion before his own question even finished, leapt from the front seat, swung open the back door, and slid in beside Luciana.

—Listen, Nuna. I think I've figured it out. It's gotta be the Yin and Yang for our stablecoin!

Luciana let him in because the look in his eyes wasn't one of a boyfriend trying to patch things up but a man who had made a groundbreaking discovery, something beyond the ordinary rush of ideas.

—Yes, we might be different. We're *different*. That much is true.

He stammered, his words spilling out in fragments, thoughts unformed but insistent.

—…Okay?...

—But that's a good thing. It's a great thing. It's the only way we can make this work.

—*This?*

—Our stablecoin. And… maybe our relationship too.

—…Okay. Talk about the coin first?

Luciana noticed how he mentioned *our stablecoin* before *our relationship*. Strangely, his sequencing of the sentence carried an intimacy.

—We've been chasing this ghost—a single coin that would miraculously solve everything. For those unimaginative stablecoins like Tether and BUSD, the single-coin approach could work because they have the luxury of collateral—dollars, bitcoins, whatever. Easy stuff. But our revolutionary stablecoin must be based purely on an algorithm, not a collateral, right?

—Yes. That's exactly where we've been stuck.

—Exactly. But you see, we've been trapped—in our own thinking.

—How do you mean?

—What if we made *coins*?

—You mean… more than one single coin?

—Exactly. We are going to make two coins. One will be the stablecoin, and the other will be the collateral coin—but in a very different way. They're going to be like Yin and Yang. Like you and me.

Luciana stared at her boyfriend, still perplexed about where he was going with this. Do continued.

—We're different, but like Mrs. Susan here said, we're also relative to each other. No, scratch that. We're interdependent. Listen, Nuna—I'm going to be the *LunaCoin*.

He pointed to himself, eyes blazing with conviction.

—You're…the LunaCoin?

—Yes, Nuna. I'm the Luna. You are going to be something else. *The better half.* The more stable half.

Do replied to etch the idea into existence.

—What… would that be?

—You'll be the *TerraCoin*. You'll be the stable Yin.

—TerraCoin. You mean Terra as in the earth? Like the land?…

—Yes, remember when we first met in Berkeley? You said you wanted to be like Wozniak, keeping your feet to the ground? The TerraCoin would be a befitting concept for that.

—Aha... so I am going to be the stablecoin?

Her expression shifted. She began to feel the gravity of the names he'd chosen.

—Yes, and I am going to be the LunaCoin, burning itself to maintain the peg—the volatile, fiery Yang.

—Maintaining the pegging... by burning. Oh, oh!

As Do guided her into this discovery, Luciana stepped into the same realization.

—You see where I'm getting at, Nuna?

—Yes, yes. That's how it could work! We've been fixated on this static pegging—keeping it at one dollar at all the time, but it doesn't have to be like that. Yes, you are right! The peg can fluctuate! I mean, even the U.S. dollar fluctuates. That's how it's supposed to work—with *the interplay of two coins*!

—Yes, exactly! I knew you'd get it. The algorithm! The arbitrage between LunaCoin and TerraCoin!

They were both ecstatic, filling the red Prius with a renewed sense of purpose. They skipped past the part where they should've been reconciling, but that was fine in light of such a monumental eureka.

—Do, that's... I gotta say, that's fucking genius. That's fucking genius! That is genius!!

—Think you can code it?

—I'll start the moment we get back.

Yes, Luciana was that kind of person too. In the presence of undeniable ambition, Do could always count on her to be even more ambitious than he was. Their love wasn't built on sweet nothings. Their love was intellectual, a love shaped by ideas, by the interplay of opposing yet complementary forces of Yin and Yang. It was the kind of love that could only exist in the triangular relationship of Do, Luciana, and their shared ambition—an abstract deity they both gazed upward, allowing them to begin loving each other all over again.

•

As Mrs. Susan watched the two young lovers chat excitedly, she felt genuinely happy for them. Of course, she couldn't understand half the jargon they were using—LunaCoin, TerraCoin, pegging—it sounded like some alien language. So let us pause for a moment to explain the mechanism of these two coins. We owe her at least that:

The mechanism of LunaCoin and TerraCoin is like the relationship between Yin and Yang—interdependent, maintaining balance through each other's existence. Simply put, TerraCoin is the $1 coin. LunaCoin? Its price can rise as high as it can.

The TerraCoin (Ticker: $TERRA) represents stability and balance, the "Yin."

The LunaCoin (Ticker: $LUNA) represents volatility and energy, the "Yang."

TerraCoin is pegged to the dollar and relies on LunaCoin to maintain its value. The system works through the interaction of the two coins, maintaining balance autonomously.

They use supply and demand, similar to how central banks regulate the value of a currency. When the dollar becomes too strong, more money is printed, increasing the supply. When it becomes too weak, the supply is reduced. Think of TerraCoin as the one dollar bill. The only difference is George Washington's portrait on the paper and Do-Luciana's couple portrait on the coins.

If the value of TerraCoin exceeds $1 and rises to $1.10, it signals that demand has outstripped supply. At this point, new TerraCoins are minted, and LunaCoins are burned. The burning of LunaCoin increases the supply of TerraCoin, bringing the value back down to $1. As the demand for LunaCoin rises, so does its value. Arbitrage opportunities drive traders to mint TerraCoin by burning LunaCoin, profiting from the price difference and restoring the peg. LunaCoin sacrifices itself to stabilize TerraCoin, ensuring the system's balance.

If the value of TerraCoin drops below $1 to $0.90, it signals an oversupply. LunaCoins are minted to purchase TerraCoins, increasing demand for TerraCoin and bringing its value back to $1. This process increases the supply of LunaCoin, potentially lowering its value, but TerraCoin regains its stability. LunaCoin absorbs the volatility to maintain TerraCoin's peg to $1. The two coins work in tandem, constantly rebalancing each other.

Here's what's especially radical about this pair of coins. Everything is driven by an algorithm, not by any individual or institution. It's not just another dollar-pegged stablecoin. The system works in harmony, rebalancing autonomously.

Trust isn't necessary. Permission isn't required. The trust and permission are programmed by Do and Luciana—but they will not be the masters.

Phew, I think that's enough of an explanation. Let's return to the architects of this creation.

•

—Nuna.

—Yup.

—I want to say this before it's too late. Thank you for telling me that you care.

Do's voice, far softer and gentler now, took on a sincerity that only emerged when they were side by side.

—…Yeah.

Luciana replied, her own voice calmer.

—And you know how much I care about you.

—I do.

—I admit that we have our differences at times, yes. But… that's also why we're drawn to each other. Like the Earth and the moon.

—Heh, yup.

—Hah, I'm sorry. I am so overusing this Earth-Moon, Terra-Luna metaphor. I shouldn't be mixing up work and love like this.

—It's alright. This is the kind of discovery you can't stop thinking about. It's the kind of epiphany that lives on. And honestly, I don't mind mixing work and love.

—Thank you, Nuna. And even though we might have come from different places, I want to believe we are heading to the same place. I want to go to the moon—with you. Shoot, I had to make that moon metaphor.

—I'll happily give you a pass, since you've always been cheesy and lame, heh. I'm glad that your surname at least makes it a little less lame.

—Very kind of you to say that, madam.

—You're very welcome, mister.

They exchanged a glance, a warmth rekindling between them.

—And Do, thank you for saying that. I mean it, too. Though when we get back, instead of undressing, we'll need to open our laptops.

—Of course! What do you take me for? You know what, I'll actually start coding right here, on our way back.

—Sure, you go head first.

—But before that, just one kiss, please. Love you, Nuna.

—I love you.

With the two lovebirds entwined in the backseat, Mrs. Susan's weary red Prius sped down the Bay Bridge, clinging precariously to its front bumper as if by some minor miracle. They passed through the tunnel and burst forth onto the open road, where the waters of Emeryville's bay shimmered on either side like liquid sapphires. Yet, Do scarcely registered the shift in light; his mind was adrift, submerged in the delicate gestation of their invention. LunaCoin was finding its form here—inside this weathered chariot, his fingers dancing like possessed spirits over the keys of his Macbook Air.

The coin that would ripple across the world was stirring into existence. And soon, when they reached the dorm to bestow the final touches upon this sudden revelation, LunaCoin would be cut free, severed from its nascent cord, to begin the first lines of its own genesis.

Act II

chapter block
09.0

[real-time dashboard]

LunaCoin ($LUNA) / Price: $62.25,
Market Cap: $14.5M, 24h Volume: $3.2M
TerraCoin ($TERRA) / Price: $1.00,
Market Cap: $234K, 24h Volume: $1.1M

—Hi, I'm here to extend my leave of absence?

—Name, please?

The Stanford International Center staffer asked back nonchalantly.

—First name, Do-hyung. Last name, Moon.

—Sorry, Hee-young?

It always startled Do how Americans managed to find the most creative way to pronounce *hyung*.

—No, just search for D-O? Like the extinct Dodo bird.

—Ah, Do Moon. Okay, may I see your ID?

—You can just google him. No need to check his ID.

Nik cut in with a laugh.

—Do, you know we are throwing a graduation party at Angelica's place tonight, right? You gotta come.

—I'm not even a senior, dude. I just extended my leave so that I can stay as a sophomore forever. Do laughed.

—That's perfectly fine, because half the seniors graduating will be working for you one day.

—Hah, you better stick around too.

Do returned to Stanford to extend his leave of absence. He wouldn't have returned unless it was to celebrate a heroic victory. LunaCoin hadn't quite shaken the world yet, but it had successfully completed its ICO with more than a buzz. A stablecoin powered purely by an algorithm—the Silicon Valley had taken notice. And his story fit the Valley's ideal narrative—a Stanford computer science major dropout to start the next big thing. In the coin or the creator, the future of LunaCoin seemed blindingly bright.

Do decided to make an appearance at the party. He hadn't even properly completed his sophomore year, yet he was already a star. As he surveyed the room, he caught glimpses of people toasting to his success, subtly edging closer. Gosh, the world was such a beautiful place for the successful. And right on cue, the one person he wanted to impress the most—or the second most—walked past.

—Hey, June.

He greeted his ex first.

—Oh, Do. Hey, it's been a while.

—Yeah, it has. I haven't been around campus.

—I heard.

June paused, and Do's anticipation surged. You heard what, June? Come on, tell me.

—So, uh, congratulations on your coin venture.

Everyone, did you just hear this painfully understated, sparing acknowledgment? She's trying! It made Do smile with a perverted sense of victory. But then, Do glanced at her left hand. It's still that Swarovski ring still clinging to her finger.

—Thank you, thank you. I heard you applied to law schools. Where are you headed?

—Oh, Columbia.

—That's fantastic. Congrats. And congratulations on your graduation, too. You got into Stanford before me, and now you're leaving before me.

—Oh, it's nothing, haha. I wish you all the best with the LunaCoin.

—Yeah, so—

—Oh, sorry, Do. I've got to go.

Abruptly, she turned and walked off. And after a few steps, she linked arms with that same blockchain club guy and disappeared from view. A familiar resentment bubbled up in Do's chest. Sure, that same tacky silver ring all these years? And you, the glorified Mr. VP of the Stanford Blockchain Club. How do you like your cute role-playing as coin experts in a school club, gathering every week to study the very coin I created? And June, stop pretending you're cool and above it all. Soon enough, you'll be paying for date nights with my coin. *Good luck living in the world I'm building.*

Do brushed away the creeping discomfort like tossing out trash.

—Hey, hey, superstar.

It was Aaron, fresh out of the Navy. Turned out, he hadn't decided to swim across the Pacific to abandon his duty halfway through his service. What an unpleasant surprise.

—Oh, hey.

Do acknowledged him with the bare minimum of interest.

—I've been back at school for a while, but I haven't seen you around, man. Only in the news these days, haha.

—Come on. It's not like that.

—By the way, you haven't met the new KSA freshmen, have you? I told them about you, and they were dying to meet you.

The two underclassmen stood nervously, like they'd been granted rare backstage access to some K-pop star.

—Pleasure to meet you, *sunbae-nim*. Wow... can't believe it's real. I went to Sudo High too, and I've heard so much about you.

—Nice to meet you.

Their nervousness was almost cute, and they seemed bright enough. But Do was riding too high to pay attention to such trivial connections.

—So, man, it feels like a lifetime ago, but remember when I said I'd want to invest in your project if it took off? Aaron interjected again.

—Ha, Yeah.

—Well, while I was stuck in the military, you went ahead and built the whole new thing... kinda feels a bit unfair, haha.

Aaron tossed out his trademark jab—sneering just enough to test the waters, but not quite enough to cross the line. Do, however, didn't hesitate for even a second to crush him.

—That's funny. You think you could've done the same if you hadn't gone to the military?

Do looked down at Aaron, squashing the jealousy dressed in friendly barb. Success had honed his social skills in a novel way. Where most would stew in delayed irritation, rehearsing clever retorts that would never see the light—*I should've said this and that*—he had risen above those reflexes. Most people are bound to an automatic courtesy. But Do, now one of those larger-than-life figures, saw no need to maintain that courtesy anymore. So when Aaron dared to play at his level, Do casually but firmly stomped him out.

—Oh, no... nah... haha, I know I'm not as talented as you, haha...

Aaron quickly backed down. And Do smiled, reassured of his standing.

—And LunaCoin is too big now for my kind of investment... But I know a guy back in Korea. He's a big shot, to say the least. And when I met him last summer he seemed to be pretty... interested in your project.

—He's an investor?

—Yeah, sort of.

—More investment wouldn't hurt. But if it's just some trust-fund baby's dumb money, I'm not interested.

—Come on, Do, haha. You think I'd bring dumb money to the hottest startup in the Valley?

—Well, who's the investor?

—Damien Jin. The founder of CouponMaster. Ring a bell?

Damien Jin. *That* Damien Jin? Do felt a flash of surprise but kept his expression blank.

—Oh... yeah, I know him. Really? He's interested in LunaCoin? How do you know him?

—Our dads are friends. But seriously, with Jin, a lot of good things will come your way. Should I set it up? You could meet him next time you're in Korea.

—Hmm... Yeah, sounds good. Thanks, Aaron.

—Hey, no problem. You're a big deal now. Gotta hang with the big players.

Grand compliments don't feel like empty flattery anymore— they ring with truth. Yeah, I'm done dwelling on old, useless relationships. Everyone's dying to be part of me now, and the only integral constituent is—*Nuna.*

•

Venture capitalists in Silicon Valley casually wield billions. They live in their little enclave along the Sand Hill Road. Unlike the towering buildings of Wall Street, you won't find any taller than a three-story office here. These minimalist offices, resembling modest homes, are where seasoned VCs, dressed in their ever-present Patagonia vests, greet entrepreneurs with an easy, friendly smile.

—Finally, the golden boy of crypto is here! Mr. Moon. Do— can I call you that? Oh, please, call me John.

It's not because they're your friends. They've stripped away all formality, so they expect you to do the same. No dressing up— just raw talent on display. You might walk in, glance around the office, and feel underwhelmed. When you begin your pitch, however, their incisive questions will cut you bare, the slow disintegration of your dreams.

—Do, thank you for the pitch. But it seems like there are still quite a few rough edges. This might sound cliché, but pretend I'm a 10-year-old and explain why we need stablecoins, please?

—Oh, of course. Absolutely.

—Ah, and maybe you should close your eyes, since I doubt my wrinkles will help you imagine me as a 10-year-old, haha.

—Haha, not at all, sir. I mean, John. So, uh, the clearest advantage of a stablecoin is that it enables seamless cross-border payments. It helps everyone—from parents sending tuition to their kids to Silicon Valley engineers sending money back home to their families in India. And not just individuals. Think of companies that conduct international business—if they use our coin for transactions, the scale would be unimaginable. And banks too! We could build new financial products...

—Yeah, that's all very well. But why would anyone use the stablecoin instead of the dollar? Just to save on fees?

Do had prepared himself for this kind of battle.

—Well, PayPal and now Stripe—they both started with the simple premise of saving fees. And look at them now. PayPal is a global standard, and Stripe is a $50 billion company.

—True that.

—Convenient payments, fee minimization—both companies launched on those seemingly insignificant premises. But I don't think someone with your insight, who's backed both PayPal and Stripe, would need me to explain the significance of dominating the payment systems of the cryptocurrency world.

—Well, you've done your homework.

The VC smiled. Sensing momentum, Do pressed on.

—And it's not just that! The era of cryptocurrency is coming whether people like it or not. In that new era, to move money through blockchain, what you need most is not Bitcoin or Ethereum. You need TerraCoin and Lunacoin.

—I'll agree with you there. But what about your competitors, like Tether?

—To be blunt, I don't consider Tether a real stablecoin. If a coin requires dollars to exist, it's not a coin at all. Our coin, with enough liquidity, operates on an algorithm alone.

—Yes, regulating supply algorithmically between TerraCoin and LunaCoin to maintain the price... It's indeed a once-in-a-generation idea.

—Thank you!

—But.

—Yes?

—I'm still not sold on the entire cryptocurrency market itself. Blockchain is an amazing technology. It cuts to the heart of what money is. But making the new money isn't just about that. Yours is an... audacious project.

—...I'll take "audacious" as a compliment.

—It was meant as one. But if audacity doesn't lead to success, it's just recklessness.

—With my algorithm and the talented developers working alongside—

—I want to ask about *you*. Just you. Because you *are* the LunaCoin. So here's my concern. How ready are you to knock down the walls in front of you?

—I can assure you, sir, that I've always knocked down any walls standing in my way.

And Do meant every word. That was his very essence.

—Do, readiness is one thing. Fighting it out till the end is quite another. PayPal had to fight the credit card companies. Uber had to battle taxi unions and the governments protecting them—in New York! Think about that. That fight was grueling, and only Travis and his investors know how tough it was.

—Yes, I agree.

—And look at Tesla. Do you know how many oil barons and the ghosts of Henry Ford are out to strangle Tesla? But it's Elon at the helm, so we know we could count on him. On the other hand... Do, you're smart, but this fight isn't about brains. It's about grit.

—I understand. And I think I'm—

The VC, still polite but unflinchingly direct, cut Do off.

—For your stablecoin to succeed, you will be up against the presidents and the treasury secretaries of the world defending their national currencies. Oh, and let's not forget Buffett, Munger, and a slew of Wall Street billionaires like Jamie Dimon and Ken Greenspan whose fortune is all in dollars and none in crypto. Are you *actually* prepared to take them on?

—I...

—You see, Do, neither I nor my colleagues care about nationality, race, or gender. In fact, entrepreneurs who come from disadvantaged backgrounds tend to perform better because they're tougher.

—That's true, yes.

—But LunaCoin has to beat the US dollar. Are you prepared to handle all those lawsuits while you're here on a student visa?

The VC's words landed heavily, and Do wondered when they'd dug into his background so thoroughly.

—That's...

—Oh, sorry, Do. I just remembered I have another meeting. We'll leave it here for today. It was an intriguing conversation. Feel free to reach out again when you have more tangible results.

•

Clinging to his battered pride, Do exited Sand Hill Road and headed to another VC office, this time in San Francisco.

—Did I miss something here? What's... LunaCoin? It's a pretty name, but why do we need it?

—Oh, sure. Let me explain again. The stablecoins—

—No, when you say, "Let me explain again," you're implying I didn't get it the first time.

—Oh... I'm sorry.

—It's not your explanation. It's the clarity of the product itself. Your coin has to be so intuitive and easy to understand that a 10-year-old would get it the first time.

—Yes... I apologize. So, the stablecoins—

—How can we trust a company or a coin to be stable when its founder clearly isn't? Anyway, if you have more tangible results in the future, feel free to reach out again.

•

Next, a meeting at another reputable VC firm—not quite Sequoia or Kleiner Perkins, but perhaps with a better shot at success for that very reason. Do hadn't eaten all day, but his stomach was already heavy. After the disastrous meeting in San Francisco, he rushed back to Sand Hill Road.

—Hello, I'm Do Moon, founder of LunaCoin? I had an appointment with Dana at six.

—Oh, Dana had a last-minute engagement. She left a note for you.

—Wh...what? So the meeting's canceled?

—Yes, but I'm sure the note will cover what you need.

Do unfolded the note handed to him.

I'm sorry I had to cancel. Feel free to reach out again when you have more tangible results.

•

Fuck this!

He returned home-office much earlier than planned, slamming his bag onto the floor before collapsing onto the barren mattress—the only furniture in the room aside from the clutter of laptops and monitors. The LunaCoin basecamp was situated in their neutral DMZ ground, the San Francisco Mission Bay. It was their battlefield where dreams collide violently with the inevitable frustrations. The rent was steep, but the profits from LunaCoin were more than enough to cover it. That wasn't the endgame, though. No, their ultimate goal was to pay the rent not with dollar bills but with LunaCoin.

When he and Luciana first moved in, they decided to assemble the flatpack bed later when they had time. Months had passed, and the bed assemblages were still untouched, scattered like unfinished thoughts. Every ounce of their energy was funneled into their creations.

Fuck this...

What kind of delusion was I under? Do brooded. Showing up at meaningless parties, acting like I've already made it... The second I feel the temptation to live a little, I'll end up right back where I was during college admissions or in the fucking DMZ post.

—Do?

Luciana's tone was soft but laced with concern as she took in his unexpectedly early return and slumped posture.

—Nuna. The VC meetings… they… phew. I'm sorry.

He barely whispered the endearment with a mixture of affection and apology. He sighed, dragging a hand through his hair.

—Yeah…

Luciana didn't offer platitudes or try to dismiss his frustration. Do's face tightened. *Yeah?* Perhaps he'd secretly hoped she would say something like "It's okay," despite hating that meaningless combination of words more than anyone else. A part of him paradoxically craved that empty reassurance.

—You know, Nuna. It's starting to feel disturbingly familiar… just like when I messed up my college admissions. These asshole VCs—they're no different from college admissions officers. They paint themselves as open-minded but won't believe you until you show them something undeniable. But once you do, they will fucking believe everything without question.

Luciana, ever the pragmatist, shifted gears—which wasn't what Do particularly wanted at this moment.

—Well, Do. If it's any consolation, the dev team made a breakthrough yesterday. You know we need smart contracts for our ecosystem to really take off. So I thought we could use LevelDB to give each contract its own keyspace—

—Nuna.

Do cut her off sharply.

—Hm?

—Our coin is complete, right? Like, it's technically waterproof?

—I wouldn't say that yet, but it's getting close enough—

—If you think it's close enough, it means it's perfect.

—It's… it's premature in my opinion, Do.

His gaze, intense and unwavering, nevertheless locked onto hers.

—Look, I can't let this devolve into another failed endeavor, like my old college application. This isn't about getting into Harvard or Stanford. TerraCoin and LunaCoin—our brilliant creations—they don't live or die whether VCs grant us their approval. We don't need their fucking permission. So let's move forward with the Anchor Protocol.

—No. Do. We're not ready for that yet.

Luciana's expression hardened as the words *Anchor Protocol* registered. She adamantly refused his proposal.

—Why?

His voice rose, tinged with the same desperation that had driven him through every stage of his life. He pressed on.

—The Anchor Protocol is the only way forward. We have to go bigger. That's how we will incentivize people to buy our coin. Stablecoins—people don't understand the beauty of them like we do. They don't make money fast enough. If this were some shit scam coin that soared 1000% one day and crashed 2000% the next, people would still throw their money at it. Fuck, why do I keep forgetting that most people on this planet are idiots? They don't even know what they want until it's shoved in front of their faces. So let's *show them* with the Anchor Protocol.

We'll delve into the specifics of this Anchor Protocol a little later. Let's remain anchored in the present.

—Yeah, fuck the VCs.

—Yes, Nuna, exactly! Fuck the VCs—time to show the world our Anchor Protocol!

—But *not* the Anchor Protocol.

Luciana's emphasis on the word cut through the air with a steely resolve.

—What...? Why? His momentum suddenly checked.

—I can't approve the Anchor Protocol. If we go down that path, our coin will just become another obscene token.

—Then give me a goddamn alternative!

What nerve had been struck in Do? Was it her outright rejection of the Anchor Protocol? Or was it Luciana's choice of words—*can't approve*? But this brief crack in his composure is quickly overshadowed by the immediate problem at hand.

—I agree with you that our coin doesn't need anyone's permission to succeed. But we can still prove our use case without jumping into the Anchor Protocol. We should start with... I don't know, using our coin to buy something simple, like pizza?

—Pizza?

—Something mundane. We cannot and should not promise people they'll get rich off our coin. That was never our purpose to begin with. And you, Do, more than anyone, understand that.

Luciana continued, determined to bring his soaring ambition back to earth.

—Yeah, I get it. I... okay. I won't jump into Anchor now.

—Thank you. Let's start small. Let people know they can buy pizza, or pens, or calculators with our coin. Let's run a proof of concept first—maybe on a small e-commerce site.

The CTO[9] steadied the CEO's impulses while guiding him towards a more pragmatic path.

—You are right... our coin could work that way first. I've actually got a meeting with someone back in Korea. Do you know CouponMaster? Do began, the gears turning in his mind.

—Oh, yeah! Isn't that like the Korean version of Amazon? I remember reading about it in a Haas business case series.

—Exactly. It's like a Korean Amazon—or more like Korean Groupon. But Groupon's dead, so they've pivoted to be more like Amazon now.

—You're meeting CouponMaster's CEO? When?

—As soon as possible.

—That could really work. Do, you're the CEO, and I trust your judgment. But let's keep our focus on making this simple proof of concept happen.

—Thank you, Nuna... and should I just ditch the VCs now? Do you think we need to hire more engineers for the dev team?

—No need. We have a good team already, and we'll scrap together what we need. And yes, fuck the VCs. When you apply to all eight Ivy League colleges, you're not planning to attend them all. You are just trying to increase your chances, right? And when

---

[9] Chief Technology Officer

you get that letter from Harvard, that's where you'll go. We don't need every VC in town in our pocket.

—That's... that's a brilliant analogy, haha.

The CEO had always respected the coding prowess of his CTO slash girlfriend, but her strategic insights consistently took him by surprise. You don't often hear about couples who build empires together. They, however, do exist: Eventbrite, VMware, Houzz. They may not be the gods of Silicon Valley, but they certainly are demigods. *And I admire and love you so much that I might even be okay with being demigods together*, Do thought for a brief moment.

—Nuna, you're absolutely right. Thank you... for reminding me. We're not the nobodies we once were. We've got a kickass pair of stablecoins with us now.

—We sure do.

—Rome wasn't built in a day, so before we take on the U.S. market, I will go to Korea and prove that people can actually buy real stuff in the real world with our stablecoin.

Do gripped Luciana's hand firmly as he spoke.

—Good. When are you leaving for Korea?

—Probably tomorrow. Late night.

—You shouldn't bother texting before you leave. I'll be up all night or catching a nap with the dev team anyway.

She squeezed his hand back, a gentle assurance.

—Thank you. I love you. And... I'm sorry.

Do wanted to bring up the Anchor Protocol again, but he couldn't bring himself to undermine the support and belief of someone who held him up so completely.

—Don't say sorry. Do, as I always tell you—I'm not obsessed with reaching some colossal success. But I do believe, realistically, that this project is bound to succeed in its own right.

He smiled and nodded, though he couldn't fully agree with her. For him, anything less than colossal success simply wouldn't be enough.

chapter block
10.0

[real-time dashboard]

LunaCoin ($LUNA) / Price: $200.12,
Market Cap: $185.4M, 24h Volume: $32.6M
TerraCoin ($TERRA) / Price: $1.01,
Market Cap: $50.1M, 24h Volume: $3.8M

The fragrance of the wind at Incheon Airport always carried a distinct difference after time spent abroad. It was a scent only those returning from foreign lands could sense. A hint of briny air if you'd come from somewhere fresh, a hint of rejuvenating air if you'd come from somewhere stale.

Do slid into a taxi headed straight home and promptly rolled up the window. He focused on reviewing the notes for the upcoming meeting.

Damien Jin.

Graduated from UPenn, founded CouponMaster. *Underlined.*

Grandfather was the attorney general and the CIA chief under the military regime. *Underlined.*

Nationality: American. Damn, he probably never served in the military. *Lucky bastard. Underlined.*

Could Do really win over a man like this? Desperation and confidence, after all, are two different things. He needed to keep the former buried deep but present the latter with ease. Just like applying to college—you prepare as though your life depends on getting in. When you actually submit the application, however, you exude nonchalance as if you couldn't care less about their permission.

After a string of cold rejections from haughty VCs, Do's confidence had taken a hit. He stopped reading about Damien Jin and returned to rehearsing his pitch.

Ahem, ahem. CouponMaster is one of the largest e-commerce companies in Korea... Supporting SMBs[10] is essential... Many SMBs face cash flow issues and need immediate working capital... But in Korea, it takes seven days for electronic payments to process... However, with our stablecoin, payments are completed in seven seconds... our stablecoin can lower fees in the long run... Most importantly, using our blockchain for transactions and issuing your own cryptocurrency can unlock the seigniorage effect... CouponMaster is an e-commerce giant in Korea, but not the only one... With TerraCoin and LunaCoin, you simplify payments, save on costs, and offer additional discounts through seigniorage. It's like becoming the central bank of e-commerce... Blah blah blah.

The fundamentals were rock solid, no doubt about that. But still, he pondered—what extra touch could he bring to the meeting? Should he get a new cologne?

Ding. His newly reinstalled Korean Whatsapp chimed with a message.

```
@theyohanlee: Yoooo Mundo!
@theyohanlee: Woah it's been ages mannnn. you
back in korea?
```

The first direct message since landing, and it's from Private Yohan Lee. The nickname *Mundo* tugged a faint smile from Do, although his military days were now a faded blur. With so much competing for his attention now, trivial memories didn't often resurface. He nearly ignored the message.

---

[10] Small and medium-sized businesses

When he briefly lowered the window, the air that filled the taxi carried a haunting familiarity—a scent of his homeland, a trace of the DMZ. He remembered Yohan's discharge day, when he'd hugged him like a brother. So Do decided to reply.

@do_llarmoon: hey man. long time no see
@do_llarmoon: loll how do you know im back
@theyohanlee: Your profile just popped up fresh
@theyohanlee: Got time for lunch tomorrow? My treat!

Ugh. Do groaned. *Should've just ignored it.*

•

Still, Do agreed to meet Yohan for lunch. The reasons were unremarkable: 1) the meeting place was right by his place, and 2) sometimes, those chance meetings with seemingly useless people lead to useful discoveries.

Do showed up five minutes late to the so-called high-end ramen shop in Gangnam. Let's ignore that it was barely a five-minute walk from his apartment. Let's also ignore the inherent contradiction of high-end ramen.

Through the large glass windows of the ramen shop, he spotted Yohan, looking every bit the throwback with wired earphones dangling from his ears, like some Gen X time traveler caught in the wrong decade. Yohan was scanning the fancy decor with a slightly lost expression. They'd only ever known each other in uniform, both sporting buzz cuts, stiff postures, and the look of young soldiers. This was their first reunion as civilians, but one glance was enough to tell it was still the same Yohan—the unmistakable kindness, bordering on naivete, in his face.

—Yo, Mundo! Here! Woah, it's been forever, man.

—Yeah, long time no see. It's been ages since anyone called me *Mundo* since discharge, haha.

—This is the first time we've met in civilian life. Feels strange even saying that, doesn't it? We're both miles away from those days now.

—Ha, you're right.

—I see you on Instagram now and then. Stanford, huh? Damn, I always knew you were smart, but that's on a different level. I have never even traveled to America.

—Haha, thanks. What's with the… wired earphones? Retro look? Looks pretty cool, haha.

—Oh, these? They were a gift. Yohan smiled, a touch of bashfulness in his expression.

—Ah, from a girlfriend?

Wired earphones, hmm. Do could see the charm. A bit nostalgic against all the sleek wireless tech of today. The cord as a tangible connection between the couple. Come to think of it, he realized that he and Luciana had never exchanged couple rings. The only thing they ever truly shared was their grand ambition. Of course, he wanted something beyond an ordinary pair of couple rings. He wanted a special token, proportional to the ever-increasing market cap of LunaCoin every day.

I should get something on my way back to San Francisco. There Do sat, adrift in thoughts of Luciana half an atlas away, even as Yohan sat across from him.

—Nah, from my mom, actually. Yohan grinned.

—Ah.

—Yeah, you know the tradition—red thermal underwear for the parents with our first paycheck. The thermals alone felt a bit bare, so I added the earphones. But when mom found out my earphones weren't as nice as my gift, she decided to go out and get me a pair to match, haha.

—You're a good son, Private Lee, haha.

First paycheck. A concept Do barely related to. He was engineering the money itself, yet he'd never earned a paycheck in the traditional sense.

—You must've done some internships back in school, right? I bet an intern's paycheck in Silicon Valley is double what a full-time salary is in Korea, haha.

—Haha, maybe.

Their conversation could barely stretch beyond a couple of sentences before hitting a wall. It made sense—they had little, almost nothing in common beyond their fables from the DMZ. Do's mind drifted back to LunaCoin and his upcoming meeting with Damien Jin.

—So, Mundo... erm, speaking of paychecks, haha, I've been seriously looking into jobs in America lately. Thought I might get some advice...

—Haha, that's not bad.

Do, lost in his own thoughts, gave an offhand reply.

—Hmm?

—Oh... nevermind. Sorry, come again? I didn't catch it.

—Oh, no problem. I was just thinking about getting jobs in America. I know my English isn't great, but... I'm willing to work my ass off. Or maybe I could start here, join a company with overseas branches, and work my way up to some international experience...

Yohan went on to describe his plan in detail, but Do barely registered any of it, letting the words flow in one ear and drift right out the other.

—I see, haha. But yeah, it's tough in the U.S. too.

—Of course, of course. But... like, at least in the U.S., it feels like things are always building up, like there's some kind of progress.

—Haha, yeah...

You have to understand, Do isn't some totally ungrateful guy dismissing a senior who looked out for him during military service. In his defense, when your daily life revolves around questions like, *How can I replace the U.S. dollar?* or *How can I create a completely new financial system?*—it's sort of hard to empathize with the everyday struggles of Yohan. Scientists have even claimed that the brains of powerful people undergo physical changes, diminishing their capacity for empathy, haven't they?

—These days, nobody wants to work anymore. Everyone's just chasing quick money—stocks, crypto. It's the same at my company.

—Yup. People have lost their sense of the value of labor. Meanwhile, the value of capital is exponentially multiplying. So who can blame them? Unless *someone* breaks Wall Street and makes a new one.

—Oh, man, that's deep. You really are a Stanford guy.

—No, I just read Piketty in my freshman year, haha.

—Pickets?

—Oh... erm, it's nothing, haha.

—Yeah, I remember those pickets scattered around at our DMZ post. Oh, and remember? In the barracks, I told you to buy Bitcoin before your first leave.

—I remember that, of course, haha. Didn't you sell all your Bitcoin?

Now that Yohan was talking about cryptocurrency, Do finally started to listen—just a bit.

—Yeah, yeah. You even bought me a book about Bitcoin when you came back.

—I fondly remember that. Good times.

—God, I want to punch myself. I sold most of my Bitcoin before it started to really take off. When it did, I had only two left in my wallet. Did sell them for like 5 million won[11] each, but that just stings more. I had hundreds of Bitcoins back when I was a Private. What about you? Did you keep your coins?

—Ah... I didn't buy that much Bitcoin back then. Maybe around 20 million worth now.

His old senior's eyes widened at the casual mention of such a sum.

—Twenty mil?! You mean in won, not in dollars, right?

—Oh, oh, yeah, in won.

---

[11] Approx. USD 5,000.

Do didn't mention that his current Bitcoin holdings were worth easily more than twenty mil—and, of course, in *dollars*. But no need to shock Yohan further.

—You say that like it's pocket change! Damn... I'm jealous, haha. You should sell the rest before Bitcoin crashes though. Altcoins—that's where people actually make money.

—So are you back into crypto now?

—When something's hot, you gotta go all in.

—Which altcoins are you into? Ethereum? Ripple?

—Ripple's wild swing is fun. But actually, I got a tip from a friend last night.

—Oh yeah? What's the tip?

—Shit, I feel like if I tell you this, you'll be the one raking in all the profit, haha. Nah, just kidding. He told me about this thing called stablecoin.

Wow. Do suppressed a smirk, amusement secretly simmering beneath the surface. *Yohan, there really must be some cosmic thread tying us together,* he mused.

—Oh really? What's a stablecoin? I'm so curious.

Do leaned in with a playful grin, feigning interest with the poise of a god who already knew every line in the script. And Yohan was still blissfully unaware.

—Well, the stablecoin's just like a one-dollar bill. It stays pegged to the value of one dollar.

—Mmhmm. So which stablecoins did you buy? Tether?

—Oh, wow. You already know a bit about it too, huh? But here's the lessons I've learned from stocks and crypto, Mundo.

Yohan perked up, impressed.

—What are those lessons?

—If you're only looking at what's hot right now, you're already behind. To stay ahead, you've gotta look to the future. Tether? It's yesterday's news. You know Tether, I know Tether, right? You've gotta invest in coins people haven't caught onto yet.

—I do agree with that.

—So, if stablecoin is the future, I'm getting in on it. But then I asked my friend, "If it stays at one dollar, how do you make any money?"

—Yeah, exactly. How?

Do continued to play along.

—Well, he explained some algorithmic stuff, which I didn't really understand, haha. But basically, there are some special stablecoins made up of not one—but two coins. So the first coin stays at one dollar, but if you buy the second coin, that's the one where the price goes up. That's the one you gotta buy.

—Ah-ha. What's the name of that special coin? I'm curious.

Yohan leaned in, clearly thrilled to be the bearer of hot news.

—Okay, I'm not holding anything back from my DMZ comrade, haha. Listen up, it's called *LunaCoin*. Write it down. Luna-Coin. It's gonna blow up, dude. My friend said it's the hottest thing in Silicon Valley right now.

This meeting was worth it, Do thought. He hadn't discovered some miraculous revelation, but he now had the confidence he needed for his upcoming meeting with Damien Jin.

—I even like the name, too. LunaCoin. They say having a pretty name is an important price factor—like Stellar Lumens, Avalanche. I hope this LunaCoin soars like them one day.

—…Yohan, I guess this is what people say something is meant to be. Thank you. You might not realize it, but you've been a big help.

—Heh, glad you're catching on now. Since you've made twenty million won off Bitcoin, you're buying lunch today.

—Haha, I would gladly do that. And Yohan, send me your wallet address, please?

—You mean my crypto wallet address?

—Yeah.

—Uh, okay.

Yohan had no clue why Do wanted his wallet address—maybe he's sending lunch money in Bitcoin?

His crypto wallet currently displayed:

Wallet Summary
Total Balance: ₩9,340 (~$7.14 USD)
Portfolio:
• Bitcoin (BTC): 0.000024
• Ethereum (ETH): 0.00074
• Ripple (XRP): 0.96
Last Transaction: Received 0.5 XRP from 0x8f...a1b7

A grand total net worth of about seven bucks. But then a minute later, his near-empty crypto wallet pinged with a notification—a hundred million won had been deposited.

Now, his wallet displayed:

Wallet Summary
Total Balance: ₩23,009,340 (~$20,006.34 USD)
Portfolio:
• Bitcoin (BTC): 0.000024
• Ethereum (ETH): 0.00074
• Ripple (XRP): 0.96
• LunaCoin (LUNA): 100
Last Transaction: Received 100 LUNA from 0x3a...2ba2

Yohan stared at his phone, dumbfounded.

—Mundo! Did you just send me LunaCoin?!...

—I did.

—Dude, lunch was like 10,000 won[12] each. You added like, three extra zeroes. I'm sending it back now.

—Oh, no need. Remember those ramen ppogeuli you'd whip up for me after DMZ shifts? Think of this as a thank you. Besides, that's not twenty million won.

—Huh? But it says...

—It's not twenty million won. *It's a hundred LunaCoins.*

---

[12] Approx. USD 10.

—Yeah, man. That too. Shoot, Mundo. Why'd you send it in LunaCoin? I mean… I'm the one who just said it's gonna go up, but already buying so much? What if it crashes, like, tomorrow?

Yohan thinks Do had just bought LunaCoin and sent it over. His innocence was almost endearing.

—Don't worry, Yohan. Truth is, I actually knew about LunaCoin before you brought it up, and I've been holding onto *a lot* of it already. Sorry for not mentioning it sooner, haha. I wanted to see what people really think of LunaCoin.

—Oh, you already knew about it?… Dang, I guess being in the States keeps you ahead of the game… haha.

Yohan said, though the reality of it still didn't seem to fully register with him.

—And LunaCoin will never crash. So no worries.

—Still, be careful, you know? There's no such thing as "never" in crypto…

—I agree. But I can assure you LunaCoin will never crash.

Because I trust myself more than the coin itself. He left the latter part unspoken. With a bemused Yohan still processing it all, Do stood up, ready to leave.

—Yohan, I have an important meeting tomorrow, so I should get going. It was good catching up.

—Oh, okay. Uh… you sure you don't need the coffee or drinks after? Starbucks, maybe?

—I'm all set. It was good to see you, man. Take care.

—Good to see you too, Mundo. Thanks for coming. And, uh, are you sure it's okay for me to keep this many LunaCoins…?

—Of course. We are DMZ comrades, like you said.

—Mundo?

Yohan hesitated, then asked, eyes glinting with curiosity.

—Yeah?

—Sorry, I just had to ask. How long ago did you buy in on LunaCoin? My friend says it's still at a sweet spot, so I'm debating myself how much I should put in.

—I didn't buy it.

—Huh? What do you mean you didn't buy it…?

And with the calm, benevolent smile of a creator, Do gathered his things and replied.

—I created it.

•

In seemingly purposeless encounters, one often discovers the purpose unknown even to oneself. As Do departed the ramen shop, he exchanged one more glance with Yohan through the glass façade —a mirrored tableau revealing more than mere reflection.

By virtue of Yohan's gaze, Do felt himself elevated and transfigured into a divinity, cast as both idol and myth. Let us explore this phenomenon more closely.

Typically, a gaze of admiration is the province of strangers. It is the gaze of Sudo High juniors as they cast their awe upon the one who made it to Stanford. It is the look in the eyes of Silicon Valley peers as they regard the architect of LunaCoin. Yet those who have weathered the grueling ascent to success know a darker truth: they aren't looking at us. What they admire is but a mannequin, a flawless and lifeless likeness, placed on display to play the part of success.

Those who have tasted the bitter elixir of triumph rarely savor the sweetness. The bitterness overshadows it. The acid of relentless ambition dissolves it. And so we shatter the mannequins and sculptures we've become, pressing onward, down a path strewn with the thorns of ceaseless doubt.

The admirers come, dutifully, to pay respects at the mannequin exhibition, touching the shell I abandoned long ago, nodding as if to say, "So this is how success looks." In doing so, they only deepen my emptiness.

In a profound void, in the dead of night, when the hollowness stretches to its zenith, we inevitably seek out those who once knew us in our obscurity and insignificance. We return to old classmates, childhood friends, comrades from the military who bore witness to our unadorned selves. We seek them, inquiring if they might hold some uncelebrated vestige of our former self.

With luck, we might find a humbler version of our mannequin—one untainted by the spotlight, within which the heart of desperation and struggle still beats. We need a heart transplant.

Yohan had not scaled Do's heights and never would, yet this former comrade was still capable of measuring those heights with unfailing accuracy. And Yohan, above all, was a good man.

—*I created it.*

With this statement, and a parting glance through the glass window, Do saw the gaze Yohan directed upon him—a gaze free from envy, radiant with complete reverence. It was a gaze that preserved and cherished a memory unblemished, directed not at the polished exterior of the mannequin of success but at the heart primed for revival. That gaze transmuted to embrace the present, ascendant self of Mundo.

Thus, the transplant began: Yohan, the unlikely surgeon, and Do, the patient. The surgeon, through his gaze, threaded together the hollow mannequin and stitched together the lost organs, breathing life once more into Do, imbuing him with a heart pulsing with desperation and struggle.

With his heart reborn, Do could not help but believe—to believe that he was indeed a god—the chosen creator to reform old money and summon forth the new money into existence, not with the brute weight of law or vested interest, but through the silent order of mathematics and the purity of algorithms, a benevolent overseer shepherding cryptocurrency.

His first disciple and beneficiary? Private Yohan Lee. Soon he shall buy his meals, pay his fare, cover his rent, and bring gifts to his beloved mother. All shall be paid with the LunaCoin bestowed upon him by its creator. And in reflecting upon this, Do realized there was nothing he could not accomplish. So let's fucking go.

•

—Nice to meet you. I'm Damien.

—It's an honor, Mr. Jin. I'm Do-hyung Moon. Thank you for taking the time.

After a few rounds of sizing each other up, they cut right to the chase. Synergy between CouponMaster and LunaCoin, payment completed in seven seconds, the seigniorage effect—Do ran through the points he had carefully rehearsed. But both men understood that these words were mere formality.

—Thank you for the impressive pitch. We've discussed it internally, and if the synergy you described can be realized, I think we could become good partners.

When initial responses are favorable, that's when the real tension begins.

—However, the seigniorage effect you described... it's something we'd only benefit from if we went far together, isn't it? E-commerce and cryptocurrency, it's an intriguing combination. But I am skeptical if it could be a lasting one.

Of course, the customary resistance. Yet this time, Do held his ground. He knew that investor meetings were less about selling the product and more about selling the person. The due diligence can be done without so much as a glimpse of the founder. They bring you in to observe the person in the flesh.

Did the signals Do had cast into the air find their mark? Would Damien Jin detect the inferno blazing beneath his polished, controlled LunaCoin pitch?

—But... hmm. Mr. Moon.

Jin began, leaning in with a hint of intrigue.

—Yes, sir.

—It seems like you have something more you'd like to say. Why don't you tell me what it is you really want?

Here it was—the moment.

—Mr. Jin. I actually need your permission more than your money.

—Permission? Jin arched an eyebrow.

—Yes, your permission.

—Haha, as if I wield such power. If our goals align and we break new ground together...

Jin stopped, cutting the superficial courtesies short. Interesting kid. Not quite what Aaron described. Yes, there was an air of ego, but that ego wasn't idle; it was relentlessly proving itself through action, refusing to stand still or complacent. That's the quality of a real founder.

—I created LunaCoin because I want to live in a world without permission. Do added.

—Then why ask for mine? Jin replied.

—Because getting your permission is like getting permission from ten thousand others.

—Haha, you don't need to butter me up. If the terms are right, we'll invest. If not…

—Do you see this as flattery?

Do's gaze held firm, his words piercing through the formalities with raw clarity.

—… No, I suppose not.

The CouponMaster CEO weighed if it was time to drop his social mask and finally speak to this kid on equal terms, cutting past the pretense.

—Your permission would be the first and last permission LunaCoin will ever need. If we can use CouponMaster to prove LunaCoin's product-market fit to the world, we will never need another permission.

—So are you saying CouponMaster is just a stepping stone for LunaCoin?

Damien Jin's tone was rather teasing, yet Do's expression didn't waver.

—That's not the intention, but if you see it that way, I wouldn't argue.

—Haha, well, it's clear you're not trying to flatter me.

Jin regarded the young man before him. Look at this kid— he's onto something big, no matter what brand of game he chooses to conquer.

And Do sensed it, too. He was on the verge of earning Jin's permission. Now was the time to seal it.

—Mr. Jin, I'm not merely creating a new kind of online shopping money. And I don't believe you see your CouponMaster as just a convenient e-commerce website, either.

—Go on.

Jin responded, his tone slightly haughty as still wore his mask.

—The value of CouponMaster isn't just about selling goods online or delivering them faster.

—Then what do you think it is? Jin prods, putting Do to a final test.

—The true value of CouponMaster…

Do paused to reflect and regurgitate the answer he's about to put forth.

—…is *increasing the GDP of the internet*, I would say. And by doing that, you come to understand how people consume. CouponMaster could therefore shape the demand, not just the supply—what people buy, what they eat—that's where the real power lies.

Wow, this kid gets it. He sees the world from the same vantage point as I do. That cocky certitude—that he had already mastered every chain of causality despite barely scraping together his first real investment. Foolhardy, maybe, but it held the spark of something monumental. Jin was secretly yet completely taken by Do.

A great investor reads a founder's ambition, because ambition never betrays. The simple ambition to get rich and famous—it's straightforward, easy to handle, yet it burns out fast. Do's ambition was something else entirely, the kind that never burns out. Akin to a messianic drive, a conviction that only he alone could birth a new currency.

Isn't that a bad thing? No, not at all. People misunderstand messianic beliefs. Do not picture the old aristocrats of the Joseon Dynasty—left hand behind their backs, right hand twirling their mustaches, chins tilted upward with that timeless disdain. Hubris is not how you believe you are the chosen one.

Picture the Jewish people instead—humiliated, persecuted, and yet firm in their conviction that they alone are the truly chosen ones. That's what it means to believe. Because when you genuinely believe you're chosen, you don't waste a second looking down on others. You devote every moment to anchoring your belief in a system. The aristocrats of Joseon die away with history; Jewish financiers govern the wealth of nations.

And Jin could see that in this kid.

—Mr. Moon.

Jin's tone shifted, settling into something closer to his true pitch.

—Yes, Mr. Jin.

—I'd like to make a counteroffer. Actually, I'd like to accept your offer and add a counteroffer of my own.

—Of what kind...?

—I want to join the LunaCoin team.

—Excuse me?

—Of course, our priority would be to establish LunaCoin as a payment method in my CouponMaster.

Ah, yes! I made it. The deal is sealed. A surge of excitement silently coursed through Do, his neck trembling with barely contained exhilaration. He quickly stifled the impulse, though, and added a cautionary measure to secure his position in this proposal that seemed almost too good to be true.

—...If someone like you joins our team, it would be an honor

—I appreciate it.

—However, before you do, I'll need safeguards to ensure that I retain majority control. With all due respect, Mr. Jin, I don't want to end up like Jobs bringing in Sculley.

—Haha, come on, that's ancient history. But I get your point. How about—think of me as Eric Schmidt instead of John Sculley. You and, uh, Ms. Luciana Kim here? You guys would be Larry and Sergey of it all.

—A fine analogy, Mr. Jin.

Do relaxed just a little, allowing himself a professional smile. Big deals always come with big risks, and he remained vigilant, guarding against the smallest possibility of LunaCoin being devoured by whales.

—Now, I'm sure you've read up on me. My late grandfather built the laws and politics of this country, although some ignorant people spew nonsense about dictatorship and whatnot.

—Uh, yes, yes. I've read about him. A remarkable figure indeed.

—I'm not bringing this up to boast about it, but do you know why I didn't go into politics like my grandfather?

Because you're an American and didn't even finish the mandatory military service? Do kept this line to himself.

—Erm... no clue, sir.

—Because a true democracy, my friend, exists in corporate democracy. Political democracy is one person, one vote. But the fact that we, who are clearly different from the hoi polloi, only get one vote—that contradicts the essence of true democracy. In corporations, the more important you are, the more votes you get. That's the true democracy, isn't it?

Jin said, his mask now completely cast aside.

Surprisingly, his answer turned out to be more intriguing than expected.

—I totally agree, sir.

Do, indeed, totally agreed.

—You're the architect of LunaCoin, and it's only right that you have the most votes. I'll only cast votes in proportion to my shares. The true president will always be you.

—Yes, sir.

—But know this. When you become president, everyone will try to impeach you. So, I count on you to do your best. And I'll be there to support you, so you can count on me as well.

—I will. Thank you for saying that.

Do knew, however, that men like Jin would be the first to secure their spot on the best lifeboat if the ship were to sink.

Still, Do made it. The scrappy LunaCoin boat, hitherto sailed without a penny of investment, will soon become as grand as the Titanic with Jin's blessing. Excitement tempered control—a fresh reaffirmation that he alone was the master of LunaCoin, and no one else could fulfill this mandate.

—Let's go celebrate, Do. I've got some excellent wine on hand. Jin said with a benevolent smile.

—My pleasure, Mr. Jin.

Jin made a call, and judging by his familiar tone and lines like, "Prepare a vintage Petrus, remind me, which year..." it was clear he didn't rely on Yelp or Opentable to book restaurants. Though he ran a billion-dollar tech company, it wouldn't be surprising if he had butlers in traditional tuxedos handling his errands. People like him—how many invisible connections must they be born into, connections the rest of us can't even fathom? Do thoughts run adrift. Then, suddenly, a thought struck him—something completely unrelated to business.

—Uh, Mr. Jin, this is totally random, but...

—Hmm?

—Do you happen to know any antique dealers?

chapter block
11.0

[real-time dashboard]

LunaCoin ($LUNA) / Price: $228.54,
Market Cap: $244.5M, 24h Volume: $52.4M
TerraCoin ($TERRA) / Price: $1.00,
Market Cap: $75.8M, 24h Volume: $13.4M

"This man is redefining what money means."
"The new wonder boy of Silicon Valley"
"Even his last name is destined for greatness."
"Will LunaCoin overthrow the reign of Bitcoin?"
"10 billion dollars of cryptocurrency at his fingertips... Who is this twenty-something Korean boy?"

These aren't mere patriotic odes from the Korean press, eager to celebrate a rising descendant. This is a global fascination. *The Wall Street Journal, Bloomberg, Wired, Forbes, Fast Company—* the world is transfixed by Do-hyung Moon.

One door opens, and another follows. With Jin's permission, LunaCoin became the legal tender of Korean e-commerce. Customers enjoyed additional discounts, sellers received instant payments, Jin earned substantial commissions, and Do proved to the world that LunaCoin could replace his homeland's national currency, the won.

He was the real deal. Elizabeth Holmes might have also secured permissions from powerful patrons, but she never had a

156

truly great product. Look at me. Build a great product, and the permissions of the powerful naturally follow.

There was a certain sign that LunaCoin had now become a giant. Employees in t-shirts bearing the company logo, their ID badges swinging as they walked. They all knew my face, yet I knew none of theirs. They gazed at me with that peculiar reverence, like acolytes in the presence of a modern oracle. And it wasn't just here in the office. Whether it was at Stanford lecture halls or Nobu Palo Alto—VCs, developers, professors—they all glanced my way.

Today at the company town hall meeting, Do's voice rang out with a conviction that left no room for self-doubt.

—Who is our competitor? Is it Tether? Is it Iron? Other stablecoins whose names we don't even care to know?

He paused deliberately and then subsequently let his voice crescendo.

—No! Our competitor is the *dollar*. The Benjamin Franklin! Our competitor is the global reserve currency. We have already proven in Korea that our coin is no mere token—we replaced the Korean won! A monumental feat we have accomplished together. So, do we stop here? Do we grow complacent and rest on these laurels?

The audience roared back in unison—No!

—Never! Do's voice thundered. We must not stop here. We will never stop here! When people buy tacos at the food truck outside, when they fill up their gas tanks on the way home, they should be using the LunaCoin, not the dollar. And so, I introduce our next moon to reach. I call this the "Anchor Protocol."

The hall exploded in applause. Yet, in the shadows of the room, standing in the dark corner, was the CTO, Luciana. She remained still, distant, watching the spectacle unfold. The fervor, the money—she couldn't help but to feel rather... *obscene*. The raw ambition of it all left a knot in her chest, an unnamed discomfort that sat heavy inside her. Only out of an allegiance to her boyfriend and CEO, she stayed until the last word of his speech, knowing that loyalty can blind as much as it can bind.

—This is the second step of LunaCoin and TerraCoin beyond a mere payment tool. It's straightforward. When our users deposit the TerraCoin in the Anchor Protocol, they'll earn a steady, fat return.

A hand shot up from the sea of employees, momentarily disrupting the cadence of his speech.

—So, is this like a…?

—A bank? Yes, you might call it that. But we are not going to offer a pathetic 0.45% like Bank of America. We will offer a 20% annual return.

20%? Is that even possible? But Do skillfully drowned out any trickle of doubt with the flood of ambition.

—Do you think that's an impossibility? We're going to be so much more than "a bank." I have no intention of running some small regional bank. I have every intention to become the *Federal Reserve of the Internet.* And if the SEC or the Fed were to hear me say that, they'd lose their minds. He leaned in, his voice electric. But haven't we already shown the pigs of Wall Street that stablecoins can replace fiat? We're simply redefining, redrawing the boundaries of what is possible and impossible—again.

Cheers resounded. This had always been Do's singular gift: the ability to crystallize a grand vision, presenting it so boldly it all but demanded reality conform to his will. And, most critically, he possessed the rare talent to make it seem almost within reach. It was what drew everyone—Luciana, Nik, the entire company, and soon, the world of LunaCoin users—to feel that undeniable, Steve Jobs-like magnetism in Do.

Do, re, mi, fa, so, la, ti, do! So, Do!
The crowd chanted his name like Do-Re-Mi.

Still standing apart from the frenzy, the quiet architect behind this new crypto empire could only manage a faint, uncertain smile. Luciana wanted to ask Wozniack. Woz, when your creation became larger than life and your partner became someone else, how did you feel? She didn't need to ask what choice Woz had made during his final chapter at Apple; that much was already clear in the history books of Silicon Valley.

•

—Our supreme leader, we thank you for your speech.

Nik delivered a mock salute with a grin.

—Hahaha, gosh, shut the hell up, Nik. How did the dev meeting for the Anchor go last night?

—Debate, quarrels, and coding through the night, as expected.

—How's the timeline shaping up?

—There are a few skeptics, but when haven't there been? We're pushing ahead.

—Good.

—Oh, and PR contacted me earlier. Forbes wants to shoot your cover for their 30 Under 30. Congrats, Do.

—Thanks, but I'll probably just skip it. Just do the interview, maybe. I already have one with Institutional Investor today.

—True. Forbes should at least give you Entrepreneur of the Year, not the 30 under 30.

—Haha, same difference. Anyway, I'll join the Anchor Protocol meeting tonight too, so see you then.

—Great. Should I get the full team?

—No, just you and Luciana.

—Only the CEO, CTO, and CPO[13]—sounds about right.

Wherever Do walked, he commanded attention and admiration—silent, reverent, and constant. He had mastered the art of walking with his gaze forward, never meeting the awestruck eyes that lingered on him.

—Do.

But of course, there was one exception.

—Hey, Nuuuna.

Do stretched the familiar endearment, elongating it with unmistakable warmth, an intimacy embedded within each syllable.

---

[13] Chief Product Officer

On the other hand, Luciana's greeting was clipped, severing the air between them with quiet intensity.

—Hey, erm, can we talk?

—Anytime. Oh, and Nuna.

Do's tone remained buoyant, untouched by her coolness. With a playful flourish, he reached into his inner pocket.

—Ta-da! I got you a gift from Korea.

Do held out two coins, polished and gleaming with the patina of centuries-old oriental tradition, the kind of relics you'd expect to see encased in glass at a prestigious national history museum.

—What's this?

Luciana arched a brow.

—This might not be the most romantic gift in the world, but it's the most fitting one for the two of us. This coin dates back a few centuries to the Joseon Dynasty. And guess what—I got a pair.

Do gestured with exaggerated pride.

—Wow, Joseon Dynasty… how did you even get this? Is it for sale? I mean, nevermind.

Luciana quickly stopped herself, not wanting to pry too much into a gift.

—Well, there are auctions for this sort of thing. I tried different routes, haha.

And Do indeed did. Damien Jin introduced him to a few cryptic antique dealers, who then introduced Do to the labyrinth of antique dealers, which he had painstakingly navigated to finally get ahold of these two ancient Korean coins.

The price for the pair exceeded six figures. The dealer gleefully emphasized their rarity. Only a few remained worldwide —the kind the British Museum would covet. Since a Korean national had purchased them, the cryptic dealer claimed, both the buyer and seller were fulfilling a patriotic duty. Of course, if Luciana knew the full story, she'd never accept the gift, so Do simply introduced them as rare coins.

—Nuna, you know we never went for matching couple rings? But given our profession, I thought *couple coins* would suit us better than *couple rings*.

—That makes sense, haha… thank you, Do.

Luciana appreciated his gift and the gesture. Yet, the whole thing—those ancient rare coins and the lengths he'd gone to obtain it—felt almost like something from a story about English nobility in a tabloid—remote, disconnected from her reality.

—And I didn't know you had such a profound love for honoring Korean history.

She added with a fleeting smile.

—Of course I do. You always call me grandpa when I start referencing those old Korean idioms.

—Right, true that.

Luciana couldn't help but recall the simpler days when their sole focus was on making their creation more formidable. She, too, had come a long way and accomplished much with her significant other. And yet, she was the only one who kept looking back, increasingly wary of what their creation might truly become.

Because she cared. She hadn't yet lost touch on what it means to be the user, not just the creator, of this new order. But it was still so difficult for her to digest so much ambition, to let it settle inside her without turning sour. Sometimes, she resented herself for that.

Not too long ago, Do would have noticed her inner turmoil without her saying a word. But now, he was drenched in the seawater of success. He was perpetually dehydrated, constantly craving the next high.

—Nuna, the face value of this coin was exactly half a dollar dating back to the 18th century. Although, of course, its real value today must be astronomical. Like I said, these are couple coins. So you keep one, I keep the other. We will match. *And together, we will complete a dollar, heh.*

—…Thank you, it means a lot. And it's beautiful.

Luciana's underwhelming reaction, though appreciative, didn't quite match his enthusiasm.

—It's my pleasure. And lucky for us, these ancient Korean coins already came with a hole in the middle. So we can thread it

and wear it around. If you ever want to wear it as a necklace…
haha, it could be one stylish option.

Do handed the coin and a refined white jewelry chain over
proudly, as if offering a rare diamond salvaged from the depths of
the ocean like in that Britney Spears song.

—The necklace is from Van Cleef, though I'll admit, a
Joseon coin and Van Cleef may not be the most seamless pairing.

—What's van cliff…? Luciana asked.

—Oh, just erm—never mind. Anyway, you look even more
stunning with it on.

—Thank you. I'll wear it every day, babe.

—Love you, Nuna.

They share a reserved laugh—one worth slightly less than a
dollar.

•

The laughter soon faded, and in the silence that followed,
tension lingered—stretching between them like a bridge drawn too
long. As mentioned before, co-founders and co-lovers were
conflicting concepts. Do had hoped that the success of LunaCoin
would wash away the discomfort clinging to him like stubborn
grains of sand. And for a time, it did. But, much like dipping his
feet into the ocean, the sand inevitably found its way back, sticking
with each new wave.

It was Luciana who finally broke the silence.

—Listen, Do. I… erm, I need to talk to you about that Anchor
Protocol.

—Yeah… yeah. Definitely.

An empty conference room. A scattering of chairs. They
leaned toward each other, yet neither could meet the other's gaze,
both fixated instead on the shapes their hands made. Do had always
wanted to look into her eyes—back then, it had been easier. Not
that he loved her any less. Absolutely not. Perhaps blame it on the
overwhelming success of LunaCoin. If asked how love could
change, he'd insist it hadn't. It was only that—how to put this

delicately—love was always the dependent variable; success, the independent variable.

•

Now, back to business. Why do we need this Anchor Protocol? For the LunaCoin ecosystem to work as planned, a meager interest from college kids and crypto enthusiasts wasn't enough. They needed a sea of liquidity. They needed people who knew or cared little for cryptocurrency—moms, dads, grandmas, and grandpas of the world. Where did they put their savings? A bank. So what must Do become? A bank. It was a simple, logical goal.

Yet, achieving that simple and logical goal demanded nothing short of Herculean risk. Moms, dads, grandmas and grandpas of the world trusted cryptocurrency even less than those miracle health supplements sold on late night TV. No, I take that back. If only they believed in cryptocurrency even half as much as they did in those scam supplements, Do wouldn't have had to worry at all. Winning them over required more than persuasion; it demanded an outrageous offer: a 20% annual return.

No, you didn't read that wrong. *20%*. The Anchor Protocol promised to make this outlandish claim a reality. Here's how it would work: moms, dads, grandmas, grandpas purchase TerraCoin, deposit it in the Anchor Protocol, and collect a hefty 20% return.

How is such a high return possible? The Anchor Protocol would stake LunaCoin against TerraCoin as collateral to generate rewards, consolidating profits from a myriad of blockchain networks. These profits would be the source of the interest paid to depositors. Essentially, rewards from network activity and returns from DeFi[14] protocols would sustain this lofty annual return—in theory.

A 20% return, hundreds of times higher than what banks offered—does it sound like an absurd plan?

---

[14] Decentralized Finance

—Do, I'll say it. I'll need to bring out the elephant in the room. It's a completely absurd plan.

Luciana said firmly.

—Nuna, startups are all about making absurd plans happen. And if we are talking absurdity, it's the fat cats at the Fed adjusting rates from their oversized chairs however they damn well please.

—I don't care about the Fed. The Anchor is just mathematically impossible.

—What's with the sudden change of heart? Has Professor Janet Yellen graced your office with a visit?

Do's voice carried a teasing lilt, but it only deepened the tension in the air.

—Not funny, Do. And it's not sudden. You know that a 20% annual return is nonsense!

—I'll admit it, though. I do miss our chats back at Berkeley. We were both ambitious back then, weren't we?

—Do! Are you hearing me? Stop trying to dodge this!

—Who's dodging? I am going to make the Anchor Protocol happen and prove everyone wrong again.

—You can't ignore all the potential disasters waiting to happen. Anchor isn't a side project. If it fails, it could mean the end of it.

—End of what?

—End of everything. The algorithm sustaining LunaCoin and TerraCoin could unravel completely—it might depeg!

—…Nuna, I need you to know that I'm not taking your concerns lightly. We did the math.

—I don't remember doing it?

—Nik and the other dev team did. And I reviewed it, too.

—So you're bypassing me now? On something this important?

—You were working on the Mirror Protocol. I didn't want to…

—Oh, you know that's bullshit.

—We'll bleed in the short term, sure, but that's business. Platforms are winner-take-all. Once we're on top, those short-term losses will be trivial. Besides, I've already announced the Anchor Protocol to the entire company. How could I backtrack now?

—It wasn't an official announcement. If we go further, there'll be no turning back.

—When we first talked at Berkeley about these coins… Nuna, I can't help but feel nostalgic. Remember?

—…I remember.

—Think about it… the daydreams we had back then are now our reality. We're living in the reality we created. Forget the annual return. Forget the math. I want to keep building our reality and live in it—with you, Nuna.

Knock… knock… His assistant tapped cautiously at the door.

—Mr. Moon, your next appointment is in five minutes.

—What appointment? Is it an interview or another investor meeting or what?!

Do snapped.

—Uh, it's an interview first, and an investor meeting at seven.

—Ah, damn. Sorry, Nuna. I can't skip this. We'll talk later. I promise we'll talk this Anchor Protocol through.

—…Will you?

Do nodded, his gestures quick before slipping out the door. Luciana knew he's nearly at the point where he needed no one's permission anymore—save, perhaps, from the Treasury Secretary or the Fed Chairman. He could easily reschedule an interview or an investor meeting if it suited him. She knew he was deflecting. And yet, as she recalled that evening at Berkeley when they first kissed, the memory softened her. So she didn't—couldn't stop him.

•

As you might have guessed, Do considered press interviews mostly a nuisance. Just as legacy currencies persist in the world of crypto, so too do legacy media interviews in the age of social platforms. Still, he stuck to his talking points because saying so aloud would waste even more of his time. Or maybe because the reporter was rather attractive.

—So, Mr. Moon. Here's a potentially uncomfortable question for you.

—Yes, yes. By all means. Thank you.

—You're very active on Twitter, Mr. Moon. But recently, you got into a debate about the Anchor Protocol and tweeted "I don't talk to poor people"—which certainly sparked some controversy. Do you still stand by that?

—First of all, precise wording matters, especially given your profession. I didn't say I don't talk to them, I said I don't *debate* them.

—Sure, but the person you dismissed, who said the Anchor Protocol would fail, turned out to be an economics PhD. Did you know that?

—I didn't, and I don't really care. Frankly, I see little correlation between studying economics and understanding money.

—Ho, there's another headline.

—I don't think so. I admit that "poor people" was a bit much, but I meant those who lack any real understanding of money.

—Hm, so should we avoid criticizing Steph Curry if we can't shoot like him?

—No, you can criticize his game if you like. But no one goes up to him mid-training to lecture him on how to shoot three-pointers, because no one understands that better than Steph. Go warriors by the way.

—Hmm, not a bad point.

—The point is this. Just as Curry missed his final shot in Game 6 against the Raptors, you can criticize me if I ultimately fail. I don't run away from criticisms. But a random streetballer drains a few shots and starts telling Curry his form is off? Well, that's just laughable. So I'll say it again. Mr. PhD in economics, you are a nobody.

The reporter found Do's audacity both grating and magnetic, a man certainly engineered for headlines.

—Would you say that arrogance is a trait inherent to all geniuses?

—Do you think I'm arrogant?

—Do you think you are a genius?

—Haha, touché.

—Some people love you, some hate you, but they mostly agree you're arrogant.

—Well… if you felt that way, I won't debate it. Honestly, though? I don't consider myself arrogant.

—You don't?

—Arrogant people sit back, arms crossed, convinced they're right—and then they do nothing. Does that sound like me? I argue on Twitter every single day, don't I?

—Hmm, fair point.

—Thank you. Arrogant people are afraid to be wrong, so they do nothing. I'm the opposite. I'd rather die than be wrong, which is precisely why I'm out here proving I'm right, moment by moment. I'm not arrogant. I'm just *right*.

—I have to admit, you certainly have a character. But don't you think it's inefficient to spend so much time proving yourself on Twitter, now that you're the CEO of a major company?

Do didn't yield a single word, his expression unchanging.

—This morning, Forbes asked me to do a cover shoot, and I ignored their request. If I were a poser, like Elizabeth Holmes, afraid of being exposed as wrong, I'd be fixated on how to look cool in front of the camera. Instead, I'm sitting here, debating with you—a journalist from a respectable publication, but with a subscriber base way smaller than Forbes by many.

—Ouch, that stings a little.

—My apologies, haha. But the point is this. I could've been posing for Forbes, yet here I am, still proving I'm right. Cryptocurrency is math. It's algorithms. It isn't smoke and mirrors; it's unforgivingly real. You can't fool people forever with image-making. And users know that. So even if people think I'm arrogant, they're still using LunaCoin.

—You know, you're quite compelling. Not the kind of person I'd want to date at a fancy restaurant, but you're certainly someone I'd believe if you told me you were rewriting the rules of money.

—I'll take that as a compliment, though I might regret not asking you out. Thanks for keeping me on my toes.

—You're amusing, I'll give you that. And no problem. This has been… illuminating. Thank you for your time, Mr. Moon. And I wish you a good luck.

—Thank you, though I won't need that.

•

His assistant, again visibly afraid, cautiously knocked at the door of the now-emptied meeting room as the reporter left.

—Mr. Moon, we've got two VC meetings lined up for seven and nine this evening.

—Can't we do them both at once? I need to pull an all-nighter with the dev team.

—Um… the schedule's already set, so it might be hard to…

—The team for the 7 o'clock meeting is here, right? Tell them to come in now. And cancel the 9 o'clock meeting—tell them to reschedule.

—Yes, yes, Mr. Moon. I'll reach out immediately.

Do no longer needed to chase investors. No, the tables had turned—investors must chase him, begging to take their money.

—Hello, Mr. Moon. I'm Sung Lee, President of December Ventures. This is SVP, Haocheng Pang.

These executives looked at least two or three times Do's age, with their resumes just as lengthy.

—Thank you for taking the time to meet with us, Mr. Moon. We went over the materials you sent us. On page 22, you briefly mentioned the Anchor Protocol and Mirror Protocol. Fascinating concepts. Could you expand on that a little?

The younger one asked.

—Isn't it all written in the IR materials?

—Well, yes, but…

—Listen, I appreciate smart people challenging me. Do responded, taking a line directly from Ken Greenspan's book. I don't appreciate is people wasting time with stupid questions. With all due respect, I'm not your babysitter. Do I need to teach you how to read?

Though annoyed, Do was more than ready to break down any critiques of his invention, prepared to counter every point if they dare to bring up one. But the older executive quickly stepped in, silencing his subordinate.

—Oh no, of course not. Mr. Moon, we're here because we want to invest in LunaCoin.

Ah, Boring. They were quick to backtrack, too worried about ruffling his feathers. Now, he understood Ken Greenspan's disdain. College kids, although they say stupid things most of the time, were refreshingly fearless compared to these executives afraid to challenge him.

—Leave the term sheet, then.

—Yes, sir. Thank you, Mr. Moon. We'll await your response.

Do could cancel meetings at the last minute and hurl insults, and investors would still grovel, desperate for him to accept their money. He remembered Hoffman's class, where the Silicon Valley titans—Google, Facebook, Netflix—had perched uneasily on plastic chairs, coming down from their Olympian heights to share their gospel. We the students, mere mortals then, could only marvel, imagining the vast chasm that lay between us and those gods. But Do was the only one musing—perhaps that chasm isn't quite so vast if you're willing to jump?

Don't be delusional, people would say. If you graduate, if you are fortunate to land a job at Google or Facebook, you'll realize just how unreachable the gods of Silicon Valley really are.

Do never accepted that brand of defeatist wisdom. The boundary between human and god? It was far more crossable than anyone dared to believe. And those who insisted otherwise? They'd never even approached it. Who were they to speak of a boundary they'd never breached?

So, where am I now? Do thought. Right here, on the other side of the table.

•

It wasn't until nightfall that the CEO, CTO, and CPO of LunaCoin finally convened.

Beyond the glass walls, the lights of San Francisco stretched beneath them, a sprawling, glittering reminder of the world they sought to alter. The space around them was as pristine as it was severe—minimalist to the edge of sterility. Potted succulents dotted the room, Edward Hopper paintings exuded a sense of isolation, and a vast expanse of blackboards waited for Do's vision. He picked up a marker and began sketching the plan.

—Alright, let's talk bAssets, which is the most crucial element for our protocol. The bonded assets that'll yield block rewards... The architecture itself will rest on Web Assembly smart contracts...

Do's tone was clipped, almost clinical, lacking the charisma he'd displayed earlier in the day. Luciana and Nik listened in silence, both acutely aware that their CEO was sidestepping the elephant in the room. So the CTO had to break in again.

—Do, I hate to interrupt but there's only one question that matters tonight. Is the Anchor Protocol's 20% annual return sustainable? Sorry to sound like a congressman at a hearing, but if we don't get this right, a Congressional hearing will be the least of our concerns.

Luciana tried to tread lightly.

—Right, okay. I'm open to discussion. But let me lay out the numbers for the Anchor first. They look pretty good. Nik?

Do passed the baton to Nik, who was unusually quiet tonight as well. The CPO cleared his throat, a bit unsteady as he prepared to lay out the projections.

—So, erm, here's the setup. We're looking at an annual return of exactly 19.46%, with governance votes set to adjust monthly, capped at a 1.5% swing. Oops, excuse me.

Nik coughed again, almost stalling. He slowly started sketching intricate equations and symbols across the blackboard.

—Take this formula, for instance. (% Earn Rate Change) = min(abs(1.5%, ((YR % Change))). If our yield reserve increases by 5% in a month, the formula would be: X = min(abs(1.5%, (5% - 3%))) = min(1.5%, 2%) = 1.5%. The earn rate increases by 1.5%...

He continued scrawling out indecipherable symbols across the board. Of course, Luciana had no problem deciphering it. She stared at the math for several minutes, but they seemed only to reinforce her skepticism.

—Nik, I trust your calculations. But these projections... they rest on one towering assumption—that we have enough reserves, right?

Yeah, come on, guys. Who are we fooling here?

Nik looked to Do, hoping he'd answer. But when the CEO averted his gaze, the CPO had to speak.

—...True, Luciana. We do need a lot of reserves. Nik admitted.

—And what's your estimate for those reserves? Luciana asked.

—450 million dollars. To start. Do partly admitted as well, his voice flat.

—To start?

Luciana's eyebrow shot up, her incredulity—a rare visitor—made its presence known.

—Don't worry. We'll gauge how much more we need as we go.

Do replied, brushing her skepticism aside with alarming nonchalance.

—Do.

—Yeah?

—I'm not saying the Anchor Protocol is a bad idea. But I just don't think it's sustainable.

—Well, you might as well say that.

Do retorted, his tone clipped. Silence hung heavy between them, pressing down like the weight of everything unsaid. Luciana's expression also hardened.

—Alright then. If you think locking up 70% of TerraCoin's supply and offering a hundred times the return of a normal bank is somehow feasible, then I really don't know what to say!

—Hew… okay, okay. Listen, Nuna. I know your concerns are valid. And if I can't convince you, there's no point.

He paused, sensing the moment to shift tactics, unveiling a solution he'd kept under wraps.

—I've come up with another solution to make Anchor work. It's called the *Luna Foundation Guard*. LFG, for short.

Do erased his earlier notes from the board with swift strokes, his voice regaining a spark of fervor as he explained his latest brainchild.

—The Luna Foundation Guard is a reserve backed by Bitcoin. A massive amount of it. Think of Bitcoin as another protective layer for TerraCoin's $1 peg. While Lunacoin continues to manage the regular mint-and-burn process to maintain TerraCoin's $1 value, Bitcoin will now serve as a reserve to stabilize TerraCoin during extreme market swings, preventing excessive LunaCoin minting.

His movements were decisive, as though every word were building the very structure of another complex interplay of TerraCoin, LunaCoin, and now, Bitcoin.

—If TerraCoin drops below $1, the LFG can sell some of its Bitcoin reserves for cash, using that cash to buy TerraCoin, boosting demand and raising its value back to $1. Conversely, if TerraCoin rises above $1, we can mint more TerraCoin and sell it for Bitcoin or other assets, increasing supply and bringing the price back down to $1. This will help us maintain the peg to the dollar.

The city lights reflected in the glass, as if all of San Francisco held its breath, waiting to see if his ambition would materialize or implode.

•

—That is… genius. I didn't know you had such plan in mind, Do.

Nik's voice held a tinge of awe. Luciana, too, felt a glimmer of excitement—though hers was tempered with caution.

—This is the first time I'm sharing it. I wanted you two to hear it first.

Do said, glancing at both of them, his confidence blooming under their attention.

Luciana again felt a pang of nostalgia. It transported her back to the red Prius when he sketched out the LunaCoin-TerraCoin mechanism. It wasn't so long ago, but so much changed. They weren't just college students chasing a dream, free from consequence. Now, people bought groceries, paid rent, measured wealth, and traded lives—all with the money they'd created.

—Thank you for the pitch, Do. I think this can definitely work! Nik said.

—Thank you. Then, with the LFG in place, there's no issue launching Anchor, right?

Do said, his eyes alight with the answer he expected to hear.

—Wait, but you omitted an important number… How much of Bitcoin are we talking about for the LFG? Half a billion

Luciana asked, and Do paused.

—…No.

—More?

—We are going to secure enough Bitcoin for the LFG.

—Do, how much is that "enough"?

—…*10 billion dollars*. Approximately.

Their jaws dropped. The weight of that number—absurd, yet spoken with such certainty. Nik glanced at Luciana, both of their minds racing, each calculating the madness of what their CEO was proposing.

—Erm… I don't know, Do… Is this even possible?

Nik, who had been riding the wave of excitement just moments ago, looked deflated.

—Don't get cold fucking feet, Nik. This was never meant to be a small project. Once the Anchor is fully functional, we will truly be too big to fail.

—*Too big to fail*—that's hell of a phrase. Are you even serious now?!

Luciana let out a dry laugh, her cynicism hardening the room's tension.

—Oh, but those too-big-to-fail banks survived—no, they thrived even after the subprime mortgage crisis, or did I miss a chapter of history?

Do shot back, his voice simmering with exasperation.

Luciana knew she had to stop him before things spiraled further, before Do's ambition grew even more catastrophic.

—No.

—No what?

—I can't do it. I won't do it. If the Anchor depletes the reserve, causing the depegging—

—You keep bringing up the depegging! Our peg is built by math. *Your m*ath, Nuna!

—That's why I know! Listen! Depegging isn't just the end. What about the death spiral that comes after?

—Death spiral, hah. You sound like one of those doomsayers on social media. What's going on with you?

Do echoed, dismissively.

—I don't care if I sound apocalyptic, because if the Anchor Protocol fails, it will trigger an actual fucking apocalypse.

For the first time, Do's face contorted, even toward Luciana.

—…Nuna, can you please tell me why you're being so discouraging and apocalyptic all of a sudden? And I hope you have a good reason.

—Your idea of using Bitcoin to back the LFG is brilliant, sure. But even if we pull this off—can we still claim we are an algorithmic stablecoin? With 10 billion dollars in Bitcoin backing our entire existence? Really?

—I was the first and only one to believe in pure algorithmic stablecoins. Don't lecture me on what it means, thank you.

He shot back, his voice tight.

—I'm not lecturing you on anything!

—Then let me actually do some lecturing. Businesses lie to people all the time. Netflix encouraged people to share their Netflix accounts at first, and now they're cracking down. That's why we don't share our accounts anymore? So Nuna, tell me the real fucking reason you are against Anchor Protocol.

When Luciana answered with silence, Do's irritation bubbled over, spilling into his words.

—I mean, the reserve with Bitcoin is still decentralized! We won't be at the mercy or permission of the Fed or any government...

Oh my god. *Permission.* That word set Luciana off. She had enough of his obsession with permission—or the lack thereof.

—Oh gosh, you and your permission! Your permission can go fuck itself!

Luciana's voice cracked with sharp frustration.

—Then tell me your real reas—

—Because it's obscene!

She finally gave him the real reason.

—*Obscene...?* How is our coin obscene? We are the revolutionaries. We are everything the financial establishment is against.

Do replied, plainly confused.

—Robespierre was obscene, too. If Anchor protocol ever goes wrong, it will create another subprime fucking mortgage crisis. Have you watched the movies about it? *The Margin Call*? *The Big Short*?

—I've never watched them, and I won't, because I don't intend to be one of those failures. He scoffed.

—You should. We might be too young to have lived through it, but just watching them would show you that this is not a fucking game, Do. It's real money, real lives, real consequences.

—Nuna, financial products succeed and fail catastrophically all the time. That's why there's a disclaimer—invest at your own fucking risk?

—Do. Will you please listen to me carefully, just once?

—…Alright, I'm listening.

—Do you know why subprime—and potentially our Anchor Protocol—are especially obscene?

—Please, enlighten me.

—Because subprime toyed with people's fucking homes! Because our Anchor will toy with people's fucking savings!

Luciana's voice rose, charged with fury. She continued.

—There are some things in this world, Do, that you cannot afford to betray. Homes should be where we feel safe with our families. Savings should be where we safely store the fruits of our labor. They are never meant to be traded, swapped, or gambled away in some financial experiment!

As the passion of her words faded, Luciana exhaled, nearly drained. Nik, caught in the crossfire, nodded instinctively but refrained from speaking, unsure where his loyalties lay. Do, after a moment of silence, however, chose to show the worst side of him.

—So, Nuna, are you playing, what, Brad Pitt in that movie now? Ben Rickert or whatever his name was? The morally righteous guy lecturing everyone while making a fortune from the collapse?

—So you did watch it.

—Beside the point.

Oh, Do perfectly registered every word she said. He just refused to understand it. Luciana seethed at his feigned ignorance.

—Then let me get to the goddamn point. It's my name on the coin, Do. My name. *Luciana Nuna*. And I'll have no part in screwing over our users.

—So that's what it's actually about, huh?

—Of course it is! Why did you say you named the coin after me anyway? When I heard the name at that crazy Paguk restaurant, I thought it meant you valued me, my contribution. I thought you value*d us*.

—And I still do!

—No, when you make reckless, obscene decisions like this, it's no different from naming an expensive yacht after some girl on your arm.

—Wow.

—Do, if you won't back down on Anchor, I'm done. I'm leaving.

Luciana's voice was steady, but the ultimatum it carried was clear.

—What?... You can't be serious, Nuna, are you? You—you are going to leave it all?

—I mean… yes. At the very least, I refuse to be anywhere near the Anchor Protocol.

Luciana saw the flicker of vulnerability in his posture, and it softened her resolve, if only for a moment. She decided to take a step back, trying once more to reason with him, hoping to find the man she once knew beneath this thick ambition-fueled façade.

—Do, listen. If we proceed with the Anchor Protocol, I swear, we will be doing something far more obscene than those Wall Street guys did in 2008.

—I just don't understand why you keep saying that. How so? They tried to profit off people. We are trying to give people an entirely new currency—

—…Because in those films, they only profited off the crisis. But we—*we will be the ones to start a crisis*. Knowingly, with our own hands.

—…Start a financial crisis.

—Yes, Do. With our own hands. It will destroy the economy. There is no undoing. Can you live with that?

Luciana had spoken from the depths of her soul, and Do sat in silence momentarily. That pregnant silence was her last hope. *Please, let my words break through your ambition.*

•

Hahaha…

Instead, her hope shattered in an instant as Do began to laugh —a chilling, hollow, eerie laugh.

—Do… are you laughing?…

Luciana didn't recognize the man in front of her. She was scared.

—Stop it, Do.

Nik interjected, an alarm in his voice as well.

—How can I not laugh?

Do's grin widened as if he'd just had a revelation. He continued.

—Nuna, you said it yourself. Don't you see what this means?

—…No, I don't. I don't understand how you can laugh at this moment, at any of this.

—Those Wall Street guys? They simply *profited off from* the crisis. But me? *I* could *start* it.

Luciana was at a loss for words.

She didn't know this man anymore, this man who could find humor in the prospect of catastrophe. She was terrorized. And the laughter dissolved from Do's face, replaced by something darker— an unsettling seriousness that bordered on manic elation.

—You just made me realize. *I* am the one who pulls the trigger. If LunaCoin succeeds, I'll forever change what money means. If LunaCoin fails, I'll crush the entire economy. The world needs *my* permission now. Ha…! I don't need anyone else's permission anymore. Oh my gosh, isn't that beautiful?

Nik watched his friend in horrified silence. Luciana, dismayed, took an instinctive step back.

A monster. She had always known his relentless ambition ran deep, but now, it had consumed him. And the monster looked at her, as though inviting her to join the chilling dance.

Luciana. Lux. My light. He seemed to say with a twisted tenderness. You're my cofounder. You're my lover—the one who will also never need permission from anyone.

…The light had left. The light *within* him had gone out.

chapter block
12.0

[real-time dashboard]

LunaCoin ($LUNA) / Price: $1987.28,
Market Cap: $2.16B, 24h Volume: $282.0M
TerraCoin ($TERRA) / Price: $1.00,
Market Cap: $188.3M, 24h Volume: $23.9M

—Today, we're joined by Tisa Underwood from *Institutional Investor* to discuss the latest on LunaCoin. Welcome, Tisa.

—Thanks for having me.

—So, LunaCoin's price has been skyrocketing since the Anchor Protocol announcement. As we speak, the market cap has just surged by another billion dollars.

—Yes, and it's no exaggeration to call this the hottest startup in crypto right now. These crypto companies feel more like celebrities than traditional businesses, with their enormous fanbase.

—Exactly. These fan cultures really contribute to the growth of the company. LunaCoin also has a massive fanbase, doesn't it?

—Yes, indeed. They call themselves "Lunatics" and they follow the CEO, Do-hyung Moon with unwavering devotion.

—Lunatics—ho, that's quite a name.

—Both online and offline, from students to billionaires, these Lunatics revel in being a part of this audacious crypto experiment. Here, take a look at this photo.

—Oh good lord. Is that a tattoo on an arm?

—Yes, indeed. And not just any arm—this belongs to Michael Novogratz, the famous Bitcoin billionaire. Obviously, he's invested heavily in LunaCoin and proudly proclaims himself a Lunatic.

—I have to say—and sorry Mr. Novogratz—but that's not the prettiest tattoo in the world, haha. But despite all the hype and fanfare, there are criticisms of LunaCoin too.

—Yes, some claim that LunaCoin, especially the Anchor Protocol at the center of this buzz, is nothing more than a Ponzi scheme.

—Plus, there are major players in Wall Street looking to short LunaCoin.

—Nothing is confirmed, but it does appear that a few significant hedge funds may be setting their sights on LunaCoin.

Do clicked off the TV, a smirk pulling at his lips. The reporter—yes, the one with the sharp wit and sharper looks. Last time they'd spoken, she was just beginning to grasp the intricacies of LunaCoin; now, it seemed she was fluent in the language of his creation.

Under his leadership, the Anchor Protocol had ignited a frenzy, sending LunaCoin's ecosystem surging at a breakneck speed his competitors could only envy, thanks to the outrageous 20% annual return.

The world thrummed with the name of LunaCoin and its faithful Lunatics. It echoed on Twitter, reverberated through news headlines, and cascaded across the digital landscape. As the reporter had shown, even a billionaire investor tattooed LunaCoin onto his own flesh.

Think about it—an American billionaire tattooing the creation of a college kid from Korea on his own body. That was a whole new level. This wasn't just a product anymore. It was a cult.

Buoyed by the praise, Do opened Twitter, reposted one of the hundreds articles celebrating LunaCoin's success, and typed:

`@do_llarmoon: Terra is the largest decentralized money in crypto, period.`

One tweet alone could hardly contain his gleeful megalomania, so he quickly followed with another.

@do_llarmoon: and we are going to make it with you, LUNAtics.

•

—Nice tweet, haha.

Nik teased.

—Gosh, Nik. Friends aren't supposed to mention each other's social media. Like, never.

Do replied with a laugh, his voice light, pride unmistakable beneath the surface.

The main conference room at LunaCoin HQ was no longer just a gathering of peers. The place was packed with men in suits, their expressions flat, eyes calculating, their voices a measured weight of authority.

—Do, we need to go over a few admin matters. There's the SEC subpoena. We're working on it, but—

Meet LunaCoin's new chief legal officer—Mr. Berg, a Jewish lawyer with a resume sharp as his Yale degree and a steady, methodical voice to match.

Speaking of lawyers, Do thought of someone he almost managed to forget. If June graduated from Columbia Law and was fortunate enough to land a job at a decent law firm a few years down the line, her boss's boss would probably report to someone like Mr. Berg—who now reported to Do.

The young CEO still took every aspect of LunaCoin's daily operations as seriously as he should. But for a man who once loathed needing permission, he'd grown comfortably accustomed to being the one who granted it.

—By the way, Nik. I checked out June's LinkedIn yesterday.

Do dropped the comment with casual irreverence, mid-meeting.

—What? You guys follow each other on LinkedIn?

—No way, haha. I wouldn't give her that satisfaction. She'd have to wait in line for that honor. But yeah, she's doing a summer internship at Bird & Simone LLP? Mr. Berg, you know that firm?

—…Yes, they are small but quite promising.

—Right, right. Oh, and about that SEC subpoena. You're handling it well, right? No major issues?

—We are, but there are still a few unresolved matters—

—Then, for this case, we could hire an intern, right? She's just a 2L.

—An intern…? An intern, sir?

The legal chief seemed astonished at the silliness of the suggestion.

—Yes, yes. She's pretty smart. Used to invent all kinds of things in high school, so she must be good with patent law or something. Also sharp with numbers.

—Actually, she's his first love. Do dated her since high school. Nik teased.

—Ayo, shut up, haha. She wasn't my first love, just an ex. But, you know, trust is key in a lawyer-client relationship, and she's someone I know well. Her name's June Ma. Stanford, now at Columbia Law.

—…I'll look into it, though bringing someone over from another firm may be complicated.

It was a ridiculous idea. The mercurial CEO retracted with a smirk.

—Ah, sorry. Mr. Berg. Forget it. I take that back. No need to hire her or anything.

—Good idea. We don't want to tack a harassment case onto your docket. Nik quipped, grinning.

—Oh, get the hell out of here bro, haha. June and I are on good terms. But, sorry. I wasn't serious about the proposal.

—…Understood. I'll keep you updated on the SEC matter as we make progress. Mr. Berg replied, maintaining his professionalism.

It wasn't that Do particularly missed June. It was more the thrill of his new position—that intoxicating power where even his whims could materialize simply because he willed it. The young *Crypto Christ*, fickle and mercurial, amused by the sway he held over those who once held authority in the old world.

As for Mr. Berg, he found the whole Silicon Valley culture insufferable. Especially this crypto scene—with its reckless energy and arrogance, bordered on obscene in his eyes. But he reminded himself that he could have had it worse. Some of his colleagues dealt with that Sam Bankman-something of FTX, who played League of Legends in board meetings.

—Alright, Nik. Enough jokes from me. Let's talk business. We need to migrate to a bigger pool—the 4-pool.

Do shifted the mood in the room to a bit more serious and vigilant.

—Sorry, what's the 4-pool, Mr. Moon?

A young lawyer under Mr. Berg asked, his tone tentative.

—It's—we're migrating to a bigger pool because we need more liquidity for Anchor. Legal doesn't need to worry about this, so you're dismissed. Thank you for your time.

—Uh, well, if it could lead to any legal issues, we should probably—

—I said thank you for your time, guys.

Do brushed them off with a wave, already back in his element, ready to leap forward without a second thought.

The legal team exited with a sense of unease, leaving the CEO and CPO alone in the vast meeting room.

So, what is the 4-pool? Since Do won't explain it to that poor young lawyer, allow me to elaborate.

The Anchor Protocol was a colossal success. But it brought with it the colossal obligation of paying out that infamous 20% annual return promised to its depositors. Do and his crew were far from capable of generating returns like other traditional market makers. So where would the money come from?

1. The obvious, safe path: lower the promised annual return gradually. Do's ego might take a small scratch, but it would be a prudent, realistic choice. The payouts would become manageable.

2. The daring, risky path: create another use case to drive demand for TerraCoin. And that's where stablecoin currency swaps came into play. Imagine a "pool" where stablecoins could be exchanged seamlessly—an eternal source of liquidity and stability. There was already the "3-pool," composed of USDC, USDT, and DAI. Do wanted to topple this competitor 3-pool by introducing the "4-pool" composed of USDC, USDT, FRAX, and his own TerraCoin. The 4-pool would be a grander pool designed to bolster TerraCoin's liquidity and entrench its place as the supreme stablecoin. It was an urgent move to boost TerraCoin's liquidity— because otherwise, the Lunatics will go lunatic when they don't get the 20% return they were promised.

—Yes, fuck those SEC and those useless rubber stampers. All they do is latch onto serious businesses and drag them down.

Nik's uncharacteristically emphatic statement made Do laugh.

—That's true. But let's not call ourselves a "serious business." Like, never. Haha, good thing legal wasn't here to hear that.

—Alright, even I cringed a bit after saying it.

Nik chuckled along.

—Haha, right. Okay, first things first. The 4-pool. Where are we on the migration?

—Yes, about that. The timing is a bit—

—The right timing is now. Do cut Nik off.

—...It's premature, I have to say.

—It may be, from a technical perspective. But remember? We're too big to fail now. Look at the billionaire who tattooed my creation. While they're happy, I want to get this done.

—Do, but... we could be very vulnerable during the 4-pool migration. There's a lot of risk, as you know. Nik took a breath.

—I'm acutely aware. But we have market momentum now. We have investor confidence now. But that won't last forever. Do shrugged, the weight of urgency clear in his expression.

—Even the tattoo?

—Even the tattoo won't last forever, haha. When those Lunatics don't get the 20% from Anchor, they'll actually go lunatics. They'll start a revolution and behead me like I'm Robespierre.

Do inadvertently invoked one of Luciana's own metaphors despite his deliberate efforts to ignore her absence. Her words hung around him like ghosts, a constant reminder. He quickly pushed forward.

—We have to understand just how mercurial the masses can be. And if they lose interest, they will turn on us. And the investors will, too. Even Novogratz will then strangle me with his LunaCoin-tattooed arm.

—...Okay, haha. That's scary to think about. He's pretty ripped.

—Yeah, and I bet he got a whole crew of bodyguards hired just to do the strangling for him. But seriously, the 4-pool migration—ASAP. You handle that, and I'll keep working on building the Bitcoin reserves for the LFG.

—Got it. Where are we on the Bitcoin reserve? Nik masked his anxiety with trust in Do.

—Passed the billion mark yesterday.

—Wow, gosh. I still can't wrap my head around a billion fucking dollars, haha. I mean, three of us, splurging on an extra orange chicken at Stanford cafeteria... Oh shit, I'm sorry.

Nik broke off, realizing his slip. It should have two, not three. Do glared at him for a moment, but was it Nik's fault? It was a telling sign that the CPO, like everyone else, felt the CTO's absence. While the world was filled with LunaCoin and Lunatics, the *Luna Nuna*—whose name and contribution had become inseparable from their success—was conspicuously missing.

—I should be able to secure another 225 mil. No, if the meeting goes well, 250 extra million for the LFG. That should provide a decent failsafe for us. But the migration has to be quick, secretive, and discreet.

—Of course. I will work on it with the team starting today.

—And Luciana isn't here. That's not gonna change anytime soon. So I'm trusting you with this, Nik.

—Roger that.

Nik straightened, meeting Do's gaze with a resolve.

—Good. This is how it's supposed to be. Lions like us don't belong caged in a zoo.

●

When a friend makes a thousand bucks, you feel a twinge of jealousy. When a friend makes a million, envy. So goes the Korean proverb. But there's no proverb to describe what happens when a friend makes a billion—like Mundo.

Yohan had been chewed out at work yet again for no reason. His days bled into one another in this monotonous, visionless job. Even payday had lost its luster. The pay was a pittance, drained further by goddamn taxes. How did Uncle Sam—or rather, King Sejong—always manage to take so much? Crypto, on the other hand, had no taxes whatsoever. Just pure, undiluted gain.

So Yohan's routine began to shift. Twitter, Reddit, Binance, FTX. He deepened his dive into the world of coins, struggling through r/cryptocurrency posts with the help of a clunky translation app. Everywhere on the internet, people were talking about his old DMZ comrade.

The hundred LunaCoins its creator had bestowed on Yohan multiplied tenfold in weeks—now a 200 million won[15]. That day, Yohan felt his heart racing in a way it hadn't in years. He became a *Lunatic* before there was such a term. He couldn't invest billions in LunaCoin or adorn himself with Lunatic tattoos like Novogratz, but he, too, wanted to change his life. Ambition is an infectious thing. And even for a gentle, grounded soul person like Yohan, ambition

---

[15] Approx. USD 200,000.

—or a feverish delusion of grandeur—kicked in and shook him to his core for the very first time.

After enduring another tirade from his shitty mustached boss on a dreary Friday evening, Yohan bought another million won's worth of LunaCoin on his way home. When he woke up the next morning, that million had turned into 1.3 million.

So when he got to the office the next Monday, he looked at the stubbly mustache perched on his boss's ugly upper lip with a newfound glee. The world suddenly looked so beautiful that he even felt the urge to kiss that lip and bite it off. He restrained himself, fortunately. This blissful LunaCoin investor floated through the morning as if he were walking on the moon, and by lunchtime, he ran to the bank to take out a loan to buy more LunaCoins.

LunaCoin's price kept climbing. On television, American billionaires and celebrity journalists debated Do's every move. Sure, there are other famous Koreans known to the world—K-pop idols maybe. But people merely paid for concert tickets to see them. Do? He was rewriting the very currency people used to buy those tickets, the drinks, the ice cream, the fan merchandise—he was shaping reality itself.

To Yohan, therefore, Do was a God, the rightful Crypto Christ—as he was to many in the world of cryptocurrency. And what of the tithe required by most faiths? Well, in this new religion, Lunatics didn't give offerings; they instead received them. The 20% annual returns from the Anchor Protocol was the divine dividend of this new faith, making it the most lucrative religion in the world!

Thousands had faith in Do. Yet they had only seen him through screens. But Yohan? He had known Do far before he was *the Do*—when he was just another face in a crowd. Even then, however, Yohan had known that Do would amount to something extraordinary.

John the Baptist—yes. It would hardly be an exaggeration to say that Yohan believed himself to be the John the Baptist to the Crypto Christ, one of the first to recognize his messianic purpose.

Yohan, or John, became convinced that their bond wasn't mere happenstance but destiny. And he was certain that LunaCoin was the hinge upon which his life would turn.

A month later, he emptied his savings, took out another loan, borrowed from his parents, and funneled every last won into LunaCoin.

Again. And again. Yohan could not stop.

•

Mrs. Susan didn't have to drive Uber or UberEats anymore. Her modest investment in LunaCoin, which she bought out of mere curiosity months before, had soared high enough to cover her daughter's tuition, afford a brand-new car, and even a camper for weekend escapes.

How did it begin? Well, it all began with a young Korean couple she'd driven from San Francisco to Berkeley. She grew so curious about their cryptic conversation—*Luciana, Nuna, LunaCoin.* Had the name "Luna" not been so pretty and memorable, she would've forgotten about it. She thought it was some girl's name, but they spoke of it like it was some treasured artifact. So she looked it up. They were talking about a coin, but not a cent or a quarter you'd find lost in the couch cushions. According to the Internet, LunaCoin was like a digital cent or a quarter.

Of course, Mrs. Susan knew nothing about crypto wallets. She, however, had the initiative to stop at a gas station, ask the young cashier how she might buy some of this LunaCoin, and eventually purchase a few at a crypto ATM. She bought a few not to make a fortune but to keep a few commemorative digital coins for her daughter. But the price of those commemorative coins started rising faster than any other Nasdaq stocks, and well, she simply couldn't resist buying a little more. Soon enough, her portfolio was more than comfortably padded.

She was grateful to those young passengers, though it was she who had unintentionally provided the valuable hint of Yin and

Yang. Her newfound gain, therefore, was a very inexpensive reward for her contribution, really.

Mrs. Susan wasn't naive. She knew easy money could be lost just as easily. It wasn't fear so much as the wisdom that comes with age. She wanted to convert her overnight LunaCoin profits into something safer—like a good old bank deposit. But in this era of near-zero interest rates, where could she park her money safely with a decent annual return?

One morning, driving south on the San Francisco freeway after dropping her daughter off, she spotted a massive billboard: "Anchor Protocol: Deposit your coin and earn 20% return!" The promise seemed too good to be true. Yet, in the corner of the billboard, she noticed a familiar face. *It's that Korean friend!* Turns out, the same company behind LunaCoin also made this Anchor thing, and she trusted the young couple behind the venture. Plus, any company that could afford this expensive billboard in San Francisco had to be trustworthy, right?

So back at home, she called Anchor's customer service, half-expecting someone to sell her snake oil. Instead, the customer representative was as gracious as he was patient. He explained Anchor Protocol in the simplest of terms. When Mrs. Susan mentioned she was a LunaCoin holder, he became even warmer, gently guiding her as she deposited her first TerraCoin in the Anchor Protocol. Mrs. Susan didn't understand everything, but it wasn't that different from putting money in a bank savings account.

She subsequently downloaded the Binance app with help from her tech-savvy neighbor, a software developer in a struggling Silicon Valley startup. Together with that Good Samaritan, Mrs. Susan bought more TerraCoins as instructed and deposited more of them in the Anchor Protocol. At first, it was only $100. That 20% return still sounded like a scam, so she figured that $100 was as good as lost.

To her surprise, her account balance after a month had grown just as Anchor had promised. She withdrew the funds, half-expecting some hidden fee or delay. Yet, cash in hand, she was stunned. Anchor had delivered, no strings attached. Unlike the incomprehensible coins she could barely follow, Anchor Protocol was straightforward. It was intuitive. It was a damn bank. *The Bank of Moon.*

And let's face it. This new "bank" was a lot more pleasant than her local B of A, with its ticket numbers, worn tellers, and endless lines. Anchor had become her bank, and because of that, Mrs. Susan, too, began to *believe.*

As Jobs once said—and as Do always believed—people only know what they want once they actually see it. The following week, she drove off in a brand-new camper. And instead of stashing her daughter's college fund in the vaults of Bank of America or Wells Fargo, she entrusted it to her new digital bank with the promise of 20% annual return.

•

—Chairman.

—Yes, how was San Fran?

—The fog was thick over the city.

—Good. And the details?

—We've been quietly accumulating TerraCoin over the past few weeks. Our Bitcoin acquisitions are moving along, albeit slower. They're planning to migrate to the 4-pool soon—liquidity will be at its tightest then. That's when we strike and short.

—Good. But the timing has to be precise. And needless to say, if they try to expedite their 4-pool migration, all the better.

—Understood, sir. You know how these computer guys are—always so eager to prove they're the smartest in the room. I gave one of LunaCoin's senior developers that satisfaction, and he nearly sang about their plans.

—Cross-checked?

—Yes. I was rather surprised at how lax the security is, even for a company founded by an inexperienced boy wonder.

—Because boy wonders also think they are the smartest in the room—and they actually are. But that's precisely when they start to miss the obvious.

—Couldn't agree more, sir.

—What the kid created is a brilliant invention. But it's never going to replace the dollar. That's the allure, though, isn't it? That's why people are flocking to it in droves. And that's why we'll make even more money—by wrecking it.

—Indeed, haha. Frankly speaking, I didn't expect the boy to get this far. I pegged him for just another overreaching brat, but you were right, sir. You said you met him at Stanford?

—Yes. I even offered him to come see me when his venture was ready to be listed on Nasdaq.

—Haha, and he didn't even realize that was his first and last opportunity of a lifetime.

—Kids like him don't see it as an opportunity if it's handed to them. It has to be something they believe they've carved out themselves.

—Classic Silicon Valley wonder boy.

—I do respect him for that. He just chose the wrong field. If he'd built AI pizza robots, this wouldn't be happening. But he chose to create money instead.

—Like you said, sir, people in the Valley here mix too much emotion with money.

—That's why this will serve as a lesson. Keep your focus sharp. Be vigilant. Watch and listen for the very moment they begin that 4-pool migration.

—Yes, sir. I'll make sure of it.

chapter block
13.0

LunaCoin ($LUNA) / Price: $5299.91,
Market Cap: $8.41B, 24h Volume: $392.8M
TerraCoin ($TERRA) / Price: $1.00,
Market Cap: $1.66B, 24h Volume: $197.0M

—Everyone!

The voice rang out, a clarion call that instantly seized the room's attention.

—LunaCoin has just hit a new all-time high at $5300!

Clapping, popping, cheers erupted.

—And our total market cap has officially surpassed $10 billion. No, wait—since TerraCoin will soon replace the dollar, we should probably say 10 billion TerraCoin!

Curiously, this monumental announcement didn't come from their CEO. It was his COO[16]. His name was—let's actually skip over insignificant details. The true figure of interest, our CEO Mr. Do-hyung Moon was here. He sat quietly in a smaller room off to the side with Nik, watching LunaCoin's meteoric rise on a monitor. His gaze, however, held no trace of joy.

A ton more people signed up for Anchor Protocol, which meant a ton more of TerraCoin was locked into the Protocol, straining liquidity. As a consequence, the vast reservoir of Bitcoin

---

[16] Chief Operating Officer

within the LFG, arduously procured from investors, was draining like sand through an hourglass.

No matter how sharp the intellect, there is something deeply visceral about watching wealth diminish from your coffers. Up until now, Do had never truly felt the cruel weight of that reality—his fortunes had only ever soared. But now, as he gazed upon the numbers, the same lingering question gnawed at him: *is this sustainable?*

—You look concerned.

Nik observed, furrowing his brow in an echo of unease.

—I am.

Do confessed.

—No, not because I think we've miscalculated, but because we've done everything too well. I expected some bleeding, but everything has been so smooth. If there had been just one hiccup, it would have put my mind at ease.

—Do, you brought us this far. Maybe you should relax and enjoy it.

The CPO, however, was also feeling the same discomfort lurking beneath their success. There was something unnerving in perfection.

—Nik, did you get into Stanford on your first try?

A question so out of time and context.

—Uh... yeah?

—Mmhmm, I thought so. For kids raised here, getting into college is still difficult, sure. But even if you don't get in, it's not like it shatters your life.

—That's actually true, haha.

—Unfortunately, it wasn't the case for Korean kids. You know—Harvard, Stanford, Yale, Princeton—all those motherfuckers slammed their doors in my face the first time I applied.

—Oh, shoot. I, erm, I didn't know that.

—I know. You're wondering why I'd even care to bring this up now. I am now controlling billions of crypto. I am on the verge of changing the very concept of money. And yet, here I am, suddenly crying about what happened in high school.

—I mean… early experiences always hit harder.

—Yeah, the reason those memories are hitting me now is that I was so unprepared. I was completely blindsided.

—How do you mean, Do?

—I wasn't—how should I put it—*paranoid enough* back then. I wasn't unprepared, but I just… never entertained the possibility of rejections from all those fucking schools. It was like crossing a street at a green light and getting hit by a perfectly sober dump truck driver.

—Wow, that's…

—Ever since then, I've had to account for every worst-case scenario. I imagine them, suffer through them in my mind, and prepare myself in advance. If I ever let myself again to simply fold my arms, to do nothing and let life come as it may, I wouldn't be able to live with it. Never.

Do's gaze fixed on the LunaCoin price chart, rising higher and higher, a burden akin to the weight of his own soul.

—This coin is *me*. I won't let the past repeat itself. I must strike first. I must press forward.

—Whatever you need, I'm here, man.

—Thank you, Nik. Let's expedite the migration to the 4-pool.

—Huh? Move it up—like, even sooner?

—Very soon.

—Uh… I thought you wanted, erm, I don't know. A more sustainable approach?...

—Nik, "sustainable" isn't synonymous with "slow." If we just leave our blockchain like this, it'll bleed the Bitcoin reserve dry. A slow death. There's nothing worse than a slow death. We've come so far, but we're still flailing underwater. If we don't keep progressing, we'll drown.

—Okay… noted.

—Your tone doesn't sound very promising. What else is on your mind?

—Ben told me about… some institution, probably Wall Street market makers, has been buying up a ton of TerraCoin lately. Just in case they…

—Who's Ben?

—Our CFO[17]?…

—Ah, Mr. Powell. I didn't care to know his first name, and there's too many fucking Bens in our company—Benjamin, Benedict, Benson—anyways, so?

—Well, Ben says this buy order of this size is unusual, even by Wall Street standards. And there's a small chance that they might…

—Dump it to short our coin? Nik, you know better that shorting our coin only works if their timing is exquisitely precise.

Do's voice carried a blend of amusement and contempt.

—…Yeah, true. Shorting alone wouldn't inflict such significant damage.

—Significant fucking damage… of course, Nik. My gosh. Elon hates Tesla's short sellers, but he hates them like he hates mosquitoes. Same for me. They are just a nuisance. Or perhaps they are just another good-hearted Lunatics, for all we know.

But his own words from just moments earlier echoed back: the determination to leave no possibility unchecked, to predict and prepare for every worst-case scenario with unrelenting paranoia. Do therefore felt an even greater urge to take preemptive action.

—Fine. Since you brought it up and since I don't want any anxieties hovering over our heads, put together a team to investigate. If some institution bought in that deep, we could reverse engineer them, right?

His ingrained paranoia naturally took the reins again, though this time he took some effort to mask it as a task for Nik's peace of mind.

—Erm… but Do, we don't have a team for this kind of matter…

---

[17] Chief Financial Officer

—The hell are you talking about? We just hired, like, 20 engineers yesterday.

—Yeah, but this kind of work requires C-level clearance and, of course, very specialized programming skills. Luciana handled all of it herself until now...

Nik's voice grew quieter as he cautiously brought up the former CTO. If it wasn't so personal, Do would have the issue dealt with just as any other normal CEO would.

—That's just wonderful.

—Sorry, Do.

—All the more reason to speed up our 4-pool migration, because they would have no idea when we would start it. Though I want to make clear—this decision has nothing to do with whatever petty schemes those Wall Street vultures are trying to pull. We'll begin once I return from Chicago next week. We should have another 200 mil Bitcoin in the LFG if the Windy City meeting goes well.

—Two hundred mil... got it.

—Nik, I know liquidity is going to get really tight, but we can handle it, right?

At this point, neither man expected anything beyond a perfunctory reassurance of "we'll be fine."

—...We'll be fine. But I will run the numbers again and let you know.

—Good. Thanks.

—And Do, one last thing... Sorry to bring this up again but... we'll need Luciana, especially if we're doing the migration soon. But erm, if you're uncomfortable, I can—

—No worries. We need her. Yup, I understand. And Nuna and I are not—*uncomfortable*. She won't ignore my call. I still love her. And... she probably feels the same. I'll call her.

—Okay, thanks. I'll go speak with the dev team. We'll be ready for the migration when you are back.

The weary CPO departed, leaving the CEO alone in the expansive room, a silence settling over him like an invisible fog.

Do pulled out his phone to call Luciana but hesitated. Was he calling her as a cofounder or… as a lover?

A messenger app felt too casual. A phone call felt too exposed. He opted for a text instead.

+1 510 906 1991: nuna, how have you been? sorry I couldn't call you
+1 510 906 1991: listen—can we talk? about the 4-pool migration.
+1 510 906 1991: I need you nuna. will you please come over?

No, that's too vulnerable. Scratch that. I should've written "we" instead of "I" in case Nuna says no. I barely have any emotional capital left for your rejection. *Backspace, backspace, backspace.*

+1 510 906 1991: we need you nuna. will you please come over?

Satisfied. No typos. Sent.

Oh, gosh. Luciana was immediately typing something back. Her typing bubble appeared. The floating three ellipses—the dreaded suspense. Why does iMessage even have this feature? Why should we endure this torment every time we text?

Do couldn't bear the sight of those ellipses lingering any longer. He turned off his phone, sank back into his chair, and waited for the reply he wasn't entirely sure he was ready to read.

chapter block
14.0

[real-time dashboard]

LunaCoin ($LUNA) / Price: $10081.49,
Market Cap: $32.5B, 24h Volume: $3.08B
TerraCoin ($TERRA) / Price: $1.00,
Market Cap: $25.2B, 24h Volume: $944.2M

Just days before the 4-pool migration was set to unfurl and soar, something uncanny began to stir in the heavens. Meteorologists were forecasting a lunar eclipse, set to occur on May 15, 2022, 20:29:02 Pacific Standard Time in San Francisco. The Earth would drift into place precisely between the Sun and the Moon, painting the night in hues of copper and blood red.

Yet, unbeknownst to all, another *luna* eclipse was looming, an omen unnoticed, even by the one who had set it in motion. Do's attention was elsewhere—focused entirely on the perfect metamorphosis of his creation.

•

@do_llarmoon: Curve wars are over, all emissions are going to the 4-pool.

The moment Do posted the tweet, the global crypto market erupted into action. Is this what the Fed Chair must feel like every quarter announcing the interest rate? He finally got to taste this heady exhilaration.

For weeks, the dev team had prepared tirelessly for this operation, hardly setting foot inside their homes. But no one was complaining. Their wallets were already brimming with the currency of the new world. Moreover, it's like they were programming their own paychecks, an experience not even Google or Microsoft could offer.

—We're really doing this?

Nik's voice carried a blend of awe and trepidation.

—We're really doing this.

Do confirmed, as if speaking an incantation.

And so it began! The team commenced the precarious migration from the existing 3-pool to the newly forged 4-pool.

Great migrations are at their most vulnerable, exposed to attack. Like hedgehogs, they curled inward, bristling with spines— cautious, deliberate, inching forward. It was a scene out of *The Chronicles of Chu-Han War.* Liu Bang fled from Xiang Yu, traversing an impassable plank road, so-called the "ladders to heaven," on the arduous Road to reach Bashu. When Liu Bang eventually returned, however, he returned with an empire rich with a thriving empire, rich lands, loyal subjects, and Han Xin's formidable army at his back. So Do pressed forward.

—Nik. How's the situation?

The tense atmosphere in the sparse meeting room was palpable. Every digit of every block number glared back from the screens, demanding scrutiny. The team was on edge. Cactus plants, austere and prickly, filled the corners—today, their presence felt profoundly appropriate.

—Liquidity is… tight. Really tight.

—Still within our estimates, though.

—True. Nothing out of the ordinary. Do, you've been up since yesterday. You should get some rest.

—No, not at all. You guys should get some rest. I won't be able to sleep until the migration is complete.

—It's going to take over a week.

—And I'll happily stay awake for every second of it.

If only a gunshot had marked the beginning of this war, it might have been simpler. If only a radar could track the lurking enemy, it might have been bearable. But here, the only sound was the relentless clatter of keyboards—the sound of this quiet, invisible war that would carry on, without any clear start or foreseeable end.

•

The LunaCoin team operated like a finely tuned 4-part orchestra, each section harmonizing to compose the grand symphony of the 4-pool migration.

First quartet: *Smart Contract Deployment and Upgrades.* They handled deploying and upgrading the smart contracts that governed the 4-pool, ensuring seamless integration with the platform. Their work involved crafting Solidity code with the precision of a maestro—managing liquidity pools, token swaps, and intricate incentive mechanisms.

Second quartet: *Liquidity Migration Scripts.* They automated the migration of liquidity from existing 3-pool to the 4-pool, ensuring that the rewards flowed like a steady stream and that transaction fees functioned without a hitch during the delicate transition.

Third quartet: *Governance Adjustments.* They managed governance-related smart contracts and shifted CRV token voting power toward the 4-pool, aligning incentives and securing voting on liquidity emissions.

Fourth quartet: *Monitoring and Security Enhancements.* They observed the migration's progress with hawk-like vigilance. They stood sentinel over the movement of funds, ensuring the integrity of the system, ready to confront any discord that might appear and threaten the liquidity or security of the 4-pool.

No one truly understood the entirety of the symphony. The music was alive, a creature unto itself—unpredictable, at times discordant, capable of silencing the room with a single errant note or abruptly halting when least expected.

In the program handed to the Lunatic audience, the credits read:

```
The Master Conductor: Moon, Do-hyung.
Principal Cellist: Petrakis, Nikitas
```

Wait—wasn't there someone missing in between?

```
Concertmaster: Vacant.
```

•

The music progressed each day, albeit tentatively. Each note rang out smoothly, yet the sensation beneath their feet was like walking on the thinnest, smoothest ice—an operation perilously fragile. Mistakes surfaced, discordant notes struck, and as exhaustion blanketed the team, more dissonance emerged. Yet the music did not stop—not yet.

Outside, the city of San Francisco dimmed. The lights withdrew into the backdrop, while the faint moonlight, ever ethereal, reflected off the windows of nearby buildings. It cast a pale glow into the office, as if mirroring the delicacy of their efforts—a precariously played *Moonlight Sonata*.

—No strange signals yet, right?

Nik's voice, laden with weariness, asked Developer No. 1, who barely had the stamina to respond.

—Yeah, all smooth so far.

Developer No. 2, equally drained, answered instead.

—Wait.

Then came Developer No. 3's voice, a sudden, desperate gasp. A wrong note, a sour chord of terror striking through the symphony. His octave sent ripples through the room, shifting the entire tone. Everyone snapped awake.

—What's wrong?

Do rushed to Developer No. 3's side, urgency breaking his composure.

—Someone just dumped a massive amount of Terra.

—How much?

—200... 285 million. 285 million. Oh my...

—Who the hell...?

The smooth ice beneath the music cracked. Do, Nik, and the senior developers gathered around Developer No.3's monitor. The chart showed a sharp downward spike. Dumps had happened before, but never at such a seismic scale. And with liquidity so tight due to the 4-pool migration, this was no trivial disturbance. *This could stop the music.*

—How's the peg? It hasn't dropped below 98 cents, has it?

Nik asked anxiously, almost praying with his own eyes glued to his screen.

Ninety-eight cents—that was the final line of defense. A breach below that would spell disaster.

—It's at 98.6 cents now. Damn it. No, this can't be happening.

Developer No.2 replied, his tone a grim waver.

—It's still...

—But people are going to think the peg is breaking!... Oh no, look. The sell orders are pouring in.

—It's not just on Curve. Binance, FTX—sell orders are everywhere!

Developer No.4 screamed, intensifying the frenzy.

Chaos rippled through the team, yet the CEO, the young master conductor did not lose his composure. Partly because he knew better, but mostly because he had rehearsed such worst-case scenarios in his mind too many times to falter now. In his vast theater of imagined disasters, this wasn't beyond the pale. So what's his job now? Amidst the migration, a true commander discerns real threats from mere circling vultures swooping in on a perceived weakness.

—Don't panic. We expected this level of attack. Let the market correct itself.

Do ordered, his voice a calm, cutting blade in the storm.

—But Do…

—I'm not going to waste the LFG's war chest every time these scavengers decide to feast. Let it be.

Half an hour ticked by, each minute stretching under the weight of collective anxiety. It felt more like half a day to all the developers—and rightly so, for LunaCoin's transactions poured in relentlessly, compressing a day's volume into thirty intense minutes. But just as Do had foreseen…

—Okay, okay! The market is responding. Buy orders are coming in too.

Developer No. 1 announced, relief breaking the tension.

—Yes, it's recovering to one dollar! Echoed Developer No. 2.

The music slowly returned to its original key, its tempo restored. Market participants stepped in to buy TerraCoin and LunaCoin at a discount, confident in its return to the dollar. Faith in their coins had become its own currency, much like the faith placed in Nasdaq. Even when it occasionally crashes, buyers swooped in to scoop up the bargains. The same held true here. Good, endure a just while more to see this migration through.

Do had rehearsed far worse in the theater of his mind, where catastrophes unfolded in grotesque detail, each one conjured and conquered in vivid detail. In spite of his outward calm, even his resilience felt worn, fatigue gnawed at his bones. And Luciana— still nowhere to be seen—remained a phantom in his mind, her absence louder than any market fluctuation.

While the rest of the team basked in the temporary calm, Do quietly withdrew to the bathroom. Cold water splashed across his face, a vain attempt to stay awake. As the water dried, exhaustion wrapped its arms around him, dragging him under. Like Francis Underwood once said, sleep puts even the most powerful men on their backs.

When the Crypto Christ surrendered to the pull of unconsciousness, however, the true enemy began to stir, lurking unseen, ready to strike from the shadows.

•

On the other side of the world, in a small, dimly lit studio in Seoul, Korea, Yohan stared at his screen in disbelief.

What the... 98 cents? TerraCoin dropped by 2 cents?

Yohan felt as if he had been flung into another dimension. If the dollar bill in your pocket morphed into 98 cents, or every crisp $10 bill slipped to $9.80, or that sacred $100 stashed away shrank to $98, you wouldn't need an economics degree to feel the ground shifting beneath you.

Since last night, something suspicious had been haunting the charts of TerraCoin and LunaCoin. Yohan had barely managed a bite of food, staying wide awake with bloodshot eyes, glued to his crypto exchange app under an unblinking, fevered stare.

The peg—meant to be an unbreakable dollar—was now slipping. The tectonic plates of TerraCoin were shifting, and the lights of LunaCoin were fading into darkness. He couldn't care less about tomorrow's work.

He fought against sleep until 4 a.m., his eyelids heavy, but at least the peg seemed to crawl back up toward 99 cents. Maybe things will hold out. Maybe I can make it to work tomorrow. Or take the morning off...

Just as sleep almost pulled him into its embrace, however, the stablecoin's price chart painted an enormous, blood-red bar as it plummeted—the magnitude of an avalanche unmatched since Do first gifted him them. An invisible hand pounced on the kingdom of TerraCoin and LunaCoin, riling up even more non-believers.

94 cents.

94 fucking cents?

Lunatics around the world must have shouted W-T-F from their respective corners of the globe. No one had seen anything like this before.

Some abandoned their faith as swiftly as they could, hammering the Sell button in a frenzy. With such a significant proportion of belief evaporating at once, the values of TerraCoin and Lunacoin had also collapsed to an unprecedented low.

But how could Yohan the Baptist abandon his faith like those opportunistic Lunatics? He had spread his faith to his friends and family. He had led them to repentance and prepared them to embrace their Crypto Christ and LunaCoin as the currency of a promised land. Sure, even Yohan's belief faltered at the brutal reality of 94 cents. The Christ had promised a dollar but now it was at 94 cents. Lunatics were panicking, and the panic sell drove off the price further.

Yohan picked up his phone. Obviously, he didn't have Do's direct line, but he tried Korean Whatsapp to send a direct message to the Crypto Christ himself.

@theyohanlee: Art thou he that should come, or do we look for another? (Matthew 11:3)

He stared at the Buy and Sell buttons, waiting. There was only silence, however. Do had long ago erased the Korean messenger app from his phone, severing himself from anything or anyone that tethered him to accountability.

And faith alone did little to soothe a pounding heart or a shrinking wallet. Yohan's chest heaved, his hands trembled. His fingers, slick with sweat, danced over the phone's screen, his mind frantically searching for an update—any sign of reassurance. News, YouTube—nothing yet. The world was still nestled in slumber, waking slowly to the sound of birds. Only Twitter was alive.

@wearesodone1991: terra/luna are crashing? just wow. if the peg breaks below $1, this thing's dead in the water
@real_kimchisoup: Yeah, forget about Bitcoin. This is why you don't buy Kimchi coins smh
@holdthefloorrr: Stop spreading FUD, guys. LunaCoin holders, let's pull together—on three, heave-ho!

Yohan's mind went blank. The work tomorrow, the throbbing capillaries in his right eye, the stale air that clawed at the last bits of oxygen in his small room—none of it mattered. The remnants of sleep still clung to his eyelids, but panic had already seized his heart. His silent scream echoed within. *What do I do? Sell? Is this the end of it?*

His sleep-deprived brain stumbled, unable to decide. When the TerraCoin hit 92 cents, however, he finally lost a significant portion of his faith. He sold 100 TerraCoins and 30 LunaCoins in a frenzy—a pitiful offering on the altar of uncertainty. Perhaps those were the very coins Do had bestowed upon him. No time to care, no time to check the hash now. Yet the moment he sold them, the price of TerraCoin ticked up—96 cents.

Fuck! Fuck! I just lost so much money! Goddamn it! Yohan's trembling hands scrambled to buy back 200 TerraCoins and 60 LunaCoins, desperately trying to undo his mistake. He had plenty more LunaCoins stashed away, but the regret was all-consuming. His fingers, shaking like leaves in a storm, alternated between the green Buy button and red Sell button, fueling the market's volatility with his panic.

The price of TerraCoin slowly crept back up, climbing three more cents—almost to a dollar again. *Yes!* He cursed himself for his earlier lapse of faith and those who sold off like blind fools, shaking his fist at the ignorant masses of defected Lunatics. *You idiots! Can't you see this is just a test of our faith? The price will rebound—no, it'll soar even higher! Never bet against the Crypto Christ.* Fueled by his newfound faith, Yohan bought an additional 220 LunaCoins with borrowed funds, leveraging his position to an extreme. As he watched his three months' salary multiply before his eyes in seconds, the buzzing phone calls from his boss didn't even register.

The Crypto Christ, my DMZ comrade, finally answered, albeit belatedly. Yohan knew Do was busy, so he sent the direct message as if he were transcribing a line from the Bible:

@theyohanlee: And blessed is he, whosoever shall not be offended in me. (Matthew 11:6).

Over the span of that night and into the next day, Yohan lived through the heights of heaven and the depths of hell, each ascension and dissension measured with LunaCoin's treacherous fluctuations.

The cruel morning came, indifferent as always. His phone buzzed again. The mustached boss. Yohan ignored it, of course. That ugly man should count his blessings—had he spoken to Yohan in that moment, blood might have been spilled. Yohan bit down hard on his shaking finger. His teeth dug into the flesh around his nail, blood seeping out, leaving a metallic tang in his mouth— tasted somewhat like a coin. But he didn't feel a thing. He was numb. Numb like the frostbitten cold he once felt on patrol in the DMZ—the kind that freezes the marrow of your bones, making you forget there was ever warmth at all.

•

Back on the other side of the Earth, at the LunaCoin office in San Francisco.

—…Do, Do! Do!! Wake up! TerraCoin fell to 91 cents!

Do awoke in a haze, the boundaries between dream and reality blurred. *91 cents? …Did I just hear that right?*

Voices clawed at him, yanking him out of a brief and fragile sleep. The music—no longer a delicate sonata—had shifted into a deafening symphony of panic, a chorus foretelling apocalypse. It all happened in the moment when the conductor's baton slipped from his grasp. But you know that ain't gravity's fault.

—The peg… the peg is fucking broken. I have… I have never seen this. It's at 91 cents.

Nik grabbed Do, his body trembling uncontrollably.

—Who? I mean, how? Wasn't it recovering?!

—Apparently not. It's all fucked up. Uh, gosh. We can't stop the depegging! It's coming from like five, six different exchanges. And the market... the market is panicking.

The peg was broken.

Before the depegging, the total market cap of the stable, one-dollar TerraCoin stood at around *18 billion dollars*. On the massive screen before them, a dollar had plummeted to 91 cents. A mere nine-cent drop caused *1.62 billion dollars'* worth of TerraCoin to vaporize in an instant. A chill swept through the room. People shuddered, seized by a visceral dread. On a side note, the market cap of LunaCoin before the depegging was *45 billion dollars*. No comment on how much of it had just vaporized.

What's worse, the 4-pool migration wasn't even halfway complete, and someone had already struck a match and set their path ablaze. Was this an orchestrated attack? Or merely the convergence of tragedies?

—We have to...

Nik stammered with a trembling voice.

—We have to use Bitcoin.

Do, though his heart felt like it had stopped, issued his orders with every shred of composure he could summon. They would figure out who caused this later. They first had to stop the what— this disaster from consuming everything.

The vast reserves of Bitcoin, painstakingly amassed across the globe, were precisely meant for this moment. By selling Bitcoin to buy up TerraCoin, Do and his team could 1) restore TerraCoin's peg to $1 and subsequently 2) limit the excessive minting of LunaCoin, which otherwise risked a rapid, uncontrolled devaluation. At least, that was supposed to be the plan.

But the ambitious CEO had pledged to create an entirely new kind of money, so the ruin took a form as singular as his ambition. When a Nasdaq stock crashes, recovery is expected—it always somehow limps back. When a Pfizer stock crashes because their new drug didn't get FDA approval, it can always rebound with the success of another. But LunaCoin was no mere security; it was an infallible algorithm, an edifice of immovable trust. When trust disintegrates, there is no salvaging it.

Nuna! Nuna... Do shouted Luciana's name in silent agony. Perhaps trust was never programmable. Or perhaps this collapse of trust was my doing—because I failed your trust. Please, answer me one thing—where the hell are you?

•

Mrs. Susan had little notion of the peril lurking behind Anchor Protocol, and why should she? Anchor had been explained to her and to thousands others as something akin to a simple savings account—and who obsessively checks their savings account balance every waking minute?

But her neighbor—the one who had kindly assisted Mrs. Susan in depositing her TerraCoin into Anchor—was a woman of vigilance. That night, under the eerie veil of the *luna eclipse*, she scrolled through Twitter before bed and felt a shiver. Something was wrong.

The dollar-pegged TerraCoin had fallen to 91 cents. She didn't fully grasp the intricacies of TerraCoin-LunaCoin's algorithmic mechanism, but she sensed that it was irrevocably broken. In a panic, she converted all her TerraCoin into LunaCoin, a reflex that set off a vicious spiral, bloating LunaCoin's supply and further rattling an already quivering market.

And she was, by all means, a good neighbor. Early the next morning, she dashed to rouse Mrs. Susan from sleep. If she didn't warn her in time, Mrs. Susan wouldn't just lose her daughter's college fund—she'd drown in debt in its place.

•

—Why isn't the peg recovering?!... Ah, Fuck!!!

Do didn't just drop the conductor's baton; he smashed it against the massive widescreen, shattering a silence that had suffocated the room. Nik's cello string had also snapped long ago, and now he clawed at his hair in despair.

Around them, one developer, then another, and then another... they began to cry. No one needed to explain the unfolding nightmare; each of them, brilliant in their own right, understood all too well.

Why wasn't the peg recovering?

Reason one: the legions of so-called Lunatics, who had never shared Yohan's steadfast loyalty and instead worshiped at the altar of profit, lost faith at the first whiff of depegging. They dumped their LunaCoin in blind, gut-churning panic, scrambling to sell at any price, accelerating LunaCoin's descent in an avalanche of desperation.

Reason two: Mrs. Susan's neighbor, who had managed to regain a semblance of composure, had swapped all her TerraCoin for LunaCoin, as mentioned above. And what did that trigger? The system burned TerraCoins and minted new LunaCoins. With the exponential increase in LunaCoin supply flooding the market, therefore, its price collapsed even further.

Reason three: Watching LunaCoin's value nosedive without mercy, even the die-hard Lunatics, like the tattooed Mr. Novogratz, stood on a harrowing precipice. With liquidity at its worst due to the ongoing 4-pool migration, they had only two choices: either clutch their LunaCoin and sink with it, or sell the coins they had bought with their savings, loans, and borrowed money—even if they were worth less than toilet paper. Most, painfully loyal as they were, chose the latter. And down went LunaCoin's price once again.

Reason four: The media began to catch wind of the collapse. The Wall Street Journal, Bloomberg, Wired, Forbes, Fast Company —all those outlets that once celebrated LunaCoin's meteoric rise now took perverse pleasure in documenting its downfall. Mrs. Susan, who had been uncertain about her neighbor's warning, couldn't ignore the torrent of news now flooding ABC and CBS. Her dream of securing her daughter's tuition through Anchor Protocol's 20% annual return was dashed, leaving behind not even a single thorn of hope. And so, Mrs. Susan sold her remaining TerraCoins, further inflating LunaCoin's supply.

Again... again... again... the whole process repeated, and the price crashed.

Hyperinflation, everywhere. The algorithm that Do so fervently believed in—the system designed to protect the peg—was now ironically triggering a fatal error. Supply kept ballooning. Demand had vanished. No one wanted LunaCoin anymore. But the algorithm didn't care and didn't stop. As more LunaCoins were minted in a macabre loop, the value of hyperinflated LunaCoin sank lower and lower.

Do's chest burned. The LFG Bitcoin reserves were being sold off at fire-sale prices in an already frozen crypto market. And we are not yet finished.

Reason five: The shock from the Bitcoin short was far more devastating than anyone had anticipated. The mysterious attacker had not only dumped a massive amount of TerraCoin but had also shorted a colossal amount of Bitcoin. Plus, when Do's LFG began selling Bitcoin to buy TerraCoin, it actually helped their cause.

What did this mean? Bitcoin—the towering titan, the unchallenged monarch and barometer of the entire crypto landscape—was wavering. It signaled market panic of the highest order. And like a colossal ship dragging a sinking fleet, Bitcoin's collapse took LunaCoin with it, pushing the spiral of destruction into overdrive.

Do and his team were trapped in the eye of the apocalypse. This was no ordinary crisis—it was a death spiral. There was no better *coinage* for it.

Half of the Lunatics of the world had abandoned LunaCoin. The other half of Lunatics—who were late to relinquish their beliefs and suffered the painful loss—were now baying for Do's blood.

And so, dear audience, that was how the music stopped.

•

Twenty-four hours later. The Blood Moon still hung low over San Francisco, its dim red light casting an eerie pall across a city blissfully unaware of the deeper darkness enveloping it.

The employees who had stepped outside for air did not return. Those who had gone to the restroom were retching, emptying their guts. The money—born from their fingertips, conjured through lines of code on their keyboards—had vanished like dust, taking with it the futures and dreams of countless souls.

They weren't mourning Silicon Valley's billionaires. No, this was far more personal. Almost all of LunaCoin's employees had genuinely believed in the mission, not just the money. They had believed in it enough to invest their own salaries, savings, mortgages, and loans.

Had it all been a gilded dream? Greed disguised as vision? Those choking on shame hunched over the cold, sterile sinks of the company's restroom; others, overcome by self-loathing, had staggered outside and slumped onto the indifferent sidewalks of Mission Street.

In the office itself, only Do, Nik, and a handful of other souls remained. The sound of keyboard typing had dwindled to a near-silent hum. The vibrations from Do's burning phone were now louder than the once-deafening keyboards. Do didn't bother to check his phone. Luciana might be among the countless names desperately reaching out to him, but no line of brilliant code could salvage this. Or he couldn't face her, couldn't bear the exposure of this ruin; his pride demanded this last shield.

Perhaps, now, there was only one thing left to do: find whoever was behind this ruin. Who was it? Who had refused to let this new currency thrive? Who had plotted to sabotage LunaCoin?

Or was Do searching for a shadowy saboteur because he couldn't admit—wouldn't admit—that he was wrong?

—Do. It could have been a hedge fund. Remember what I said? Someone had been amassing a huge amount of TerraCoin. Doesn't the timing of the initial depegging seem too... perfect?

Nik spoke, his face etched with the sorrow of a man who had lost more than money—almost a man who lost a child.

—…Yeah. Do murmured.

—They dumped all that TerraCoin at once! Those fucking bastards! And then… damn it!

—They probably shorted Bitcoin too, knowing we'd sell it off to buy TerraCoin.

Do said in a desolate voice, losing all the gumption he naturally possessed.

—Exactly! God, what do we do now…

—…It's not over yet. If someone sabotaged it, we can fix it. Let's just not—

But the CEO had already lost the indomitable will to complete his sentence. Only his hatred for the unknown enemy burned hotter with each passing second. He had to believe in that hatred to keep himself going. If this really was a carefully crafted sabotage, then maybe, just maybe, there was still a way to fix it.

chapter block
15.0

[real-time dashboard]

LunaCoin ($LUNA) / Price: $3927.11,
Market Cap: $13.1B, 24h Volume: $1.6B
TerraCoin ($TERRA) / Price: $0.91,
Market Cap: $12.2B, 24h Volume: $679.2M

@do_llarmoon: Deploying more capital—steady lads.

Do's tweet went out like a signal flare in the digital night. A mere 140 characters he released into the digital ether was met with a reaction in nanoseconds. The tides had turned. The Lunatics, once his loyal disciples, had become his fiercest adversaries. They gathered not to adore but to condemn.

@murkkedd: I already lost everything.
@LadyofCrypto1: mate, it's a stable coin, the fucking coin should be steady, not me.
@KshitizBisht: what in the world is your problem… give up now or else face the wrath.

And the wrath was real. His tweet was met with a torrent of fury, mocking Pepe the Frog memes with eyes seething in irony and rage.

As the Anchor Protocol crumbled, the devastation to the entire LunaCoin ecosystem was staggering. The combined market cap of TerraCoin and LunaCoin plummeted from billions to mere remnants.

On the first day of collapse, TerraCoin lost $6 billion and LunaCoin lost $8 billion. On the second day of collapse, TerraCoin lost another $7 billion and LunaCoin lost another $11.5 billion. Six plus eight, plus seven, plus eleven-point-five: $32.5 billion, just like that, evaporated into the void in two days.

Good thing the math was relatively easy, since it was all in *billions*.

People had placed their faith in Do, in the algorithm, in the promise of stability. Instead, their dreams, sweat, and essence distilled into their savings—gone. They were guilty of a single, fatal belief: that a simple deposit could offer safety. Mrs. Susan's daughter's college fund had vanished, Yohan's decades of salary had disappeared. The sheer magnitude of the loss defied comprehension. This wasn't just the collapse of an investment; this was the erasure of futures.

The Lunatics pleaded to the moon for just one final ascent. The moon, however, cruel and unfeeling, responded not with salvation but with the depths of a basement.

Now the LunaCoin has become death, the destroyer of worlds.

The meetings, the whitepapers, the strategies, the long nights of discussions shaping the LunaCoin—all seemed meaningless now, forgotten in the face of calamity. There were no grand exits. No time for resignation letters, debriefings, severance packages. Only the quiet terror of moral ruin, the desperate need to escape, to salvage what little remained. Employees, haunted by guilt and fear, fled, cursing the founder's name. The moon had set in the office once brimming with aspiration, leaving nothing but the creeping fingers of dawn to uncover the wreckage of shattered dreams.

The sun was now creeping in.

•

Ring. Ring. Ring.

The intercom buzzed incessantly, its sharp insistence slicing through the silence of the office. But the assistants, they too had vanished. Do, lying on the minimalist company couch, stirred slowly from a sleepless haze.

—...I asked that no one be allowed in.

His voice lacked the energy to carry the frustration.

—Yes, Mr. Moon. I know... but, uh, Ms. Luciana Kim is here to see you?...

The security guard said.

Nuna?

Do's heart stopped, then jumped to life. A brief pulse of energy surged through him. My co-founder. My love. Where have you been?—No, I won't even ask. I missed you. Can we salvage this? Is there still time?

—Yes, yes, let her in!

The words rushed out. His eyes darted around the office, desperate to find something, anything—some trace of normalcy, some vestige of the past. Snacks, the tiramisu she liked—anything. But the office, now bathed in the unforgiving sunlight of San Francisco, revealed itself to be a wasteland. The warm rays contrasted sharply with the cold desolation of his glass-walled sanctuary. The sunlight pierced through, exposing everything.

Could curtains shield this reality? Could we save ourselves from this exposure, from the glaring truth that Luna—our moon— had abandoned us?...

Do's gaze fell back to the CCTV screen, where the former CTO's silhouette took shape. Even through the grainy image, he could make out the faint gleam of the ancient Korean coin swaying right below her lovely neck. She was still wearing it.

And by virtue of that ancient coin resting against her chest, love yanked him from hope back into the cold certainty of reality.

No, I won't be able to save this. I can't save us, Nuna...

For the first time in his life, Do had to acknowledge that there was something beyond his reach, something he couldn't bend to his will. For the first time in his life, it struck him—sharp and irrevocable: *This is the end of it.*

Luciana had cleared security and was moving toward the entrance. Do urgently lunged for the intercom at full speed, his fingers trembling in a frantic blur of desperation.

—Wait, wait! Don't let her in! Do not let her in.

Do's voice cracked.

—Uh… excuse me, Mr. Moon?

The guard sounded confused by Do's sudden reversal.

—Sorry, I misspoke. Don't let her in. Ms. Kim is… no longer with the company. Just tell her that. Send her back. Please.

—Ok, sir. I'll let her know.

Do watched on the CCTV as the guard intercepted Luciana, trying to explain. She stood there, her face unreadable, her phone in hand.

—Uh… she says she needs to speak with you. Something important? Should I just send her away, sir?…

The guard's uneasy voice broke through, caught between duty and sympathy.

A text message pinged on Do's phone.

```
+1 510 221 1997: tf is this Do? Let me in
+1 510 221 1997: I need to talk to you. I know
things are bad, so let me in. im here to help
```

Dozens of messages, unread, left to pile up in a digital graveyard of missed calls and texts. His hand hovered over the phone, then he hesitated, finally reaching for the intercom again.

—Sorry, can you… can you pass her the intercom for a second? Thank you.

—As you wish, sir.

The guard handed the intercom out to Luciana. Do was afraid of what her first words would sound like. He was afraid of what her first pitch of voice would feel like. His hand shook as he braced for the unknown.

—…Do.

Her voice, a little higher than he expected, carried the weight of the moment in its deeper undertones.

—Nuna...

His voice was nearly a whisper, strained yet holding onto the familiar endearment.

—...I know things are a mess, but let me up there.

Silence.

—Do, are you still there?

—...I am.

—I want to help. Whatever I can do, I'm here for it.

Hearing his lover's voice splintered him. The tears he had held back for so long, the flood of self-pity, of self-loathing, all surged forward like an unstoppable tide. He wanted nothing more than to collapse into Nuna's arms, to cry as he never had, to confess his sins and vulnerabilities—to lay bare the weight crushing his spirit.

But he did not, as he always had not—just like that night in the DMZ, where he swallowed every tear, steeled every nerve, and locked away the part of him that wished he could be vulnerable.

—...Nuna. I'm sorry. For everything.

—Let me up, Do. We'll talk. We'll figure this out.

—When we dated, when we worked together... why did my blood always feel like it was on fire, like we were racing to the moon?"

—LunaCoin was never an easy mission. So I will be up there with you.

—This collapse... it doesn't make my blood boil anymore. I've boiled over, and I can't find the fire again.

—We don't know that yet. Come on, Do. This might be our last chance to turn things around.

—No.

He wavered under the weight of his words, yet filled with a resolute finality.

—Nuna, do not come upstairs. Do said.

—What?... Luciana asked back.

—Don't ever come back here. Don't call or text me. You understand? I'm speaking through this intercom for a reason.

Do spoke his cold words with what felt like a parting note. He said nothing further, and Lucian's voice too wavered on the edge of breaking.

—Do, what do you mean? It's not over yet. We can still—

—I need to go. Don't come back. Ever.

With that, Do cut the line. in one swift motion, he switched to the second line, connecting with the security guard again.

—Hi, it's Do Moon again. Sorry for the confusion.

—No problem, sir. Do you need anything else?

—...Please make sure she doesn't come in. She's no longer with the company.

—Noted, sir.

—And if you could, please erase the CCTV footage of her as well.

The screen went dark, plunging him back into the cold void of his empty office. The sun outside cast its indifferent glow, but inside, it felt like dusk. The room swallowed him, vast and desolate, filled only with echoes of decisions made and unmade.

Alone. Always alone.

Save, perhaps, for the ancient Korean coin necklace, nestled in his inner pocket, resting against the fabric closest to his heart.

•

Sleep eluded him for days. His body was a prisoner to exhaustion, his mind assaulted by visions of decline. His office was now a complete mausoleum. Even Nik was nowhere to be seen. He, too, must have left Do. I understand, brother.

He was left alone with the vastness of his own ruin. Silence —he feared it more than the collapse itself. It pressed against him, haunted him, suffocated him. Desperation drove him to grasp at the only noise he could summon—Twitter. In the cacophony of the digital symbols, he could drown out the deafening quiet.

@do_llarmoon: Close to announcing a recovery plan for $TerraCoin. Hang tight.

A wave of retweets and replies flooded in immediately. Thousands—most of which he refused to confront, for he lacked the courage, the time, and the will to wade through their acrid judgment. Trapped in his own hyperreality, bolstered by a weird and ungrounded surge of adrenaline, he posted again.

@do_llarmoon: Didn't mean to be so quiet – needed razor focus to deliver, thanks everyone for the support.

Not bad. Not bad! I can start it all over again, he shouted to himself. A cry into the ether. An intoxicating illusion—that words could rewrite the narrative, that sheer force of will could delay reality's unyielding tide. Confidence rekindled, a phantom of what it once was. With a renewed fervor, Do plunged headlong into his last-ditch recovery plan.

@do_llarmoon: Getting close... stay strong, Lunatics.

It read like a superhero's final rallying cry in the trailer of a doomed film. *Here comes the permissionless hero!* His hands would not stop. He fired off another tweet.

@do_llarmoon: the only path forward will be to absorb the stablecoin supply that wants to exit before $TerraCoin can start to repeg. There is no way around it.

Another tweet.

@do_llarmoon: First, we endorse the community proposal 1164 to increase basepool from 50M to 100M SDR, decrease PoolRecoveryBlock from 36 to 18. This

will increase minting capacity from $293M to
~$1200M.

Another.

@do_llarmoon: With the current on-chain
spread, peg pressure, and TerraCoin burn rate, the
supply overhang of TerraCoin (i.e., bad debt)
should continue to decrease until parity is reached
and spreads begin healing.

Another.

@do_llarmoon: As we begin to rebuild
TerraCoin, we will adjust its mechanism to be
collateralized.

And another.

@do_llarmoon: The Terra ecosystem is one of
the most vibrant in the crypto industry, with
hundreds of passionate teams building category-
defining applications within. As long as these
builders, TFL among them, continue to build – we
will come out of this together.

Oh, sorry. Did you read all that? There was really no need.
Tweet after tweet, each word a desperate gasp for air as he sank
deeper. The aftermath settled upon him—the last shudder of a
dying nerve, a dull, electric thrum pulsing through his every joint.

At last, his eyes fell upon the gigantic LunaCoin
Dashboard. The price was nearing zero. Just a breath away.

He had known. Perhaps he had always known.

This entire journey had been a simulation. The chase, nothing
more than a hunt for shadows cast by numbers and symbols.
Money had always felt abstract, a distant promise whispered on

paper and metals. But now? It was beyond abstraction, stripped even of meaning, no longer tethered to any measure of worth.

His stablecoin had once imitated the dollar, a quest to embody stability. In the end, however, it had transcended even that meager reality, evolving into a pure simulacrum—a symbol of itself, weightless and unmoored, severed from all that was tangible.

Now, ensnared in this endless loop of symbols, Do-hyung Moon the Crypto Christ was utterly, irrevocably lost.

●

+82 10 9741 7760: Hey you coming to work or quitting or what?

+82 10 0018 3579: Yohan, bro, how fucked are you with this deepshittt LunaCoin??? omg im so ready to just end it all man. no joke

+82 2 4572 1270: Sir, your loan payment is overdue. Please get in touch as soon as possible.

+82 10 3383 0236: thanks for your prudent investment advice you moron. And you said this Luna thing will change the world? lolzzz

+82 2 0755 5211: Mr. Lee, I'm reaching out because we need to clear your desk.

Yohan liked to share good things with others—whether it was a great restaurant or a lucrative crypto investment opportunity. His generous spirit, unfortunately, had now turned into an arrow aimed back at him.

One by one, cold, indifferent messages stacked up on Yohan's phone, like layers of debris piling up in his cluttered studio. Delivery containers and uneaten food lay scattered on the floor, dirty laundry strewn across the room.

Yohan should have sold his LunaCoin. He should have walked away. But he couldn't. He couldn't relinquish his belief.

Because Yohan wasn't merely another Lunatic; he was the *first*. Not the first to purchase LunaCoin, perhaps, yet the first to buy into Do-hyung Moon. The first prophet to witness and revere the weight of ambition Do bore, long before he became *Do* in the crucible of the DMZ. And just as the faithful often fail to distinguish creator from creation, so did Yohan. The Bible they started drafting together in that desolate zone reaches its final chapter here. There would be no resurrection; there would be no New Testament.

Was Yohan the Baptist wrong from the very beginning? Was Do not the Promised One but another King Herod of this obscene crypto scene?

If Do were Herod, then Yohan's own beheading was mere moments away. If Do was indeed the Crypto Christ, then Christ has fallen and the Baptist must shoulder the cross himself—not just the weight of his salary and his family's money, but the burden of the loans he took to play the leverage game with LunaCoin.

His phone rang again. Missed calls. Desperate texts.

+82 10 0427 1231: Yohan, it's Mom. Please, call me.

But Yohan could not bring himself to respond to her pleading message.

…Sorry, Mom. I should have listened to you from the start. I should have only bought those red thermal underwear with my first paycheck, like you wanted. When I splurged on those pricey earphones to give you as a gift, I really thought I'd grown up. It really meant something to me. A sense of agency. I felt… powerful, though some might laugh at the scale. I should have stopped there, with the earphones, before it turned into a greed… but it's all too late now.

Unable to bear his apartment's suffocating silence, he deleted the messenger app and requested a cab.

His destination: the Han River.

•

Mrs. Susan's daughter hadn't scored as high as she'd hoped on her SAT, but she secured a spot at a modest liberal arts college in San Diego. There was no scholarship. But she planned to work as a cashier through the summer, spend time with her boyfriend, and chip away at her looming student loans, one paycheck at a time.

Of course, it might have all been covered—the tuition, the living expenses, all of it—had Mrs. Susan not sunk her savings into the Anchor Protocol. Or perhaps even earlier, had she not dipped into LunaCoin. Or maybe—just maybe—if she'd ignored that one fateful Uber request and not picked up that bright-eyed, young Asian couple.

Her whole life she had been frugal. But she betrayed that part of herself, seduced by the siren's call of wealth, wagering her daughter's future. The guilt weighed on her, manifesting as a deep, silent illness of the soul.

Her therapist advised her to stop doing the "what ifs," to stop drowning in the sea of hypotheticals. It was the only way to cope with her overwhelming guilt.

Mrs. Susan returned to driving for Uber. She also went back to delivering food but without the warmth she once carried. Gone were the jolly greetings, the light Southern drawl she used to charm her passengers. She no longer spoke at all, even on the beautiful Redwood drive.

After one particularly long and exhausting day, she pulled into a gas station late at night. There, faintly glowing in the dark, was the cursed neon sign of a cryptocurrency ATM. Mrs. Susan's heart pounded. Her hands gripped the steering wheel tight, knuckles white, trying to steady her breath. She drove away from the neon specter and back home, back to her daughter, who was picking up extra shifts at Trader Joe's.

The next day, Mrs. Susan picked up a rare long-distance fare, from Palo Alto to Berkeley. As she drove along the highway, the Pacific stretched out to her right like a painting. Her heart ached but held steady. She pictured her daughter in a graduation cap and gown, and as that image filled her mind, Mrs. Susan drove on— slowly but steadily.

chapter block
16.0

[real-time dashboard]

LunaCoin ($LUNA) / Price: $454.46,
Market Cap: $1.7B, 24h Volume: $98.8M
TerraCoin ($TERRA) / Price: $0.69,
Market Cap: $0.4B, 24h Volume: $11.7M

@do_llarmoon: The Terra community is my
family. I will always be here, no matter how hard
it gets. Let's build it back up again—together.

With that tweet, Do deleted the Twitter app from his phone. He let out a sigh, one he hadn't been able to release in front of anyone for some time. The exhalation shattered the shards of his soul barely holding together, scattering them into an ungraspable constellation of glass, sparkling yet forever out of reach.

The silence was punctuated by a soft creak as the door opened. Do looked up, surprised. His CPO—or rather, the former CPO since the company LunaCoin was now worth nearly nothing—stood in the doorway, his face shadowed with unspoken words.

—Nik? I thought you'd already left.

And I wouldn't have blamed you if you had.

—Sorry, Do. I tried with everyone I know… even my asshole uncle at Sandhill Road, but…

Nik's face said it all. Do patted Nik on the shoulder with quiet resignation.

—It's alright. It's alright.

—And this… Do.

—What is it?

Nik's lips parted, yet no sound emerged. He instead moved silently to Do's MacBook Air, his hand trembling as he tapped open the code editor. His finger paused, pointing at the terminal: Block number 7603700.

In the world of blockchain, the system operates like a vast ledger, each entry, each transaction, documented as a "block," linked to the one before it. This chain stretches infinitely as long as the system lives. Each block is a heartbeat, a pulse that assures the world the network is alive.

But now, no more blocks were generated. Their blockchain had stopped. Their blockchain had come to an end. Block number 7603700 was their last heartbeat.

•

The Senate hearing played out like theater. Janet Yellen's face filled the screen, and on the couch sat Do and Nik—now reduced to shadows of their former selves, slouched, powerless, purposeless after years of relentless ambition. So they just needed something, anything, to fill the suffocating silence. Flicking through the channels, they landed on C-SPAN. It was far more entertaining than any entertainment channel. And it was also uncomfortably relatable.

Senator Catherine Masto (D-NV): Let me start with cryptocurrency. We do need a regulatory framework for stablecoins. The cryptocurrency market is now larger than the subprime mortgage market was before it triggered the financial crisis—nobody knows that better than us. The dynamics are startlingly similar. So my question, Madam Secretary, is this. Do you see any financial risk here?

On the name card it said:

```
The Honorable Janet L. Yellen
Secretary of the Treasury
```

Hi, Professor. Nice to see you. I feel like we know each other, thanks to Nuna. Yellen spoke.

Secretary Janet Yellen: Certainly, there are many risks associated with cryptocurrencies, and the President has asked the Treasury and FSOC to examine these risks. We will issue a comprehensive report shortly.

Of course, crypto has always been the US government's mortal enemy. Because it is the dollar's mortal enemy. Because the US government is the dollar.

Senator Catherine Masto (D-NV): Can you be more specific?

The Honorable Janet L. Yellen, Secretary of the Treasury: The President's Working Group has already outlined the risks associated with one form of crypto asset: stablecoins. They risk undermining the integrity of payment systems, and we see significant risks here.

How relatable, Do thought bitterly, sinking further into purposeless despair.

Secretary Janet Yellen: I would also note that this morning, there was a report that a stablecoin known as *Terra experienced a bank run and declined in value.*

Wait what?

Do jolted upright, knocking the remote precariously from its place on the armrest. As mentioned, he had a habit of imagining all the worst-case scenarios and running through them in his mind. This, however, was not one of them. And he partly felt the perverted ecstasy. The young Korean boy had never imagined his creation would one day be mentioned in a U.S. Senate hearing—let alone from the mouth of The Honorable Janet L. Yellen.

Secretary Janet Yellen: And I think this illustrates the risks to financial stability posed by these rapidly growing products.

You know, Professor Yellen, Nuna and I mentioned you a few times at Berkeley. Thanks for mentioning us back. Last time I saw you on TV, you were the Fed Chair—when did you even become Secretary of the Treasury?

See? You, and a select few others, control all the printed money. I wanted to change that. I wanted to control all the programmed money. So perhaps I had always wanted to become you. But I also understand that the greatest punishment isn't reserved for those who committed the worst crimes. It is reserved for those who dared to challenge the established order—and failed. I, therefore, accept my fate.

It's pretty safe to say that Do was the second most famous Korean after Kim Jong-un. His name wasn't just trending on social media; his fame had transcended the trivial. The most powerful government officials officially declared that this Korean boy to be the most lethal virus infecting the global economy. His name was whispered by Silicon Valley venture capitalists, muttered by hedge fund managers swiping corporate cards in strip clubs, and uttered by the U.S. Secretary of the Treasury in a Senate hearing!

Do here, Do there, Do everywhere. Everyone was chanting Do, Do, Do. Do-Re-Mi again—the sound of music indeed. This time, however, the pitch was notably different. It was as if the masters of global capital were composing a death melody with his name. *Do, re, mi, fa, so, la, ti, do! So, Do!*

Do did not change the world. But he upended it. No matter how historians might script this chapter of history, that was an undeniable truth.

—…Did we just get our death sentence live on TV?

Nik's voice trembled with a strange mix of fear and similarly perverse excitement, akin to a man watching the crowd gather for his own public execution.

And as if on cue, crypto investors around the world began offloading whatever TerraCoin and LunaCoin they had left after Yellen's testimony. The price plummeted, cascading toward zero.

—…Yeah, looks like it.

Do opened a Korean online news portal, seeking his own people's reaction to Yellen's address. Yet South Korea had its own justice to deliver. At the top of every website, breaking news alerts flashed like a warning siren: *LunaCoin officials under investigation.* Prosecutors had raided the LunaCoin Korea HQ and the homes of Do's family, leaving no corner untouched. Another headline confirmed the severing blow: his passport had been revoked. A message as piercing as an executioner's final pronouncement—the moment he returned to Incheon Airport, he would be seized. A man awaiting judgment, stripped of sanctuary, his fate preordained.

So this is the price I'm paying. If only he'd founded a startup making AI pizza robots. No one would have cared. But he had dared to create currency, to challenge the capitalist order, and failed. And this was his due.

•

—Nik.

—Yeah?

—I don't think I'll ever be able to go back to Korea.

—...Is it that bad?

—Unfortunately, I guess this isn't even the worst of it. Pretty soon, the U.S. prosecutors and the SEC are going to come after me. How about you, Nik? Are you going to be alright?

—Me? Well... I doubt either of us will be able to set foot in the U.S. again anytime soon. Guess I'll be heading back to Greece.

—You'll be fine there?

—My country's been bankrupt for years. One more bankrupt person returning home isn't going to tip the scales.

For the first time in weeks, Do laughed. And he knew that this would likely be the last time he laughed at his friend's familiar humor. Nik continued, a note of melancholy beneath the levity.

—You know, Do, when people reach the end of the line, they always think about when it first began.

The end of the line. Yes... this is the end. I have to admit it now. Do nodded in silence.

—I'm sorry, Do. I... I should've been a better engineer.

—Don't you say that, Nik. I couldn't have asked for a better one.

—I truly believed in this. I just never thought... I just never understood the consequences of programming money.

—It's okay, Nik. Startups succeed because they know nothing about the industry. Paypal didn't know the payment industry, and they changed it. Uber didn't care about the taxi industry, and look at what they accomplished.

—Haha... if we survive this somehow, you will make a great VC. And you already built the company of a lifetime.

—We built it.

—...Thank you, Do.

The words felt heavier than gratitude, laden with the unspoken knowledge that neither would survive this. They would spend the rest of their lives as fugitives, judged, forever haunted by their creation.

—Do, despite everything that's happened, despite what's about to happen... gosh, why am I still so sentimental and eloquent right now?

Nik's voice was quivering.

—I never regret working with you. Not for a second.

—Thank you, Nik... and take this.

Do handed Nik a USB drive.

—What's this?

—Your severance package. It's Bitcoin. I wish I could give you LunaCoin, but... well, you know. Bitcoin took a hit, but it'll recover someday. Hold on to it.

A faint, ironic smile flickered on Do's lips. Nik's face was clouded with guilt rather than gratitude. He waved it off.

—I don't need it. I bet everything on LunaCoin. With you.

—Have you watched *Titanic*?

—Of course. Yeah, there's no story more fitting for us right now.

—Before the ship sank, the guy who designed it apologized to Rose for not making it stronger… and gave her his life jacket.

Do held out the USB again.

—…So am I Rose in this analogy?

—Well, with that scruffy beard of yours, it's hard to imagine. Doesn't exactly suit the scene.

—Ha, ha.

They shared a final, rueful, bittersweet laugh before they fell into a quiet embrace, holding on as though it were their only anchor in a sea that had already swallowed them whole.

—Do, I'm the luckiest son of a bitch from Stanford's cursed Class of 2022, only and only because I met you.

—I'll miss you, bro. Actually, erm, there's one last favor I need from you.

—Anything, man. Anything.

Do hesitated before bringing up the name.

—…Can you let Luciana know to meet me at the Korean restaurant in San Francisco?

—Of course, which restaurant?

—She'll know. Tomorrow dinner. Tell her I want to pay for our final meal together with LunaCoin there. I can't… I shouldn't reach out to her directly.

Nik caught the weight of Do's words and nodded solemnly.

—And Nik… if anyone asks, Luciana was never part of our LunaCoin. She never contributed to any of this. She wasn't involved at all. Understood?

Do's expression hardened, his tone resolute. Nik held his gaze, reading between the lines.

—I understand. But Do…

—Yeah?

—What about you? Will you be, like, okay?…

Instead of answering, Do gently reached out, resting his hand on his MacBook Air where he wrote the first lines of LunaCoin's code. His fingers brushed its surface with a quiet, reverent finality —like the captain gripping the wheel as water consumed the Titanic, like the mother clutching her children in the third-class cabin, like the bandleader caressing his violin and playing *Nearer My God to Thee* as the world slipped quietly beneath the waves.

In the end, a man cannot save his creation. He can only hold it close as he goes down with it.

—Nik.

—Yeah?

—We almost made it.

—Yes, we did, Do. And no one can say otherwise.

—We were there...

chapter block
17.0

[real-time dashboard]

LunaCoin ($LUNA) / Price: $1.67,
Market Cap: $1.82M, 24h Volume: $2.3M
TerraCoin ($TERRA) / Price: $0.44,
Market Cap: $171K, 24h Volume: $62K

Hours had passed, yet still no text from her son. Yohan's mother, her face streaked with tears, dialed 119 and filed a missing person's report at the police station. Her voice cracked as she begged the officers for help.

At first, the officers didn't seem too alarmed—a healthy young man who'd gone temporarily off the radar. But the desperation in Yohan's mother's anguish, her plea for help—no one could ignore that. Even the indifferent machinery of law couldn't remain unmoved by a mother's grief.

•

Yohan stepped out of the taxi, clutching his wallet and phone as if the remnants of his life had suddenly taken on an ironic weight. After years of scrimping and saving for a future he believed secure, he finally splurged on a cab—on the day he'd chosen to walk away from it all. Until now, he only took a taxi after late nights of endless work, reimbursed at the end of each exhausting month.

A fleeting urge tempted Yohan to hand over everything in his wallet to the taxi driver—a final act of kindness, an offering of all he had left. Yet he held back, wary that such a gesture might alert the man, who, in his goodwill, might call the police and disrupt what Yohan had resolved to do. So, he stayed his hand, clinging to silence as his last, unwavering companion.

The bridge over the Han River loomed ahead, high fences lining its edge, the metal webbing like a barricade against his final act. The city of Seoul seemed to conspire in artificial mercy, offering the faint green glow of an SOS lifeline sign. A last nudge for the despondent glowed green—a verdant shade once shared by LunaCoin's skyrocketing charts, back when it knew no limits and promised endless ascent.

Yohan decided to cast away the world's money first. He emptied his wallet, watching as the 10,000-won and 1,000-won bills fluttered through the air, caught by gusts that teased their descent in playful arcs. Then came the bronze 100-won coins, tumbling down without hesitation, their descent unflinching. As he watched them vanish, he felt no relief—only an unsettling chill. The paper money danced in the wind, reluctant, defiant even, while the coins, weighty and resolute, plunged straight into the Han River's dark waters. The sight left him with a sudden, oppressive dread.

Yohan resolved next to part with Do's money. He reached into his pocket, pulling out his cellphone, tangled hopelessly in the wires of his old earphones. Those wired earphones lay in his palm like an anachronism—a relic from a time when he believed in simpler things. Too drained to untangle them, he merely turned the device over in his hands. Then, an absurd vision crossed his mind: what if, during his ride to the Han River, the U.S. government had declared LunaCoin as the new global reserve currency? What if the price of LunaCoin had shattered through the roof again somehow, vaulting him into millionaire status in a single breath? What if he had arrived at this bridge on the very eve of his salvation?

For a flickering moment, he hesitated, the hint of that old, irrational hope alighting within him. He unlocked his phone, hands trembling, and checked his crypto wallet:

```
Wallet Summary
Total Balance: ₩8,944 (~$6.68 USD)
Portfolio:
• Bitcoin (BTC): 0.000024
• Ethereum (ETH): 0.00074
• Ripple (XRP): 0.96
• LunaCoin (LUNA): 4
Last Transaction: Sent 44 LUNA to 0x1b…u2z7
```

No miracle awaited him. The U.S. government wasn't deranged. They hadn't anointed LunaCoin as the new global currency. The absurd flicker of hope had left him feeling hollow and humiliated, and Yohan, leaning against the tall iron barrier of the Han River bridge and let out a laugh tinged with bitter tears.

Once his tears had dried, only a withered anger remained— cold and brittle. Money, money, money. This cursed thing! If this was his final moment, he would let his fury fuel it. He hurled his cellphone with all his might toward the river.

That wasn't a cellular phone device to him. That was his crypto-fucking-wallet stuffed with worthless LunaCoins. The phone soared into the air, a final offering.

But—oops. It fell short, still bound to him by the tether of his tangled earphones. Great, *even this doesn't go right*, he thought bitterly. Just as it should have plummeted into the river, the wired earphones jerked it back, the cord catching on the iron barrier.

The phone dangled, swaying precariously over the water. It suspended like a pendulum of indecision. Each sway of the phone feels like time slowing down, teasing him with the idea that it could still be within his grasp. Instinctively, Yohan leaned over the rail, reaching for the phone he'd so desperately thrown away—

But with one sharp tug, the C-cable snapped free. Untethered, the phone twisted awkwardly in midair before plunging into the water below, a splash shattering the river's surface into ripples that widened, indifferent, across the dark expanse. Only the earphones remained, swaying from the barrier like some spectral reminder of what once connected him.

He saw the phone's fall. He watched the ripples fade. Then, with trembling hands, he brought the wired earphones—his only relic—back to his chest.

•

—Officer… is there any news… anything?

—Erm, ma'am. The last signal from your son's phone was traced to the Han River. The connection's gone now, so we'll need to hurry.

At the mention of the Han River, Yohan's mother felt her heart seize, a sudden stillness as if it had stopped. When it resumed its beat, the pain constricted her chest with each thud. The traffic on Yeouido Financial District's evening rush choked every inch of road. Even as the police car tore through with sirens blaring, it took them twenty extra agonizing minutes to reach the vicinity of the Han River bridge.

—There… that's the bridge, right?

—Yes, but there's no way to stop the car here. We'll have to drive around to the opposite side—

Before the officer could finish, Yohan's mother was already reaching for the door, frantic hands fumbling against the locked handle, ready to throw herself out.

—Ma'am! Ma'am! We're still on the highway! Please, just five more minutes and we'll—

—Open the door, please! I beg you, open it—now!

—Uh… Officer Kim? That person over there—isn't that him?

Yohan's mother, leaving the officers in her wake, dashed toward the faint silhouette of her son. The moonlight bathed Yohna's face in a soft glow, illuminating him as she drew near. She wrapped her arms around her son, clutching him as though he might slip away. Their bodies shook together, her own tremors merging with his, or perhaps it was the other way around.

Her hands gently brushed over his face, searching for any trace of injury. Aside from the trails of tears lining his cheeks, he bore no visible wounds. The capricious deity of fate had cast her night light to tenderly reveal her son's unscathed face. Silently, yet fervently and repeatedly, Yohan's mother gave thanks to the moon over the Han River for giving her son back.

—Mom, I'm sorry... so sorry...

—Yohan, what on earth do you have to be sorry for? If anyone's sorry, it's me. You're alive. That's all that matters. You're alive...

—I was too afraid, Mom. I could throw away all the money, but not myself... I'm sorry.

Joggers crossing the Han River bridge slowed at the sight of a mother and son entwined, weeping under the night sky. Wordlessly, they turned to the side path, leaving the two of them alone to their sanctuary of tears.

Yohan had awoken from that cryptic, nonexistent Christ he had clung to; there was only one creator—his mother, holding him now in love's embrace.

The lunar eclipse over Seoul had passed. Curious astrologers might already be charting when the next celestial rendezvous would grace the skies. But as for *the other eclipse*—well, let us linger a moment longer, until the sun of tomorrow graces us.

chapter block
18.0

[real-time dashboard]

LunaCoin ($LUNA) / Price: $0.1,
Market Cap: $2.97K, 24h Volume: $1.22K
TerraCoin ($TERRA) / Price: $0.01,
Market Cap: $0.58K, 24h Volume: $1.04K

Do steps into *Paguk San Francisco* alone.

—Good evening, sir. Do you happen to have a reservation with us today?

—Uh… no. Actually, yes. Well, no, I'm not so sure…

—May I have your name, sir?

—Oh… erm.

Do hesitates to share his name, as he should. Before he wreaked financial havoc on the American economy, no American was capable of pronouncing his full name, much less remember it.

But after his face has been emblazoned across national television, even the clumsiest tongues have mastered the syllables of *hyung*—especially if it means clawing back a few dollars of their vanished fortune.

—Sir, or perhaps I could check for you if your party has already arrived?

Unlike the brusque waiter and pretentious manager from his previous visit, this new waiter is polished and polite, almost disarmingly so.

—…Could you then try looking for Luciana, Kim?

—Of course! Let me check it for you, sir. Em, I'm sorry, sir. I unfortunately don't see any reservation under Luciana Kim. Might it be under another name?

Is Nuna running late?

—Erm... she might have used a different name. Could you please check, uh, John-Doe-Kim?

—Absolutely sir! One moment, please.

Or has she chosen not to come at all? As ever, Do cannot resist but spiral into the worst case scenario, preemptively tormenting himself. If he breaks himself now, he won't crumble when the worst actually falls.

—Oh, right here. She's already here and waiting for you. This way, please.

—Appreicate it.

The waiter leads Do to that familiar, secluded booth, nestled in the farthest corner by the window. Nuna—you're here, still remembering our seat, our little alias, carried forward asynchronously like a whispered secret between time. For a fleeting moment, the present dissolves, and Do gazes into the past, his chest tightening with bittersweet nostalgia.

—Have you visited here before?

—Uh, yeah, it's been about a year.

—Welcome back! We've upgraded the menu since then— extra depth, even more scallion flavor.

The young waiter brims with energy and optimism, his enthusiasm almost luminous.

—Oh, that's... great to hear. By the way, has the manager changed?

—Ah, yes. The previous ones moved on to other places, as far as I know.

—I see.

—I've only been working here for three months, but it's been my dream to be part of a restaurant like this. I'll do my best to make sure you have an unforgettable experience!

—Thank you...

For the first time, Do feels a pang of guilt—not for the trillions of LunaCoins lost or the millions of Lunatics, but for this one man of his age. His guilt has hitherto been vast, nebulous, abstract. He never faced the masses of Lunatics directly; they were a faceless mob, swollen with varying magnitudes of greed. This peer of his, on the other hand, brims not with delusions of grandeur but with the hope of honest labor earned day by day. The contrast feels alien, and the guilt becomes painfully specific in proportion. Against his own dark eclipse, a foreign moonlight shines and humbles Do. The shadowed moon, stripped of its glow, left only with shame—a belated lunar eclipse.

—Enjoy, sir.

In the shadowed corner booth, cloaked in obscurity, Luciana sits there, staring out at the rain that softly patters against the glass. It isn't quite Indian summer yet. The weather, however, feels fittingly out of place—no sunlight, no moonlight, only this muted gray drizzle. Do parts his lips to call her name, but she turns first, her voice beautiful, wistful.

—Do.

•

Raindrops cling to the restaurant's roof, each descending slowly, reflecting fragments of Luciana's regret.

In the end, it should have been me. I should have taken responsibility.

I was always afraid—of being thrust into a spotlight of this magnitude. I always told myself I wanted to keep my feet firmly planted on the ground. But perhaps that wasn't humility. Perhaps it was fear, masquerading as virtue.

So it came to this. It came to the worst ending imaginable. My name echoed through the halls of a U.S. Senate hearing— spoken by Professor Yellen, no, Chair Yellen, no, Secretary Yellen. Yes, my name, uttered for all the world to hear. In that moment, I felt, as Heidegger once described, thrown into a world not of my choosing, left to navigate existence.

Even in my terror, I found myself paradoxically ready—at last—to bear the weight of responsibility. As a wise comedian once said, the most liberating moment is when your fear is realized. A silver lining emerged, weathered into the warm luster of bronze—like a coin passed through countless hands. My courage was inversely proportional to the price of LunaCoin.

The footsteps of my boyfriend and my former co-founder draw near, lighter than they once were, almost hollow, as though even gravity has grown weary of holding him. Gaunt and crumpled, life peeled away layer by fragile layer.

—Do.

Luciana calls his name instinctively, her voice quivering with a tender blend of affection and emotion.

—Nuna...

His words falter. The architect of daredevil ambition fades, leaving a man weighted by the pain he both endures and has sown. The wounds he carries reflect the scars he's etched into others. A side of him unknown until now rises to the surface. A man, undone.

•

—Here's your amuse-bouche.

The same crispy, pan-fried tofu dish arrives, brimming with the unmistakable aroma of scallions. Do glances at Luciana, quietly checking if the dish still pleases her.

—...Just as good as last time, Luciana says.

—And just as packed with scallion flavor, Do echoes.

—Living up to its name, huh?

—I didn't know you knew.

—Oh, I know what *Paguk* means. Not the most appropriate name for a restaurant or its patrons, but I thought we were capable of avoiding the omen.

—...Or?

—Or maybe I jinxed it when I asked you about the name of the coin.

Luciana exhales, a soft laugh laced with exhaustion.

—Ha, even if so, the jinx was mine, so it's my fault.

Luciana has never seen him admit fault so readily. There's absolutely no catharsis in it, though.

—It's my name on the coin, so it's my fault. She says.

They share a silence. They sip that silence like wine, bitter and biting, and swallow it like the stray slivers of scallions left on their plates. Neither speaks again until the young waiter returns with their main course.

—Here you go, your medium steak—for both of you.

This time, the steaks are impeccably cooked.

—Why medium this time? Luciana asks.

—Guilt, maybe. I don't know.

—Guilt?

—I fucked up. People suffered in consequence. So I felt, I don't know, wrong to enjoy something extravagant.

—…Okay.

—No, I lied. I couldn't care less about those people.

Do exhales, a laugh slipping from his lips like a whisper of smoke fading before it fully forms.

—Do.

Luciana chides him gently, her voice barely carrying the weight of reproach.

—I mean, maybe I care a little. But I ordered medium steak in case the restaurant overlooks yours again. That I care.

His tired smile carries a trace of mischief, childlike in its selfishness yet tinged with affection. Even now, after everything, Do remains largely indifferent to the wreckage he has left in the lives of millions. For the one person sitting in front of him, however, he cares as if she is the world entire.

Luciana's chest tightens.

It's the small things, Do. It's always the small things. I love you. You love me. And yet, only our ambitions loved each other. Once, we amassed all the digital wealth in the world, but none of the emotional riches to say this.

•

Most of the steak is gone now, the juices cooling on the plate, congealing like their unspoken regrets. Do pulls his gaze away from the plate, lifting it slowly to Luciana—her neck, her necklace.

—You still wear that. He says softly.

The mismatch between the ancient Korean coin and the Van Cleef necklace remains as striking as ever, a jarring blend of the rustic and the refined.

—Because it holds us in it... at least I want to think that.

—...When people mint coins—cents, quarters, dimes—they say that more important than melting the metal is letting it cool.

—Cooling.

—Yeah.

—That sounds about right. There are those who ignite the fire and hammer the metal as one, heedless of the cooling that gives it strength.

—...I am sorry, Nuna.

—I was talking about myself, too.

—Should've given it time to cool it down.

—But to think of it... none of us, myself included, could have torn down and smelted the walls in front of us. Only you made it through.

—*Almost* made it. Then I failed, which now means nothing.

—You have brought us—and LunaCoin—this far.

—...Thank you, for trying to console me.

—I'm not trying to console you. Nothing can. I'm... sorry, Do. I shouldn't have left. I should've fought through it—with you and against you.

—It's fake, you know.

—Hmm?

Do pulls out his ancient coin from the chest pocket, gesturing toward its tarnished surface.

—Fake?

—Haha... I was just going to keep this to myself, but yeah. That coin doesn't date back centuries to the Joseon Dynasty. I tried to sell mine to buy up more LunaCoin, to protect the pegging—

however little it could. But the appraiser told me it's a fake coin. I got scammed.

Luciana's expression, however, doesn't waver at all. She gently caresses the counterfeit coin as though it holds a truth only the two of them could see.

—It doesn't change a thing.

—...I gave you a worthless coin as a gift, Nuna. I'm sorry. Sorry to keep saying sorry.

—So don't sorry. As much as I hate borrowing a page from Greenspan, the intrinsic value of this coin—well, you know what I'm about to say, don't you?

Do doesn't say anything. He either doesn't know or does want to hear it directly with his lover's caring voice.

—The intrinsic value of this... fake ancient Korean coin is the trust between us. That's what makes it valuable.

Luciana's words linger in the air as she speaks, and Do responds by tenderly touching her fingers.

—So now we're switching roles? You play the cheesy one, and I cringe at it?

—I guess we are.

They match a wistful laugh, one they know they can never truly hold onto.

•

The steak plates are cleared, and the famous matcha tiramisu arrives, lush with its signature green hue. A first for them both.

For most couples, dessert is an intermission. The pause between Act One of sharing a meal and Act Two of sharing a night.

—Well, we finally get to taste this. Do says.

For this couple, however, the dessert signifies something else entirely. The intermission before the Judgment Day. The last meal of a condemned man. The Last Supper.

And so, the tiramisu sits on their tongues like ash, weightless yet suffocating.

—…Have some, Nuna. It's really good. I secretly worried that they might have hidden a scallion inside the tiramisu, given their obsession, but no—it's just pure sweet delight.

—Yup…

—It's a shame, though—that this is the first and last time we'll share it.

Do's voice is unnervingly calm, steady in a way that makes Luciana pause.

—Why would you say that, Do?

He doesn't answer.

—Okay, Do. I came here to say difficult things. But, coward that I am, I'll borrow the sweet delight of the tiramisu and say it before it is gone.

—And I'll listen.

—You might not believe it, but we still have a chance. We made a kickass coin. Let's make it right. Let's own up to our mistakes, take responsibility, and see this through.

—Responsibility…

—Yes.

The evening rain over San Francisco begins to ease. Fewer drops fall now, but each one lands with a more deliberate resonance. Seven droplets of time pass.

—I…

Do tries to speak, but only a dry cough escapes. He takes an unfruitful sip of water, though it does nothing to loosen the tightness in his throat, as thirst wasn't the issue. Three more droplets of time fall.

—Nuna, you're right. I'll take responsibility. I have to take responsibility.

When Do finally speaks again, his voice is no longer liquid. Water crystalized to ice—solid and unyielding.

—Really?

Luciana's eyes widen at his unexpected response.

—Yes. At this point, I don't think it's up to me. I don't think I can avoid it.

—You're not someone who avoids things. Owning up takes courage, and I know you have that courage in you.

Do nods but averts his gaze, turning his head away as he speaks.

—Nuna, do you know about naming?

Luciana raises an eyebrow, a small smile forming despite the heavy air.

—Well, I know you have a peculiar tendency to ask out-of-context questions before you bring up something important.

Do smiles faintly, an echo of her wit softening the tension.

—Harvard names their buildings after dead presidents who ruled the past. Stanford names their buildings after living billionaires who rule the present.

—Sounds pretty accurate. Though I read in *The Crimson* that Ken Greenspan donated half a billion to Harvard to rename some buildings after him.

—Wow.

—I know, right?

—His lecture, though—that was our genesis.

—It indeed was. And I do thank him for that.

—They want to etch their legacy.

—Mmhmm.

—But I wanted to etch my love.

—...Do.

Luciana reaches across the table, her right hand brushing against Do's left hand with quiet intent. For a moment, it seems he might allow the connection. Yet he pulls his hand away from his co-lover and co-founder, leaving hers suspended in the air.

—Nuna, I named LunaCoin after you—Luna Nuna—*only and only* because I loved you.

Luciana notices the unlikely emphasis he places on *only and only*. The accentuation pulls at her, drawing a question to her lips.

—How do you mean, exactly?...

—You are my co-lover, but you were never my co-founder.

Do's voice now turns glacial, every word precise and cutting, like the merciless iceberg that doomed the Titanic.

—…I don't understand what you are getting at.

Luciana looks genuinely confused.

—You were never part of LunaCoin.

—What?

—You were never part of LunaCoin. This time, the former CEO emphasizes each syllable as he speaks.

—I was the co-founder and the CTO of LunaCoin.

She tries to fend off this sudden, perplexing rewrite of reality. And yet, Do remains resolute and deliberate. He shakes his head.

—No, you were never involved.

—Wait, are you doing this to protect me or something? My name is already on the coin, Do!

Her voice rises, and her disbelief escalates. His words cut through her resistance, however, striking with the inevitability of the iceberg itself.

—Nuna, let me… let me be brief.

—Brief about what?

—Here's the final version of our story: I met you. I liked you. I named a coin that didn't yet exist after you. Then I invented the algorithmic stablecoin. Then I pushed forward with the Anchor Protocol. There is no *we* in this story. Do you understand?

Do rewrites an alternative history, engraving it onto a metal coin—one destined to melt back into shapeless ore—his version, his truth. He demands her consent. She doesn't yield.

—No.

—You did once say that I named LunaCoin like "naming an expensive yacht after some girl on my arm," didn't you? Correct me if I'm wrong.

—Stop!

She shouts.

—Stop this. Stop whatever nonsense imaginary scenario you're trying to fabricate. I am just as responsible for this collapse as you are.

—You are not hearing me!

—I won't! I should have been there with you when you pushed forward with the Anchor Protocol. I got cold feet, and I fucking regret that. There's no way I am leaving you alone again.

—Nuna, Listen!

Do shouts from the visceral depths within. In the stillness that follows, he borrows a line from Mr. Andrews, the architect of *Titanic*, with chilling finality.

—The ship will sink.

—No, we still have the chance to save it.

—I'm heading back to Stanford tonight.

—Tonight?

—Yes, right after our dinner. There's a talk at the Stanford Blockchain Club. It'll be my first public appearance since the crash. And probably my last. The FBI plans to arrest me there.

—What?!

—My lawyer—well, LunaCoin's former lawyer, Mr. Berg—told me before he quit yesterday.

—And you plan to just walk in there?

—…I'm a reckless narcissist boy genius who created a stablecoin of a lifetime and named that coin after my girlfriend out of some obsession. Not that I had to spend hours conjuring up that scenario. It's a part of who I am, after all, haha.

Luciana, however, can't afford to share in his self-deprecating humor. Do, for all his bravado, is not immune to fear and emotion. His voice trembles, like a lifeboat adrift in icy waters, meant only to carry her to safety. He continues.

—I don't have much time left, Nuna. Promise me. Promise me you will go along with this version of the story.

—…No. I won't.

But Do answers with a determined stare that will not entertain "no" as an answer. Moonlight long extinguished momentarily persists as a silken trace in the dark depths of his eyes. *Nuna. This is the only way. This is why I must.*

•

—Do…

—Yes.

—You don't believe there's a way to revive LunaCoin, do you?

Luciana asks, realization dawning. Do shakes his head gently.

She lowers her gaze, tears slipping freely down her cheeks now. A quick tilt of her chin follows, an attempt to stop them from falling further. Her eyes find his again, and there, faintly, tears glimmer on his cheeks too.

Without a word, her trembling hand reaches for his. With quiet care, Do presses his fake ancient Korean coin into her palm in response. A fragment of his heart—fifty cents, to be exact.

—Nuna.

—Yeah.

—Will you… will you take my coin? Even though it's fake, it still completes our dollar.

Luciana only nods, her hand closing over the coin.

—And you're right, Nuna. Your name is on the coin. As long as I know you're out there, LunaCoin is never a failure. It lives on —with you.

With that, Do rises from his seat.

—The check's on me this time.

—…

—Take care, Nuna.

—Wait.

Luciana wipes away her tears with effort before clasping his hand tightly, one last time. Her calloused fingers entwine with his, a mirror of the wear they've both endured.

—Nuna?…

—Do, I promise to stick to your version of the story. But you have to promise me something too.

—…Of course.

—Hang in there.

His skin trembles. The *luna* eclipse has now passed, and the sun rises once more, thawing the ice that had encased his heart. The warmth pools into his eyes, threatening to overflow. He must therefore leave now; if he doesn't, he'll want to stay by her side.

—Do, I'll bring our LunaCoin back. Somehow, I'll revive it. I'll restore the people's lost money and faith—and your lost name, our lost time. I promise.

Before the tides of his sorrow swell, Do bows his head and places a fleeting kiss on her fourth finger, as if sealing an unspoken vow, then walks away to step into the shadow of his undoing.

•

—Excuse me, erm... can I get the bill please? Sorry, I've got somewhere I urgently need to be.

—Of course, sir. Hope you enjoyed our meal.

—Yeah, we really did.

Do places his credit card—one that holds little credit of any kind—on top of the bill. But wait. *Shit*. His tarnished name is embossed on the card surface: *Do-hyung Moon*.

He recoils instinctively, as if the letters have seared his fingertips. He rummages through his inner jacket pocket, searching for cash in folds of empty fabric. The act feels pitiful.

Just then, the waiter gestures to leave the card where it is.

—No need to worry about it, Mr. Moon.

Do glances up, slightly startled, his expression caught between suspicion and surprise. The professional meets his gaze with a polite, reassuring smile.

—Will be right back, sir.

•

And before long, the waiter returns and hands back the credit card along with the bill.

—Here it is, sir. All set. Enjoy the rest of your evening.

—...Thank you. And thank you for your discretion.

—My pleasure, sir.

Do studies the receipt, his pen poised above the gratuity line. He scribbles a tip, an amount meant to match his gratitude for the waiter's professionalism, for the restaurant's privacy to end his last supper in peace.

He stops, however. His pen hovers momentarily, then drifts left, tracing back toward the symbol anchoring the number he just wrote.

The Dodo bird scratches the dollar sign and scrawls a string of four characters, rewriting the currency for the closing act.

$ → LUNA

He elects to be the master of his own ruin.

Boston Book Reserve
115 Mt Auburn St, Cambridge, MA 02138
Printed in the United States of America

ISBN 979-8-9880233-2-6

LUNA NUNA:
the Romantic Ruin of the Most Celebrated Coin

www.ingramcontent.com/pod-product-compliance
Lightning Source LLC
Chambersburg PA
CBHW031308170626
46807CB00001B/332